D1495509

A
RESCUED
HOPE

can it really be happily ever after

Natalie
Replogle

Published by White Feather Press.
(www.whitefeatherpress.com)

ISBN 978-1-61808-104-9

Printed in the United States of America

Cover design created by Ron Bell of AdVision Design Group
(www.advisiondesigngroup.com)

White Feather Press

Reaffirming Faith in God, Family, and Country!

To my husband,
Gregory

In you I have found my perfect help-mate. I love experiencing life with you and the joy and laughter it brings. Thank you for leading our family by your example of hard work, faithfulness, unselfishness, and unwavering desire to pursue God with all your heart.

Acknowledgements

Thank you to God Almighty for the eternal hope you give to those who believe in You and the gift of salvation through Jesus Christ. May this novel serve to glorify you and impact your Kingdom.

Gregory – thank you for being my biggest fan and cheering me on as I pursue my dream – and for showing me an incredible love that makes writing romance easy.

Jarrett – my red-headed, handsome, growing up way-too-quickly 3rd grader. I love your tender heart, your kindness toward others, how you still fit in my arms when we snuggle, and your smile that makes your eyes shine.

Brayden – my spunky, adorable, Angry Bird and Mario-loving 1st grader. I love your hugs and kisses, your laughter that brightens my day, that you are already a prayer warrior and when asked what you want to be when you grow up you answer with "a man".

Kyla – my joyful, beautiful, miracle baby – although you aren't a baby anymore – you are 3, sniff, sniff. I love your silliness, your cute voice that makes my insides melt, how you can be a princess one moment and a tomboy the next, and that you make each day a little sweeter.

Mom – thank you for being the best mother a daughter could ask for. When I grow up, I want to be just like you!

Susan Begay – thank you doesn't seem like enough, but from the bottom of my heart, thank you! You took a clueless, wanna-be author and encouraged me, gave advice, and became a listening ear – all from the kindness that overflows from your heart. I know I said this before, but seriously, without you I wouldn't be here today.

Michael Culp – thank you for answering my unending police-related questions and scenarios. If there is any incorrect information in my book, the fault is all mine.

Darcy Holsopple of Darcy Holsopple Photography – thank you for taking my author's picture. You are so talented and I enjoy watching you use your gifts to bless and give memories to others.

To my White Feather Press family, Skip and Sara Coryell, thank you for your continued support and new-found friendship. I appreciate all you have done to help me chase after my dream!

CHAPTER ONE

KINDERGARTEN TEACHER AVA WILLIAMS DID HER BEST TO concentrate on preparing for her lesson tomorrow, but the sparkling diamond ring on her left hand kept her easily distracted. Lifting her ring finger, she wiggled it, bringing a cascade rainbow to dance across her desk from the sunlight streaming in from the window.

Ava was hopelessly, undeniably and passionately in love. A love so profound and robust she often wondered if her heart would burst through her chest. She had been engaged for the last two days – she looked down at her watch (actually forty-five hours, twenty-five minutes and fifteen seconds) – but who was counting. She was, and anticipating the minutes until she became Mrs. Ava Thompson.

She and Matt had quite the love story to tell their children someday. Two and a half years ago Ava's life came crashing down around her when her fiancé Tim never showed up for their wedding. The rejection broke her heart into thousands of pieces and she vowed to never love again.

That is, until Matt walked into her life …

She did all she could to push him away, fearful of giving her heart and trusting someone again, but his perseverance became a force she could not reckon with.

How many times in the last five months had she thanked him for not giving up on her? Countless. He was not only a man of strong character, unwavering honesty, humor that constantly kept her laughing, and her rock – but let's face it, he wasn't hard to look at.

The best part.

He loved her. Deeply.

Ava finally gave up on lesson planning … which some would call, staring out the window instead while dreaming of her tall, dark and handsome fiancé. She began sliding her papers into color-coded folders that way in the morning she would be more prepared and efficient. At least she had a few ounces of productivity today.

She absentmindedly walked around the room picking up the misplaced items and returning them to their designated spots. In her kindergarten room organization was a necessity. A cluttered room made her uptight, stressed and overwhelmed.

Crouching down onto the balls of her feet, she put the picture and reading books back in order in their branded bins to help the children find their favorites easier. She checked out the play area, pleased to see her students had done a great job of picking up at the end of the day. Returning to her desk, she began straightening up her mess, needing to be a good example. This trait didn't always come easy to her.

A tap at the door stopped her process. "Hey, beautiful."

The raspy, low voice brought an immediate full smile to Ava's lips. Glancing up from her desk, her eyes locked onto the steamy brown eyes that held so much love. "Matthew."

Matt pushed off his muscular frame from against the door jam and headed into the room toward her. She met him halfway, reaching up on her tiptoes to leave her mark on his lips.

"Hmm, it's good to see you, too. I can go back outside and we can reenact that again." His flirtatious smile crept across his face until it beamed.

"No need for you to leave." Ava reached up and stole another kiss, letting it linger longer the second round. Reminding herself of the need to stay professional, she stepped back and wiped off the shimmery pink lipstick that had transferred to his lips. Matt caught on to her cues and allowed her to slip from his arms without dispute. Quickly scanning his physique, she noticed how his short-sleeved black shirt clung to the outline of his chest in all the right places. His sling-free arm jolted her memory. "Hey, no sling. Are you here to tell me some good news?"

Over the summer Ava had helped a student's mom walk away from an abusive relationship and in doing so, marked their friendship as one that would last a lifetime. In her attempts to help Kim, Ava's life also became endangered when the boyfriend, Ray, came after her. Matt had come to her rescue while she had been held at gunpoint. Thinking she was doomed for death, an unforeseen twist at the end of the standoff proved her wrong when Matt ended up being the one shot instead of her.

The events still haunted her dreams at night. Once or twice a week she would wake up from reliving Matt's body ripple backwards from the bullet, her clothes damp with sweat and her body shaking from the illusion that teased her of reality.

Over the last month his shoulder continued to heal quickly, mostly due to his stubbornness of playing the role of Superman during his physical therapy. He was going crazy not being able to work and protect his city, and all that energy overflowed into doing everything possible to make sure he could be back in uniform in record time. His doctor's appointment this afternoon determined if the sling could come off and he could return to work.

Matt lifted his shoulder and rotated it around to show her how easy it moved and that his face didn't cringe from the movement. "I passed with flying colors and can return to work next Monday. I'll be stuck with desk duty for a few weeks pushing papers all day, but at least it's a start."

She understood his pressed smile and underlying frustration. "That's great. You'll be back to active duty before you know it." Her eyes lit up to show her excitement. "I'm thinking that calls for a celebration."

"Oh yeah. What are you thinking?"

"Dinner."

"Your cooking ... or going out?" His teasing hesitation made her laugh. It was a known fact that Ava was not a first-rate cook. She claimed it and accepted it. She easily made fun of herself about her weakness and rolled with it when others made it a punch line.

"Out, but if you're not careful you'll be sitting at my table eating macaroni and cheese from a box." She couldn't keep her grin hidden.

"Keep talking, gorgeous."

Dismissing his attempt to butter her up, she continued. "Italian. No, wait. Steak. Afterward we could stop for ice cream at our favorite place for a final visit before they close for the season."

"I like the way you celebrate. Thanks for caring." He leaned in and kissed her forehead. "I think I could add something to our evening of celebration."

"You've got my attention."

"If we hurry we can still make it to the bank before they close. How do you feel about seeing what kind of mortgage we can swing to buy a house?"

Ava felt the need to pinch herself. Everything she ever wanted stood right before her. A man who loved her and wanted to marry her – for real this time. Now, a chance to own a home and begin a long life of memories as they hopefully started a family someday.

"I'll get my purse. Try and keep up."

THE BANK CLOSED IN A HALF HOUR, BUT THE LOAN OFFICER agreed to fit them in to quickly go over options. Matt looked over at Ava as they sat crammed into the tiny office just outside of the lobby. He had been eager to bring up this idea and her reaction did not disappoint.

It made him happy to be able to give Ava the home she had always wanted. With her by his side, he'd be happy living in a shed, but a home to start their life together excited him. Except for the large number staring back at him, taunting him to panic. Was it getting hot in here or was it just him? His throat tightened as though he had a tie on, choking his airway. He mentally shook off his apprehension. The time had come to strap on his big boy boots and be in debt for what would feel like the rest of his life.

A loud shout interrupted in the lobby as screams followed.

Matt jumped up from his cushioned chair, his hand automatically going to the gun strapped to his side. He slid tactically beside the elongated window adjacent to the door that exposed the chaotic lobby. Keeping out of view, he managed to still be able to see two masked gunmen standing in the middle of the tile floor waving their guns around. The muffled sound of them shouting at the people to get down on the floor made its way into the enclosed room.

He watched the shock work its way through Ava's terrified features. Matt wished he could take a moment to comfort Ava, reassure her that everything would be okay, that he would protect her. But time did not stand on their side. One of the gunmen had already started to head toward them.

Pulling his shirt down further to ensure his gun stayed hidden, he put his plan into action. "Ava, get under the desk and call 911 after we leave." Ava scrambled around the desk and stuffed herself underneath the dark mahogany. He made eye contact with the loan officer, "Mr. Kline, I need as much in-formation about the layout of this bank as fast as you can give it to me."

CHAPTER TWO

MATT FOLLOWED THE LOAN OFFICER OUT INTO THE LOBBY AS the masked gunman trailed on his heels. Everything in him wanted to produce his gun and put these men in their place. But his years of training reminded him to keep his cool and remain a witness until he needed to step in. There were too many hostages for an unneeded stand-off. He would let the situation play out for now.

It made him sick to be separated from Ava, but she sat in the safest place she could be. The gunman never asked or checked for other people. Hopefully she had already made the 911 call and help would be here soon.

"I said, get down!" the other gunman shouted, bringing Matt's focus to where it needed to be. Matt purposefully scoped out the room checking on all exits and layout. People near him collapse to the ground with fear tightening their features. He joined them, dropping to his knees and then falling forward. The cool tile brushed against his warm face already damp with sweat. A woman next to him started to cry.

The larger man that had come into the offices to pull the people out of their seclusion stood guard, while the smaller of the men approached the counter, barking out orders to the tellers. "You two," he shouted to the tellers at the end, "come out here and get on the ground!" He pointed the gun to where he wanted them to go. They scurried around the counter and onto the floor, holding on to one another.

Jumping over the counter, he took hold of the lone red-headed teller by her shirt. "Put all the cash you can find into this bag, now!" He handed her the bag.

Matt noticed how fidgety the burly gunman behind him was getting. His body language broadcasted his nervousness. A simple assessment revealed that the man did not want to be here.

"Come on, Eddie, let's just get out of here."

"Shut up, Mike, and just do what I say. We still have time." The leader between them became easy to identify. Matt couldn't believe the slip of exchanging their names. Showing they erred on the side of being amateurs didn't lessen Matt's worry over how this robbery would end.

The gunman, Eddie, pointed his gun toward the teller and spat at her, "Let's go, do you want a bullet in your head?" The petite woman's eyes widened in horror. She let out a yelp and worked with greater speed at retrieving the money while he stood over her, helping to grab the cash.

"Come on, let's go!" Mike pleaded while pacing in front of the windows.

"All right!" Eddie grabbed the bag from the teller and motioned for her to join the rest of them. She ran out from behind the counter and dropped to the floor near the other tellers. The two gunmen worked their way to the doors but stopped short at the sound of sirens approaching.

"You idiot!" Mike hollered at Eddie, pacing again, swearing at him and calling him a few degrading names. "I told you we should've left when we had the chance."

"Shut up and let me think!" Eddie roared while rubbing his head.

The police cars arrived within seconds and from what Matt could see from his position on the floor, they had surrounded the front of the building. Matt wondered what information

Ava had given dispatch. Had she told them he was inside?

"Eddie, the cops are everywhere, what are we going to do?" Mike beseeched.

"Okay, okay." Eddie snapped. Matt became more uncomfortable by the minute as he recognized the anger building between the two men. "Go shut off the lights and I'll move everyone to the front windows."

"Why the windows?"

"So the cops won't be able to shoot at us, stupid."

Mike ran off to find where to shut the lights off, while Eddie approached the terrified group. "Everyone get over to the windows and sit down. If you try anything, I'll shoot you!"

The bank had large tinted windows that covered the front of the bank from top to bottom, facing out to the street. The entrance held an open lobby area with a half-dozen chairs surrounding a low, circular table for people to wait for a loan officer. Straight ahead in the back stood the tellers' counters and on both sides were the offices that Mike had entered to pull people out. So far, Ava remained three doors down in the left hallway. The loan officer had informed Matt that through the right hallway was the back exit for the bank. Once the SWAT team arrived, he was sure his team would be setting up camp right outside that door.

While everyone shuffled to the front windows, Matt secretively counted sixteen hostages, seventeen if he added Ava. A help desk stood in front of the windows, but Eddie went over and shoved it back to make more room for the group.

The loan officer arrived last. Eddie singled him out, frustration seeping from his words. "The police got here too quick. How did that happen?"

Matt could physically see Mr. Kline's body shudder from the fear. "I…I don't know."

Eddie put his gun up to the man's face. "Try again."

Fear gripped Matt's chest at the thought of Ava being

found out. "There is a woman, in my office, under the desk."

Traitor!

Eddie threw Mr. Kline down. His body slid across the floor until the help desk stopped his movement with a thud, penetrating the suddenly quiet room. He signaled for Mike to go retrieve Ava.

Matt struggled to regulate his breathing as Mike disappeared into the office. Everything changed with Ava coming out of hiding. He cringed when he heard her yelp. Ava's terrified eyes found his immediately as she was pushed from the office. Helplessness settled in his gut.

"Sit down," Eddie sneered.

Matt had positioned himself on the outside of the group, which made it easy for her to sit beside him without throwing up any red flags. Matt kept his attention on the gunmen, not giving them any ammunition that they were together, hoping Mike had forgotten that he'd pulled him out of the same room.

Time seemed to stand still. No one spoke as they sat in an uncomfortable and eerie silence. Eddie and Mike positioned themselves behind the group, whispering harshly to one another. The sound of tires squealing brought everyone's attention outside. The SWAT vehicles pulled up out front. Everything was falling into place.

Matt saw his team of men file out of one of the trucks and depart their separate ways. Some went behind the squad cars and others disappeared around the building or into the other truck. The final six men jumped out the back of the truck and stood at the door looking toward the bank. Matt saw his best friend and partner, Derek Brown, among the men and worked through his mixed emotions. A wave of relief washed over him that they were here and yet, he felt out of place being the hostage instead of the rescuer.

A few minutes later the phone on the help desk started ringing. The captors waited about thirty seconds to answer.

Finally Eddie walked over and picked up the receiver, silencing the shrill that echoed off the marble walls.

"What?" he barked.

The conversation was only one-sided for Matt to hear, but easy enough to understand the discussion taking place.

"You don't need my name," Eddie growled harshly.

Silence.

"Yes, everyone is fine … for now," he added, looking down at them in warning.

Silence.

"You can get me out of here, that's what you can do."

Silence.

"I'm not walking out of this building unless I'm a free man. Until you can make that happen, don't call me again," he snarled, slamming the phone down. His abruptness made the hostages jump and a few let out whimpers.

The passing time became a constant reminder that nothing was happening, but Matt had confidence that his team stayed busy. Sweat dripped down between his shoulder blades. The room was hot, too hot. Stage one completed. Make the room uncomfortable. Looking around at the other hostages, he noticed that some of the men had unbuttoned their shirts. Nearly everyone had started to sweat and become flushed in the face.

Matt allowed himself a quick glimpse in Ava's direction. Her eyes were fixed on his, tears hanging on the brim of her long lashes, threatening to drop. Sweat matted her dark hair around her temples, her cheeks glowing with a dark pink color. While the gunmen continued in deep discussion, he swiftly grabbed her hand and squeezed, allowing a faint smile to tip up the outside corners of his lips to pass along encouragement.

The phone beside them started ringing, their moment lost. He removed his hand as quickly as he'd grabbed hold.

Eddie answered the phone hastily, "This better be good."

Silence.

"Well, you must not be working on it very hard."

Silence.

"If you want to talk with someone, than you can turn the air back on. Don't forget, I'm in charge here." He slammed the phone down.

Matt figured the gunmen had been speaking with their negotiator, Jim Reynolds. He earned his position as the best and would do everything in his power to have this situation end peacefully. Within minutes the air conditioner kicked back on and it didn't take long for the refreshing cool air to sweep across the floor.

The phone began ringing shortly afterward. Eddie's eyes narrowed at Ava. "Get up and answer it since you like to talk on the phone so much. Tell them you're fine."

& & & &

A VA'S LEGS WOBBLED. HER RIGHT FOOT STUNG WITH NUMBNESS from sitting for so long on the hard floor, but she scrambled to stand up before she was disciplined for her slowness.

"Hello?" Her voice cracked while she spoke.

"Hello. This is Sergeant Jim Reynolds. I'm the negotiator with the Rockford Police Department. Who am I speaking with?"

Looking out the windows toward the SWAT truck where she guessed Jim sat in; she almost started crying when she heard his voice. Ava had met Jim at a barbecue this summer. He and Matt were good work buddies.

"Ava … Ava Williams." She didn't know if it would be a blessing or a curse that he knew she was trapped inside the time bomb.

A pause followed.

"Ava, I know you're scared, but we have everything under

control. Is everyone okay?" Jim replied back into the receiver, trying to calm her.

She glanced down at the scared faces and the love of her life. "We are all okay. No one is hurt."

The gunman that had been called Eddie snatched the phone out of her hand, "There, you have your proof. Listen, I'm getting angry. Is that what you want? Do I have to start shooting people to get your attention, because if so, that can be arranged!"

A couple of women shrieked at his declaration. Ava quickly returned to her spot on the floor and dug her head down into her knees that she had pulled up against her chest. This couldn't be happening. Her eyes pooled with tears and a sniffle escaped. Tilting her head, she caught Matt watching her, but he broke eye contact immediately.

Sure she was scared, but not for the same reason as the other hostages. Matt would keep her safe, or die trying. He had already proved that when Ray attacked her. Her fear peaked from what he would do to protect her and the others. He would never allow the situation to come to people getting shot. These hostages had no idea the sacrifice he would make to keep them safe.

She couldn't lose Matt now, not when they finally found each other. Not when they were just starting their life together. It felt like a cruel joke.

Ava could tell that Matt had been keeping his distance, not wanting to give the captors any indication that they were together, but he was just going to have to get over it for a moment. She traced his face with her eyes, soaking up each detail. His dark hair that had become slightly shaggy around his ears, to the slight wrinkles that were etched around the outside of his eyes, down to his tight jaw, and over to his lips that hadn't captured hers enough times.

Eddie's heated voice cut into her thoughts. "Fine, I'll send out ten hostages. But if I'm not out of here in half an hour, did you hear me – half an hour – someone dies." Eddie shuffled nervously. "Now tell your men to back off or someone's blood will be on your hands." He hung up the phone and stared at it.

"Eddie, do you really think they will let us walk out of here? You're crazy if you believe them. Let's just surrender," the larger gunman urged, trying to reason with him.

"Surrender is not up for discussion, Mike. Now go unlock the door and I'll send some of them out."

Mike didn't move. Tension hung between them. Watching, Ava's heartbeat pounded against her chest. Finally conceding, Mike turned and walked over to the door. She let out a breath, not realizing she held it.

How was Matt analyzing the situation and assessing how the two gunmen were acting? She couldn't read him at all, especially when he held no emotion on his face. How did he stay so calm during this evident power trip between their captors?

Eddie walked up to the group, contemplating each person. "Okay, everyone on this side can go," he said, pointing to the opposite section of where she and Matt sat.

Once the group called out left, only seven hostages remained. A man that worked at the bank, the red-headed teller, two older women, a middle-aged man, herself and Matt.

Ava looked out the window and watched the police come toward the hostages that had been released. It was a bittersweet feeling. She still sat on the hard floor, afraid for her life and Matt's, but she watched mothers, fathers and grandparents returning safely to their families.

The clock mounted on the wall became an acrid reminder that there were only ten minutes left on the deadline. Panic filled Ava's veins, causing her hands to tremble. She had unfortunately become Eddie's little buddy and didn't know if she would wager on the side where he would spare her life, or put her up on the chopping block first. Ava's nerves were on edge, pushing her to feel claustrophobic.

She needed reassurance. If these were her last moments with Matt, she wasn't going to let some gunman dictate what she could control. Slipping her hand slowly across the tile floor, her contact with Matt's hand brought his attention. She let out a deep breath and mouthed the words, "I love you."

Matt mouthed the words right back, gripping her hand tighter.

"I can't do this much longer, Eddie," Mike complained, jolting their attention back to the gunmen. "They have ten minutes to meet *your* demands before you, what again, shoot someone? I didn't agree to that."

Eddie marched up to him, clearly irritated. "We have the upper hand here, Mike. These hostages are the ticket to our freedom." He pointed the gun at them. "Now grow a spine and do your job."

"And what exactly is my job? Obeying all of your commands while preparing to murder someone? If I recall, you're the one that got us into this mess, why should I listen to you?"

Nervously Ava scooted closer to Matt and further away from the fight that seemed on the verge of launching. She caught Matt subtly shift his body to block her from the gunman.

Eddie swore, pointing his gun at Mike. He became more irrational by the second. He stepped forward but stopped when the red-headed teller stood up.

"Please let me go. I can't take it. I have to get out of here." She took off running toward the door.

"Stop!" Eddie called after her, but her stride never broke despite his demand. He yelled at her again. When she didn't stop he raised his gun and shot in her direction. She fell to the ground uninjured, lifting her hands up over her face, begging him not to shoot again.

The hostages erupted, their cries bouncing around the

room, shuffling away from the gunmen, huddling together.

Matt shoved her across the floor toward the group, stood up, his gun drawn.

"Rockford Police, get down on the ground with your hands up!" Matt's tight, firm voice, belted out over the disorder.

Mike obeyed, throwing his gun down, sprawling out on the floor with his hands above his head. Eddie turned toward Matt, raising his gun at him.

"No!" The word tore out of her throat.

"Put the gun down!" Matt yelled.

Eddie aimed toward the group of hostages. A shot rang out.

CHAPTER THREE

AVA SAT WITH HER BACK AGAINST THE OUTSIDE WALL OF THE bank, leaning her head against the unyielding brick, watching the commotion swirl around her. She had been sitting here for over forty-five minutes and still her hands shook.

It was over. Matt's shot dropped Eddie like a load of bricks. What made her uneasy was that she hadn't seen Matt yet. The SWAT team had rushed in and evacuated all the hostages. She had been checked out by the EMTs, given her statement, watched Mike come out handcuffed and Eddie in a black bag, but still Matt had not left the bank. The media had begun storming the perimeter like a pack of lions with a red meat feast in front of them. People she didn't know attempted to comfort her, but all she wanted entailed Matt's arms around her.

Pure torture. That's what it was. To help pass the time, she found a secluded spot out of sight to decompress and wait. Finally, feeling her muscles relax, her eyelids grew heavy, she held no power to stop them. A shadow cut off the warmth of the sun, causing her eyes to pop open.

Matt's silhouette stood in front of her. Before she could push herself up to stand, he dropped to his knees and pulled her face into the crevasse of his neck. "Are you okay?" His voice faltered with raw emotion.

Breathing in his woodsy scent, her body melted into his

embrace. "I am now." Her words came out muffled against his warm skin. Pulling back, she placed her hands on both sides of his face, soaking in the fact that she could finally have him in her grasp. "Are you okay?"

Matt quickly transformed to cop mode. Reading him would be nearly impossible. He had just taken someone's life, for a good reason, but he had to have crazy emotions running through him no matter the cause. Would he let her in?

He shifted backwards, away from her touch. "Yep. We better get out of here before the media gets too intense." His words sounded tired, drawn out. He was shutting down, closing her off.

Reaching out, she placed her hands on his forearms, squeezing the muscles that flexed beneath her fingertips. "Maybe if we hibernate for the winter they will just leave us alone."

A soft smirk thawed onto his face. Mission accomplished. "I'd like to marry you first before we become hermits. That sounds much more enjoyable." He winked at her, causing her cheeks to flush with heat.

"We could run away."

"That's called a honeymoon … and don't tempt me." He stood, pulling her up with him. Her hand slid into his as they shortened the distance to his Jeep Wrangler, a comfortable silence between them.

Twenty yards from the vehicle shouts erupted behind them, voices muffled from the noise of flashes going off. Ava covered her face as an instant reaction to the cameras pointing at her. Matt took hold of her arm, pulling her behind him.

"Miss Williams, can you tell us what it was like to be a hostage inside the bank?" a woman's voice asked as she approached with a microphone.

"Ava, isn't it true that you and Sergeant Thompson are engaged?" Ava's heart sank when she recognized the reporter from the paper her brother, Jake, worked at, a fellow co-worker that Jake had mentioned would go to any extent to grab a story. A man that probably knew personal details of her life from just knowing Jake. No wonder the media had such a good inside scoop.

"Sergeant Thompson, can you tell us what happened in the bank? Did you shoot the deceased in order to save your finance?" Questions continued bombarding them.

Matt turned and clutched her into his arm, ushering her toward his Jeep. "No comment," he called over his shoulder while they scurried away from the ambush.

& & & &

"**M**ATT, WHAT ARE WE GOING TO DO?" AVA SHRIEKED AS they approached his Jeep. He passed on being the gentleman he normally strived to be. Instead of opening Ava's door, he more or less lightly pushed her toward the passenger side.

He ripped his keys out of his pocket and used the key fob to unlock the door for her while rushing around to his side. He didn't know how to answer her. He wasn't sure himself what they were going to do. Matt assumed the media would get wind of their relationship, he just didn't expect it this quickly.

Matt looked back in the direction of the bank. Thankfully the media stayed back. As he started the engine he stole a glace at Ava. She sat stiff, eyes wide open in shock while clutching her bag and purse against her chest.

"Seat belt," he quietly reminded her. She looked down at the latch, realizing for the first time that it wasn't buckled.

"Oh ... yeah, thanks," she stammered in a foggy tone. Robotically she fastened her seat belt and finally glanced over at him. Her electric blue eyes had become a semblance of a deep pool. She looked fragile and he wished he had a safety harness to add for better protection.

He squeezed her hand and got the Jeep rolling before their delay sparked more unwanted attention from their fan club.

Once they drove a couple miles away, Matt finally relaxed and took his first deep breath. Ava also appeared more at ease. Her breathing had slowed down and her face regained its normal color.

"So … what are we going to do?" Ava's repeated question was quiet and held a hint of caution as it hung in the air.

"I'm thinking your earlier suggestion of running away sounds good right about now." Matt was relieved to see her smile.

She playfully shrugged her shoulders, displaying a smug grin. "I didn't think now was a good time to say 'I told you so.'"

And Ava was back.

His laughter filled the Jeep. "I appreciate your humbleness."

She joined in with her own sweet laughter. "Seriously, what just happened back there?" she asked through an eruption of giggles while she turned and pointed behind them. "It was like we were on the celebrity A-list. All that was missing was the massive paparazzi zoom lens."

Matt wasn't sure if it was really this funny to her or if she had begun the stages of an emotional meltdown. The next ten minutes would probably reveal this spirited response. Until then, he would just enjoy the show.

"I need to run to the station, finish up a few loose ends for the detective on the case. We could do a late dinner if you are still up for it?" he asked once her laughter drizzled to a stop, not sure if he was even up for it himself. A public place did not sound appealing at the moment and he held no appetite. But what mattered right now was caring for Ava's needs. What would be best for her.

"How about we just stay in tonight?" He looked over at her, lifting his eyebrows in response. She giggled. "Sorry, let me clarify. Let's get take-out and eat it at my apartment."

It came as an asset that he knew his way around the kitchen because, otherwise, once they were married, he would be gaining weight by how much they would be eating out. It wasn't like Ava was a horrible cook, she was just … simple. She didn't like to cook so she didn't put a lot of effort into improving the skill.

"Good plan."

She leaned her head back against the headrest, rotating to look at him, her black hair spilling over her shoulders with a bounce of curl at the ends. Her demeanor changed slightly, becoming more serious, clearly studying him. "You did great in the bank. Thank you for protecting me and all those people." She reached over and enclosed her small hand in his.

Her declaration held so much value. How did he end up having this woman love him when he felt so unworthy of it? Matt had felt defeated since they left the bank, wondering if deep down she was appalled by witnessing him kill someone. He did his job and held no regrets, but it didn't make ending a life any easier.

Ava's simple words weren't merely to make him feel better, she meant them. She trusted him without a hint of doubt and that truth fill him with determination.

"I will protect you until my dying breath."

"I know. I think that's what scared me the most in the bank."

His emotions caught in his throat. Needing to steer clear of this subject, he changed it. "Since I need to run to the station, why don't you call Jules and have her come stay with you?" He didn't feel comfortable with her being alone right now not knowing what lengths the media would go to for an interview or footage of Ava.

She sighed a breath of relief. He could sense she didn't want to be alone either. She pulled out her phone. "Is it okay if she stays to eat with us?"

"Sure. I'll bring food when I come back. What sounds good?"

"Chinese." She tapped her pointer finger against her chin. "Since you're paying, I'll take something with shrimp."

He laughed. "Geez, you are so high maintenance."

She winked at him while her call connected to Jules, her best friend since elementary school. He listened to the lifelong friends talk. Ava didn't have to say much. She asked. Julia came.

Ava ended the call as Matt drove up to the curb of the main entrance of her apartment complex. He scanned the perimeter, making sure they weren't going to have the same problem here as they did at the bank. He had also kept a close eye on his rearview mirror to detect if they had anyone following them. So far everything seemed clear.

"Jules will be here in ten minutes."

He finished his search and locked his eyes with hers. "Okay. I'll walk you in and wait until she gets here."

"You don't have to. I'll be fine."

"Ava, I'm staying."

❧ ❧ ❧ ❧

"THOMPSON, THIS SITUATION HAS ESCALATED MORE THAN I like." The Chief stroked his mustache while listening to Matt's summary of the media catching wind of his relationship with Ava.

The Chief's small office reined in tighter as Matt's blood pressure spiked. After he'd wrapped things up with the detective, he'd headed straight to the Chief.

It wasn't procedure to speak with Chief Miller, more of a

personal step. Chief Miller had replaced his dad as Chief of Police and they still remained close friends. Matt respected Chief Miller and wanted his opinion on the situation.

Matt sneaked a look over at Derek, hoping for some sort of encouragement, but a shrug was all he got in return. While on his way to the station, Matt had called him. Derek had become like a brother to him and he also trusted his opinion and advice. He was still at the station and agreed without hesitation to stick around. A lot of help he was now.

"I agree, Sir. I'm here for suggestions."

The Chief leaned back against his oversized leather chair, bridging his fingertips together. "Lay low. The media will stir things up for a couple days, and then it should fizzle out. Let our communication experts speak for you." The Chief pushed himself up and walked around to the front of his desk and sat down on the edge, facing the two chairs that Matt and Derek occupied.

Matt looked over at Derek, who had decided to become mute for the meeting. "What do you think?"

Derek leaned his elbows on his knees and looked down at his shoes. He looked up as he answered, "I'd agree. Keeping a low profile is the best option. Maybe have Ava take a couple days off work."

Matt sucked in a deep breath and nodded his head in reluctant admission.

"Where is Ava now?" the chief asked.

"I dropped her off at her apartment and told her not to leave until I return."

Matt had left Ava's place confident that she would be safe. Jules came prepared for the evening with a suitcase packed, ready to spend the night. It had been hard to leave Ava. The kiss he left her with was explanation enough of how he felt. Matt had departed chortling while Jules made gagging noises from the kitchen.

"Good idea. Now if the two of you will excuse me, I have a late dinner date with my wife." Chief Miller made his way back around his desk, clearly finished with the meeting at hand.

Matt stood and Derek followed suit. "Thank you, Sir."

As the partners made their way to the door, the Chief called out. "Oh Thompson, I assume you have a clean bill of health to return to work?" He pointed at his shoulder now barren of a sling.

"Yes, I can start next week."

"Great. You will continue to supervise the activities of your subordinates and your Captain will make sure your evaluation gets scheduled quickly so you can return to active duty, but with your extra free time until then, we have a position that needs filled. You will be put with Detective Bennett in the narcotics department. You can check in with him when you return."

The matter of fact statement threw Matt a curve ball. He had expected to be filing or stuck behind a computer entering data for the next couple weeks while his vision crossed. Working in narcotics sounded appealing, an area he'd never given much thought to.

The Chief looked up from his papers. "That's all. Tell your dad he still owes me a rematch golf game." He dropped his eyes back to his desk.

"Yes, Sir." Matt shut the door behind him and picked up his pace to meet up with Derek heading into the locker room.

Only a few officers remained at their desks after a long and grueling day while the night shift started to stroll in. A woman stood at the counter talking with an officer, her features frustrated as if her demands had not been met. He was thankful his desk duty would not be behind that particular counter.

Matt pushed open the door leading into the locker room and found Derek by his locker, loading up his duffle bag to leave for the day.

Derek looked up as Matt entered. "Hey, man. Congrats on the shoulder healing. I was hoping you'd be able to get back to work. I've needed someone to fill my coffee."

Matt rolled his eyes while straddling the bench that split the two sides of lockers. "Now he speaks."

"Yeah, sorry about that." He slammed his locker shut and threw his duffle over his shoulder. "Thought it would be best if I just stayed quiet, let the two of you work out the logistics."

"Well, then to make up for your sudden bout with silence, you can come with me back to the apartment and help me talk with Ava."

"Do I get dinner out of it?"

"Yeah, I'm picking up Chinese for the girls on the way home."

"Girls?"

"Jules is over at the apartment with Ava."

Derek stopped walking at the mention of Jules' name. "I don't know Matt. It didn't go so well when I met her at your engagement party this past weekend. I'm not sure she wants to see me."

Matt slapped Derek on the back. "Since when did you ever walk away from a challenge?"

CHAPTER FOUR

"WHAT DO YOU MEAN DEREK IS COMING?"

Julia Anderson spun around so quickly on the leather couch it made a high pitch squeal from the fabric rubbing against her jeans. Ava had just finished her phone call with Matt, announcing the unwelcome news. She expected Chinese, not egotistical company.

Her sharp response stopped Ava in her tracks as a cloud of confusion settled in her eyes. She tipped her head to the side. "You don't like Derek? At the engagement party it looked like you two were hitting it off."

Jules wasn't sure how to retort. The whole situation made her embarrassed and maddened, her energy building like an atom ready to explode. She let out a sigh, allowing her frustration to trickle out with her breath.

"I thought so, too."

"So what's wrong?"

Ever since Matt and Ava had started dating, she had heard all about Derek. What a noble guy he was. Charming. Good looking. Funny. A great catch for some lucky girl. Jules had been dating someone, so her interest had never been peaked to meet the infamous Derek Brown. Since she ended her relationship with Doctor Scott Henson, she had noticed Ava hinting around about them needing to meet, but she'd never pushed the subject. Jules still couldn't believe that she and

Derek had yet to cross paths. She thought for sure when Matt was recovering from his gunshot wound in the hospital where she worked that she would bump into him, but it never happened. It was as if they were meant to stay apart ... until two days ago.

Jules sat around the campfire at Matt and Ava's engagement party, roasting a marshmallow for her s'more, when Derek sat down beside her and introduced himself.

She had seen a picture of him, but the print did him no justice. His over six-foot height, tousled blond hair, strong features and muscular frame spoke of strength and confidence. His smile lit up his entire face. She could have drowned in his baby blue eyes.

Their conversation sparked immediately, as if they had known each other for years. Jules couldn't remember the last time she had laughed so hard. His quick wit and outgoing personality had summoned her heart without any rebuttal.

His flirtatious spirit toward her came across warm, not aggressive. His tender hint of interest made her feel special and appealing, a nice change since her last relationship had ended emotionally brutal for her. When Derek asked if she would have coffee with him sometime the following week, her heart sped up with excitement.

Before Jules could accept his request, the moment was crushed by a beautiful blonde woman who called his name with affection and leaned down, kissing the same lips that had been pursuing her.

Once free to talk, Derek leaned back, shock etched across his face. "Chelsea. Um ... I didn't think you were going to be able to make it?" he stammered, while stealing a quick glance in Jules' direction.

"I took an earlier flight home." She continued to talk about her day, oblivious to the conversation that she had interrupted. She looked over in Jules' direction, noticing her for

the first time.

"I'm sorry, I hope that I didn't interrupt." She stuck out her hand in Julia's space, giving her no chance to retreat. "Hi, I'm Chelsea."

Jules accepted her invitation of introductions, hoping her voice wouldn't quiver. "I'm Julia."

Her face brightened. "Ava's best friend. It's nice to finally meet you."

Jules wanted so much to not like this woman that just walked in and dropped this bomb of surprise. However, only sweetness dripped from her southern drawl. It wasn't Chelsea's fault she had fallen for a fraud. She, too, had fallen prey to his charlatan charm.

Jules stood up, brushing the dirt from her jeans. "I'll leave you two alone. Have a good evening."

As she walked away she overheard Derek excuse himself, mentioning something about getting Chelsea a drink. They were in Ava's parents' backyard, a home she practically grew up in. She spotted the back door with the porch light on, beckoning her for an escape. Making her way as quickly as she could toward her exit, she hoped she would make it before the shock wore off, revealing her trampled disposition.

Footsteps followed her. Derek called out her name but she continued into the house, pretending she couldn't hear him.

He caught up to her in the kitchen. "Jules, this isn't what it looks like."

She spun around, her arms crossing tightly across her chest. "Oh really, because it looks like your girlfriend just arrived and kissed you."

He stepped closer.

She backed up.

"Just let me explain."

"There is no need. You don't owe me anything. Oh, and about that coffee. My schedule just filled up." She twisted her

tall and slender frame back around and continued to the bathroom where she hibernated until she heard him recoil back outside.

Jules pulled herself together, giving herself a much-needed pep talk regarding the evening being about Matt and Ava, not her. She made her way back out to the party, trying her best to fly under the radar of any attention, especially that of Derek.

"Julia ... Jules!" Ava's voice broke through her memories.

"What?"

"Are you just going to sit there with a blank stare on your face or tell me what happened with Derek?" She placed her hands on her hips, her body language clearly expressing her impatience.

Jules took a deep breath. Ava didn't need this. She had just dealt with a bank robbery and the media shoved in her face, all security and privacy stolen, and here she was concerned about her. She very rarely held any information from Ava. It seemed like lately, though, her secrets had been multiplying.

Ava respected and thought highly of Derek, and Jules didn't want to be the one to taint her view of him. "It's nothing."

"Let me be the judge of that." Ava took up the spot next to her on the couch, settling in to listen.

Jules caved and started spewing all the details of two nights ago. She made sure to give only the facts and kept her words tight, refraining from embellishing on that night's storyline. Ava stayed uncommonly quiet throughout Jules's entire narrative. Usually she would interrupt with questions or input, but she sat with her hand over her mouth, eyes wide. Remorse filled Jules at having to break the news to her that Matt's best friend was a jerk, but she'd asked. When she finished, Ava sat still as a smile crept behind the hand that flashed a sparkling diamond displayed on her ring finger.

Why was she smiling? This was a no-smile zone.

Did Ava not understand what she just said?

"Oh Jules, I wish you had told me about this earlier."

"I wish you had told me about Chelsea."

"You should have let him explain."

Jules didn't hide her confusion. Did she need to repeat the part about when the happy couple had locked lips? "Ava, please stop speaking in code and just tell me what I'm missing."

Ava turned on the couch to sit cross-legged and brought her palms together, pressing her fingertips to her lips. "Okay. Yes, Derek and Chelsea had been dating." Ava put her hand up to deflect the response that sat on the tip of Jules's tongue. "However, in the last month he has been realizing that they are just not meant to be together. They had discussed it and decided to take a little break. Last week Chelsea had to go out of town for business, and he didn't feel right about breaking things off with her over the phone, so he was waiting until she returned home." She waited a moment to punch the final blow. "He broke things off with her that night after the party."

"Oh," was all she could muster.

She felt like a heel.

"Granted, he should not have asked you out before he had ended things with Chelsea." Ava's smile widened. "However, I don't think he anticipated feelings to spark so quickly between the two of you."

"It was just coffee, Ava."

"Uh-huh."

A knock at the door frayed the rest of their conversation. Matt's voice spoke on the other side of the wooden door, announcing their arrival. Derek stood less than ten feet away from her and she was in no condition to see him. She needed more than five seconds to wrap her mind around the explanation Ava had just shared.

Jules wasn't sure if she still needed to be upset by him pursuing her while, in Chelsea's eyes, still in a relationship. Her anger began to dissipate but decided that putting a wall around her heart concerning Derek Brown would be a good idea. It was best to keep him at arm's length, cordial and friendly, but at a distance. She was still trying to heal from the wake of pain Scott had left behind.

Ava patted Jules' knee while she called out that she was coming. "Go to the bathroom and take a moment," Ava whispered.

Jules released a breath and glanced down at her jeans and sweatshirt, realizing that this was the first instant since she heard that Derek was coming that she cared what she looked like.

She made it to the microscopic room Ava called a bathroom before the guys entered the apartment, letting her nerves settle. She pulled out Ava's make-up case and allowed herself the time to freshen up. Jules heard the commotion as the men stepped inside. Was Derek as nervous as she was? Their first encounter had failed miserably, but she would do her part to make sure the second would end in harmony. Dating was off the table, but maybe at least they could salvage a friendship. She opened the door, pressing a smile upon her face.

CHAPTER FIVE

THE KITCHEN NOISE INCREASED IN VOLUME AS AVA'S FAMILY trickled in for the evening. It was their traditional bi-weekly Sunday family night at her parent's house. Ava's family had always been close and her parents were determined to keep it that way. They had been doing this for years and unless it was unavoidable, no one missed.

Ava had been looking forward to tonight all week because of the extra guests joining them. Over the last month her twin older brothers, Jake and Josh, had each started to date. Tonight they chose the début of their special interests to be the same night so neither woman would feel like the center of attention.

Jake had reunited with his girlfriend from high school, Erica Miles, at a reunion over the summer. They had rekindled their old flame quickly and Ava wouldn't be surprised if Erica had a ring on her finger by Christmas.

Josh's relationship on the other hand, was more delicate and needed to move slower. He and Valerie Walker had started out as friends and were slowly testing the idea of a serious relationship. The leisureliness wasn't for the lack of feelings, but because of Valerie's assorted past.

Josh stayed tight-lipped about her journey that had brought her to Rockford, Illinois. All he elucidated was that Valerie had been married before and it ended badly. When she had asked for details, he said that Valerie would explain someday when she felt comfortable. All he would say is that he didn't care about her past or ex-husband. She had found the Lord and was giving her life to Him. "The past is the past," is the quote he stood by when he spoke gingerly of Valerie. The main cause for their hesitance centered on her three-year-old son, Aaron. This was her first time dating and she sensed caution for her son's emotions.

The family all knew Valerie from church. They liked her and were excited that she made the plunge to come tonight. Valerie couldn't have found a better man to start this journey with. However, Ava's opinion might be slightly biased.

"Lucy, what do you want me to do next?" Ava looked up from the veggie mixture of peppers, squash, onions and zucchini she had just chopped to go on the grill with the steaks their mom had splurged on for dinner.

Her younger sister shut the oven door after sticking in the pan of cheesy potatoes. She glanced around the kitchen, going through a check list. "I think that's it. Mom is finishing up the appetizers. Erica volunteered to help make dessert. Dad just went outside to fire up the grill. You are officially off kitchen duty."

Ava turned to Erica. The years since they'd last seen each other hadn't altered Ava's memory of her. Erica still had a bubbly personality and sincere spirit. Besides the golden highlights that streaked through her now long brown hair, there wasn't much of a change. "Feel privileged that she agreed you can help make something. I'm only allowed to bring drinks and cut things up."

"Ava, you know pudding made from a box is unacceptable," Lucy interjected, referring to the one and only time she gave Ava the job of bringing dessert. Lucy was a renowned chef at a restaurant downtown and was very picky about what was on the menu.

"I put them in pretty glass cups." She smiled, enjoying the

friendly banter with her younger sister.

"Yes … and a pig that lives in a palace is still a pig."

Ava threw the towel she held at Lucy while they both erupted with laughter over her comment. She and Lucy were very close but came as different as two people could be. Lucy was carefree, vibrant, cooked gourmet meals and painted exquisite paintings. Ava was more reserved, steady, cooking came from a box, and she drew stick figures.

The front door opened with Josh's voice echoing down the hallway announcing his arrival. "Well, since I'm relieved of my duties, I'll see if I'm needed elsewhere."

"I'm sure Matt could use a little TLC … it has been twenty minutes since he's seen you," Lucy called after her, with a tint of teasing in her voice.

"Nah, I hear distance makes the heart grow fonder," she countered over her shoulder while exiting.

"Hey, I heard that!" Matt hollered from the living room where he and Jake sat watching a football game.

He met her in the hallway, not allowing her to pass without a hug.

"How's the game going?"

"It's halftime and the Bears are up by a touchdown. I'm going to see if your dad wants some company at the grill."

Happiness swelled around her heart. She loved how well he got along with her family. It wasn't a show, brown-nosing or trying to prove himself to anyone. Plain and simple, he considered her family as his own. On many occasions he would call up Jake and Josh and they would end up at a table at Buffalo Wild Wings eating wings and watching the big game of the week.

"Sounds good. I'm going to go say hi to Aaron and give him the gift we brought for him. We'll meet you out back."

Ava retrieved the bag that sprouted tissue paper from the top and found Aaron sitting on the couch between Josh and

Valerie. Once she came into view of Aaron, he smiled and jumped off the couch. She knelt down to receive his hug.

"Hi Aaron, I'm glad you got to come tonight," she said, tousling his bleached blond hair. Ava taught his Sunday School class at church, which gave them a head start in their friendship.

Ava looked up at the couch. "Hi," she directed her greeting to Josh and Valerie. After they shared responses, Ava turned her attention to Valerie. "Would it be okay if Aaron and I went outside to play until dinner? Matt and I got him a few things." She lifted the bag as proof.

"Sure. He would like that. Thanks."

Ava's parents didn't have very many young guests visit and didn't hide their poke at needing grandchildren. Their gift wasn't much, just a few things to keep him entertained for the evening since her parents didn't have many treasures for a three-year-old to play with. Sidewalk chalk, a Nerf football, coloring book with crayons, a toy car and dinosaur sat in the bag waiting to be opened as she and Aaron made their way out to the back porch.

& & & &

THE OAK DINING ROOM TABLE HELD A FEW CONVERSATIONS GO-ing on at once while the ten of them scooched together, elbows touching. If their family kept growing at this rapid rate, Ava's parents were going to need a bigger table, she reflected, as she watched everyone interact. Erica and Valerie fit in quickly. It was easy to tell they felt comfortable and at ease. Aaron stole the show and giggled when everyone pretended to fight over sitting next to him.

Ava didn't hide her smugness when he chose her.

"So have things settled down since the bank robbery?" The question that her father, Steven, targeted towards Matt and Ava silenced the group.

It had been almost two weeks since the bank robbery. The first week had been uncomfortable for Ava. She had agreed to Matt's suggestion that she take a couple days off work to keep out of the public eye. Returning to the social arena proved to be difficult at first. People *noticed* her. She was no longer just a stranger in the mix. Some would just stand and gawk, while others had become more aggressive and came up to talk to her.

Last weekend Matt took her to visit Kim, who had moved in with her sister after her final brutal attack from Ray. Matt claimed the trip was a time to go and reconnect, but Ava was certain the road trip was his sly way to keep her mind off of what had happened and get them out of town for a couple days.

"Yes. Life is starting to feel normal again," Matt added, looking in her direction while she nodded her agreement.

"I'm sorry you two had to go through all that." Josh wore his concern thick across his brow.

"Me, too," Jake attached.

"The article in the paper covering the bank robbery was great," Ava confirmed to Jake. He was still beating himself up, putting the blame on himself for the media outburst over their relationship. No matter how many times Ava reassured him she wasn't upset, it didn't take away the guilt that marred his features. He made it his personal goal to make sure the newspaper handled the story with class.

"It was the least I could do."

Ava smiled, letting him know she held no hard feelings, while Erica settled her hand into Jake's, creating her own comfort.

"I still can't believe the segment the news put in about the wife of the robber … that … was killed." Lucy's voice trailed off, realizing the touchy issue she had brought up for Matt.

Her face scrunched up in remorse.

"It's okay, Lucy, we can talk about it," Matt assured her.

The news station had not only interviewed a few of the hostages, but also Eddie McCallum's wife, Sabrina. The poor woman had cried through most of the interview, adamant that her husband was a good man, just trying to provide for her since he lost his job over the summer. They were close to losing their house and desperate times produced desperate measures. It never ceased to amaze Ava what different problems had arisen when the economy dropped out years ago.

"I feel sorry for her. She seemed hopeless … but better her husband than either of you," Lucy finally added.

"I just don't understand what they were trying to achieve. Why put her through such an emotional interview and then finish by exploiting Matt and Ava's relationship and how they are happily engaged?" Erica pointed out. "It just seemed disrespectful."

Ava had been feeling the same way and often found herself praying comfort and peace over Sabrina McCallum. She couldn't imagine the heartache the woman went through daily. Did she have friends and family around to help her through this grieving process? Did she know the Lord? How was she handling her grief and loss? The questions constantly came to the surface, dredging up the past because of the present.

Stealing a peek at Aaron, she noticed Valerie keeping the young child entertained with his coloring book while the adults held their discussion. Ava couldn't help but wonder what pain and hardship Valerie had gone through in her own lifetime.

"I agree," Matt infused himself back into the conversation. "Even though the man was dangerous and his death couldn't be avoided, it doesn't take away from the fact he still had people who loved him."

"Where does the police department stand about how things

ended?" Ava's father asked, resting his forearms on top of the table.

"My Captain and IA have signed off that I handled the situation in the best professional way." He reached up to rub Ava's shoulder. "Ava did a great job handling the high stress situation with such ease."

Confirmations erupted around the table.

"Subject change. So I heard through the grapevine that you had Ava's ring quite awhile before you gave it to her. So spill it, how long?" Valerie's quiet inquiry brought much-needed laughter to the group.

Matt and Ava shared a smile before he answered, "The day after she told me she loved me."

Soft "aww's" escaped the lips of the women.

"Speaking of, have you two decided on a date yet?" Ava's mom questioned.

Ava had been waiting all evening to make their announcement. They had finally found time last night to sit down and carve out a date, agreeing that they couldn't wait long.

"December 20th."

"That's only three months away!" Lucy squealed.

"Well, if I had my choice, it would be next weekend." Laughter filled the table from Matt's confession.

"Then that doesn't leave us with much time." Ava's mom stood up, gathering the empty dishes. "Come on, girls, let's clean up. We have a wedding to plan."

CHAPTER SIX

Ava TURNED THE WINDSHIELD WIPERS UP A NOTCH AS THE RAIN increased. At the four-way stop sign she turned on the internal light to get a better look at the directions scribbled on a yellow sticky note. She had forgotten her phone charger and didn't want to deplete her battery from using the GPS. Matt had one on his, but unfortunately he wasn't with her tonight.

She tried to keep her disappointment at bay.

It wasn't working.

Since Matt had returned to work a few weeks ago he had become overly-zealous about picking up any available extra work. She never would have imagined that his "desk duty" would create such a busy schedule for him. It seemed he was trying to make up for the time while off work … for being shot.

Today marked the second Saturday in October and she and Matt planned to babysit Aaron tonight while Josh took Valerie out for her birthday. She'd received his call a half-hour before they needed to leave, explaining that he was running late and would meet her there later in the evening. He and a fellow officer were at the mall passing out brochures for drug aware-ness. Matt offered to cover the last shift so his replacement could go to his daughter's piano recital.

It was hard to be annoyed when she was marrying a man

with such a big heart. He claimed he would make it up to her. She would hold him to it. Ava began to look forward to their honeymoon, just for the fact that she would have him all to herself.

Ava placed her headlights on bright to get a better look at the numbers on the mailboxes. There was a good chance she had already missed Valerie's house with her lack of concentration. Four houses down her numbers matched. She turned left into the drive.

Josh answered the door looking spiffy in khakis and a dressy long-sleeved blue shirt that highlighted his eyes. "Wow, you look great, big brother." She leaned in to give him a hug as he shut the door behind her.

"Thanks. No Matt?"

Ava sighed from Josh unknowingly pouring salt in her wound. "He's running late."

"I don't think Aaron will be too sad to have you all to himself." As the words left his lips, Aaron bounded down the hall toward her, calling her name while clasping onto her leg, giving it a tight squeeze. "See."

She bent down, cuddling him in a hug. "Hi, Aaron."

"Hi, Awa." His little lisp got her every time.

Josh stepped forward and put his hands on the toddler's slender shoulders. "Ava, would you mind going upstairs and checking on Valerie? She's been up there for awhile."

"Sure."

Josh nudged his head towards the stairs. "Second door on the right." He leaned down to Aaron's level. "Come on, buddy, let's go find you something to eat. Who knows what you'd eat if it was left up to Ava."

Ava stuck her tongue out at her brother as she started up the stairs on her recovery mission. Pictures lined the wall that took Ava on a journey of Aaron's young life. Valerie holding him on her chest after delivery, his first birthday with chocolate cake covering his face, and the two of them sitting on the front porch in a frame that said "our first home."

She reached the second door, letting her knuckles rap lightly against the wood. It swung open from being unlatched, giving her a six-inch view of Valerie sitting on the edge of her bed staring down at her shoes, making no effort to put them on. The intrusion broke her solemn gaze and a painful smile lightly touched her lips.

"Hey, Val. Everything okay?"

"Yes … no … Oh, Ava, I'm a mess."

Ava made her way into the soft ivory and white room that Valerie claimed as hers. Ava hadn't been very far throughout Valerie's home, but what she could see affirmed that she had very good taste and a gift for decorating; hence her job as an interior decorator at a small company in the city. Wherever she and Matt decided to live, she already made mental plans to persuade Valerie to help her enhance their new place.

As Ava approached she noticed Valerie's eyes full of moisture. She made her way to Valerie's side and sat down on the bed next to her. "Well, you give new meaning to the phrase, 'a hot mess.' You look great."

Valerie wore a black skirt with a ruffled silk purple blouse that accentuated her slim figure. She had her butterscotch tinted hair pulled back as her bangs fell delicately across her forehead. As she smiled a tear escaped, "I'm just so nervous." She took a deep breath, wiping away the tear as her laughter held no humor. "This is my first time out with Josh. Alone. I haven't been out on a date in … well, a very long time."

Ava draped her arm over Valerie's shoulder. "I don't know how much Josh told you about my past, but I know how scary a first date can be after years of trying to avoid them."

"He told me. Seems like Matt was a good one to start with."

"Yeah, he's all right."

Ava's dry humor finally brought forth a genuine smile,

highlighting Valerie's cheekbones that held a rosy blush color. "I really like your brother."

"I know. He really likes you."

"I know."

Ava patted her hands on her knees and pushed herself off the bed. "Then I think you need to go touch up your make-up and get this evening started. Plus, I'm ready to have Aaron all to myself. I play a mean game of Candy Land. The poor kid won't know what hit him."

Valerie followed her cue and giggled. She slipped on her shoes and stood up. "Thanks, Ava. Tell Josh I'll be right down … and that he doesn't have to worry about me."

Ava reflected her smile. "I'll relay the message."

*& *& *& *&

VA COLLAPSED ONTO THE OVERSIZED CHAIR, RESTING HER FEET on the ottoman in front of her. The clock claimed that it was eight-thirty, but it felt like midnight. Toddlers were a lot of work. Every second of her evening with Aaron had been full of an activity. They had played two games of Candy Land, destroyed a village with dinosaurs, wrestled until Ava became short of breath, built a tent that would impress a general in the Army, gave Aaron a bath – which resulted in Ava wishing she had brought an extra change of clothes, and a snack that defeated the purpose of giving him a bath. Finally, after reading five books, she watched his eyes slowly flutter closed.

The doorbell rang as she began to wonder when Matt would arrive. Right on cue. Hopping out of the chair, all tiredness left as she rushed to the door, anticipating Matt's strong arms around her. Maybe they could raid Valerie's movie selection and spend the night cuddling on the couch.

Flinging open the door, Ava let out a quiet startle, realizing the visitor was not Matt. A man stood on the opposite side of the threshold with his jacket zipped up and his hood badly attempting to shield his hair from the downpour of rain.

His reaction appeared as shocked as hers. "Oh, I'm sorry. I must have the wrong house." He pulled out his phone, checking something on the screen, and then peered back around at the side of the door.

"Can I help you?" Ava didn't know Valerie's neighborhood well and probably wouldn't be much help for the stranger trying to find the house he wanted. It just seemed like the polite thing to say.

"Yes. I'm looking for Valerie … Walker."

"Oh, this is Valerie's house. She isn't here right now, but I'd be happy to leave a message for her."

A dark look spread across the man's features and Ava wished she had just shut the door on him earlier instead of continuing the conversation. "There's no need. I'll just wait for her."

Without warning the man pushed the door open. Ava's nerves went wild with fear. He pulled his hood back, exposing his dripping sandy blond hair while quickly scanning the living room. Ava tried to remember where she had left her phone. Panic rose in her chest. It wasn't like she could just bolt out the door. Aaron was upstairs sleeping.

And she would do all she could to protect him.

"You need to leave." Ava's words stammered as she tried to talk over the lump in her throat.

"I haven't even introduced myself. I'm Chad Taylor, Valerie's ex-husband."

His gruff, unapologetic words packed a punch that Ava didn't see coming. She didn't know much about Valerie's past, but what she did know, this man was trouble. And she believed him on who he claimed to be. Aaron was a mini version of the man standing in front of her – from the blond shaggy hair to the blue eyes and slight dimple embedded in the tip of his chin. Was it hard for Valerie to be constantly reminded of this man every time she looked at her precious son?

Had Valerie been in contact with him? By the way Josh talked, they had no communication. Valerie would have said something if she knew her ex-husband was in town or coming over for a visit. But he didn't know for sure that this was even her house. Her mind raced through the possibilities.

It didn't feel right. And the evil that sparked his eyes a deep color confirmed her fear.

"You need to leave."

"I'm not going anywhere until I see my son."

At the mention of Aaron, Ava gasped and her eyes faintly flickered up the stairs. He caught sight of her brief indication to the second floor.

"Is he here?"

Ava had to cover her tracks, and quick. *Oh Lord, give me wisdom and keep us safe!* She had to get this man out of the house before he found Aaron. Where did she leave her phone? Her panic created an inability to think rationally. She searched the entry way and the table that held the large bouquet of red roses Josh had brought for Valerie. Empty. *Think, Ava!* Matt had texted her before she went upstairs to put Aaron to bed, saying he was finishing up and would be there soon. She placed the phone on … the end table in the living room.

Distract him, Ava. Get him to leave! "No. He and Valerie went on a trip this weekend and I am just here to house-sit." As she spoke she gradually made her way into the living room. "Let me find a piece of paper and pen and you can write her a note. I'm still not real familiar with the house, so give me a sec." Ava slowly walked backwards into the room to keep her sight on the intruder.

She found her phone on the end table and slid it down to the side of the table, hopeful her sly move didn't catch his attention. With her left hand she fidgeted with the knob to open the drawer and with her right she punched in 911 on her phone. She dropped the phone onto the carpet while the drawer opened up, hoping it masked the sound.

She took a few seconds, pretending to search for those items, to let the call connect. "No paper here. Let me go check another room."

Ava's hands trembled as she slid the drawer closed. The dispatcher would be confused when only background noise could be heard. With very little information would they be able to track where her cell phone was and send someone to check out the situation? At least that was what she silently prayed for.

"I think I'll just check things out for myself." Chad held a crooked smile that made Ava's skin crawl.

She couldn't let him get upstairs. Ava scanned the living room looking for a weapon she could use if force was needed. As Chad turned around and headed toward the stairs, Ava knew there was only one thing she could do. She needed to bring his attention back to her. Reaching down, she grabbed her phone.

Her voice screeched into the phone. "Help me. There is an intruder in my house!" Ava rattled off Valerie's address to the best of her memory as quickly as she could while relief sprouted throughout her body from hearing confirmation on the other end. Ava dropped the phone. Her hands grabbed the closest object to her, a plant. It wasn't much of a weapon, but it was better than her other option of a pillow.

Chad stormed into the living room.

"Go away. The police are on their way!" She threw the plant at him and grabbed a picture frame next.

His faced turned a deep shade of red as he pointed his finger at her. "You just made a horrible mistake. I have a right to see my own son!" His voice hollered, echoing back against the deep tan walls.

Ava began to fear the worst as her silent questions bombarded her. *What if the commotion wakes up Aaron and he comes downstairs? Would this awful man take Aaron and run? Would I be able to stop him if he tried?* Nausea set in as bile caught in her throat.

His anger propelled him a step closer. Ava scurried behind the couch, giving her an exit toward the kitchen if she needed one. When cleaning up the kitchen from Aaron's snack she saw the knives displayed in a wood block by the refrigerator. Dread filled her stomach at the thought of needing a knife, but she needed to be prepared.

The frame went flying next.

"Get out of here!" Her breath became rapid and shallow. Ava wished she remembered where she'd placed her purse. Matt had given her pepper spray as a precaution when they became known all around the city. She thought he was overreacting. Now she wished she had three. Reaching over, she grabbed a candle from the bookshelf.

The sound of sirens in the distance made Chad hold up as he began to take another step closer. "*You* will regret this!" His voice burned with fury and malice as he threatened her. His eyes narrowed as he held her gaze. With a final look of disgust, he turned and ran out the door.

Ava heard the door slam. She dropped the candle and melted onto the floor.

CHAPTER SEVEN

MATT JOGGED OUT TO HIS CRUISER, ALREADY PLAGUED WITH guilt that he didn't spend the evening with Ava and Aaron, but to be this late … groveling reached first priority in his plan of action. Jumping into his driver's seat he ran his fingers through his thick brown hair as a squeegee absorbing the excess dampness from the heavy rain. Pulling out his cell phone, he tried reaching Ava again. She wasn't picking up her phone.

After her voice mail picked up for the second time, he snapped his phone back onto his holster next to his gun and decided groveling in person would be more efficient anyway. Valerie's neighborhood was located not far from the mall and by the time he'd get to an apology, he would be pulling into the drive.

Five minutes later he turned onto Valerie's street. Alarm touched his senses as he took in the flashing red and blue lights a good hundred yards down the road. Two police cruisers sat parked in front of a two-story, cottage-style house. Trepidation pushed his blood pressure higher as he spotted Josh and Ava's vehicles in the drive.

Parking his cruiser at the curb, he took off running through the yard to the front door. Without knocking he walked into the house, anxious at what he would discover.

The small entryway stood clear, but movement to the right

caught his attention. Ava sat on the couch between Josh and Officer Maze, a rookie from the station who had been placed in his unit. Officer Jones had pulled over an ottoman and had a pad of paper open for jotting down her statement, that she seemed to be in the middle of giving.

His stomach tied into knots at the look of fear imprinted across her fragile expression. The disarrayed room had objects scattered on the ground and a broken plant holder sitting in a pile of dirt. He should have been here. The guilt settled upon his shoulders like a yoke on an ox.

Since returning to work part of his desk duties included helping the narcotics unit, and his eyes had been opened to the progressing problem the city was having with a drug outburst. The crisis always rested on the brim, but in the last month it had exploded. Methamphetamine was running rampant throughout the city. It was now the drug of choice. Not only could people get their hands on the ingredients to make it themselves, but it was also extremely addictive. Passing out the pamphlets tonight felt like trying to stop a waterfall with a cork. It wouldn't do much good, but even if it brought insight to one troubled teenager, it had been worth it.

Until now.

"Ava." His voice cracked as her name caught in his throat.

"Matt!"

Josh helped her up off the couch, her legs wobbling while she rushed into his open arms. Her face crushed into his chest while his arms swaddled her. He breathed in the scent of her coconut shampoo while rubbing his chin atop her head.

"What happened?" His eyes crossed the room, directing his question to any of the three men.

Josh approached him, concern stamped between his brows. "Valerie's ex-husband, Chad, showed up. He forced himself into the house."

"Is Aaron okay?"

"Yes, Valerie is upstairs checking on him. It looks as if he slept through the whole thing," Josh reassured.

Matt pulled Ava back, giving him a chance to look into her frightened eyes. "Did he hurt you?"

She shook her head and pushed herself back into his embrace. He closed his eyes, resting in the fact that she was not hurt. Aaron was fine and not exposed to the fear that Ava experienced. He kissed the top of her head, keeping his face buried in her soft hair.

"Ava, I'm so sorry I wasn't here," he whispered, keeping lousy control over his emotions. Anger rippled throughout his muscles. He tensed, wishing for the chance to punch this Chad guy in the face. If he had been here the man never would have made it into the house and given the opportunity to scare an innocent woman.

Matt turned his attention toward his fellow officers. Even though he wore the same uniform, this was their case. "Have you finished her statement?"

"Yes, I think we have all we need from Ava," Officer Jones applied the response. He was a stocky man, a few years older than Matt and an excellent police officer. Matt struggled with not controlling the situation, but he rested in the fact that David Jones would do just as good a job, if not better, than him. "We are now waiting for Ms. Walker to give us a background on her ex-husband."

Matt wrapped Ava closer to him while her body shook. He rubbed his hands over her cold and clammy skin. "Josh, could you go make Ava some coffee while we wait for Valerie?"

"I started some brewing earlier. I'm sure it's finished. I'll be back with some mugs to go around."

❧ A Rescued Hope

❧ ❧ ❧ ❧

THE LIVING ROOM FELL SILENT AS ALL EYES FOCUSED ON VALERIE. Her hands enveloped the coffee mug, eyes lost in thought as if looking into the black murky liquid for answers. Josh sat next to her, rubbing her back in reassurance of his support. She explored each face before she began.

"I met Chad when I was a senior in college at Arizona State. After graduation we married and life seemed perfect. He was a pharmaceutical salesman and I had just finished my internship with an interior design company that offered to keep me on full time. A few months into our marriage I started to notice that he had begun to work less hours, but our finances had doubled. He explained away the extra money by saying that he found a group of doctors that contracted to use only him.

"Over the next few weeks his demeanor changed while more bizarre situations came up. In the middle of the night we would have people coming to the door. He was nervous when the phone rang and we stopped going out together."

Valerie took a sip of her coffee and looked over at Josh. He smiled tenderly and took hold of her hand, caressing her slender fingers, whispering how well she was doing. Matt pulled Ava tighter into his side. He didn't like where this was leading.

"When I found out I was pregnant with Aaron, I thought it would be the happiest time in my life. Chad was so upset and yelled at me, saying I deceived him and tried to get pregnant behind his back. His cold reaction made no sense, until the following week.

"One evening as I left work, I was cornered in the parking lot by a group of men with guns. I was told to relay a message to Chad that if he didn't give them what they needed, they would take what he loved most. Me.

"It turns out he had been working with a small-scale drug lord. Instead of giving the samples to doctors he was giving it to this group of thugs to sell on the black market. He had also started to transport other more excessive drugs for them. I begged Chad to walk away, but he said he was too far in to stop. I told him to go to the cops, but he refused. He said that they would find out and just kill him.

"I loved him, but I loved my baby more. If those men found out I was pregnant, it would just up the ante. I told him I had to leave and he agreed. For the safety of me and our child I packed my bags that night and never looked back. After the divorce I changed my last name to Walker and moved to Chicago. A huge city I could get lost in. Last year I was offered a job here in Rockford and took it, giving Aaron a chance to grow up in a smaller community."

Her eyes locked on Josh, eyes wide in terror. "I don't understand why after all this time he would track me down? Or how he even found me? What if he wants to take Aaron away from me?" She buried her face into Josh's neck and her body shook, finally allowing the fear and tears to win.

Matt tightened his grip on Ava. He had quickly skimmed her statement. If this man was desperate enough, and with his history, he would justify any means to get what he wanted. The problem was, Ava had stood in Chad's way to see Aaron and now he was furious with her. His high-tempered threat proved it. He didn't know her name or where she lived, but in listening to Valerie's account of the past, finding Ava wouldn't be a problem for the angry man. If he could find Valerie, he could easily find Ava. Especially now that her face had been highlighted across the city from the bank robbery.

He ran his hand down his face, doing his best to hide his concern. Ava didn't need to be alarmed about this now. She would be on edge enough as it was. His proof came from the slight tremors that tore through her body during Valerie's history lesson.

"So what happens now?" Josh questioned while looking back and forth between the two officers.

Officer Jones stepped forward. "We will put out an APB for his arrest. Tonight we'll keep an officer here at all times. Tomorrow I suggest Ms. Walker file a restraining order against him."

"Thank you, officer."

"We will let ourselves out. Officer Maze will be parked outside for the night if you need anything." Officer Jones shook Josh's extended hand.

"Sergeant Thompson, I assume you have things handled for Miss Williams?"

"Yes."

"If you need anything, don't hesitate to ask."

"Thanks, Dave." He nodded at Matt as he exited the living room.

It didn't feel like enough, but it was all the police could do. Matt despised the circumstances where their hands were tied. Finding this man wouldn't be easy. They knew what he looked like, but nothing more. No make or model of his car. No idea where he was staying.

However, he knew two things for sure. One, Ava would not be leaving his sight tonight. He already had plans to camp out on her couch. Two, he would not sleep well again until Chad Taylor was found.

CHAPTER EIGHT

AVA LIFTED THE POT'S LID AND LEANED OVER TO SNIFF IN THE aroma of potato soup billowing out. Next came the taste test. She dreaded this part. Grabbing a spoon from the drawer, she scooped up a small helping and lightly blew across it to help cool it down before it touched her mouth.

She chewed and swallowed. A soft smile played across her lips as she licked them. Not too bad. It wouldn't win any contests, but at least it was edible. Since she and Matt became engaged she had been trying to improve her cooking skills. In the last week she had graduated from boxed meals to fresh ingredients. Small steps, but they were steps, nonetheless.

After placing the lid back on the pot she went to the cupboard and retrieved the bowls for dinner. As she set the table she envisioned Matt's reaction to the surprise dinner. Life had been extremely stressful for them since the drama unfolded at Valerie's house. A relaxing evening together was just what they needed.

In order to keep her safe until they knew what they were dealing with in Valerie's ex-husband, she agreed to keep a low profile. She could go to work and church, but all other activities had ceased. Matt had even gone so far as to make sure someone was with her in the evenings. Between her family and friends, someone had been with her every waking moment since the dreaded night.

When Matt's plan came into action she didn't mind, looking at it in the perspective that they would be able to spend more time together. So far he had not taken a shift to stay with her since that first night, until tonight. She could barely tame her excitement.

She finished the table and went to the closet to grab a few candles for a romantic touch. After a few clicks the lighter came to a flame. She stepped back and admired her final touches.

As Ava reached the bathroom to freshen up her make-up and hair, her phone rang. She jogged back to the kitchen and picked it up off the counter.

"Hey, babe."

Matt cleared his throat. "Hi. Everything okay? Are you at your apartment?"

Always her protector. "Yes. I'm fine, but you sound exhausted. Are you on your way? I've got a surprise for you." She couldn't hide the excitement that bubbled through the end of her response.

A deep sigh answered her. "Ava … I'm really sorry to do this, but I'm not going to be able to make it tonight. Something came up at work."

Ava swallowed her lump of disappointment and forced herself not to cry. "Oh, I see." Her voice went up a notch to cover her sadness. "Would you be free to come over later tonight? We could always watch a movie or something." It wasn't her perfect plan, but as long as she got to see him, it ranked better than nothing.

His long pause told her enough. Her heart sank waiting for his response. "I don't think so. I'll probably be busy for most of the night. I called Lucy. She isn't working tonight and said she'd be happy to come over and keep you company."

She loved her sister, but she wanted Matt, not his replacement. An awkward silence deepened between them.

Matt responded before her. "Are you mad?"

She paused. "No."

"That's not very convincing." A slight irritation snipped at his words. "This is my job, Ava. Things happen, plans change."

"What do you want me to say, Matt? I'm not mad, I'm disappointed. Is it so wrong of me to want to spend some time with my fiancé?" She didn't start off mad, but that emotion grew quickly by the second.

Was he trying to pick a fight with her? She walked into the living room for more space to pace and let off some steam.

A long sigh came from his end and his earlier harsh tone turned gentle. "Ava, you know I'd rather be with you."

Did she? His actions in the last week were not a testament to that statement.

Ava strolled over to the window and looked out, hoping to see his car parked outside – that this all was just a cruel joke and he stood only a few steps away from her. An empty parking lot stared back at her.

Tears poked at her eyes. "I miss you."

"I miss you, too."

"Is there an update on the search for Chad?" Hope clung to her question. If they found him this nightmare would end and her life could get back to normal. She and Matt could get back to normal.

"No." His answer came quick and then he didn't give her any chance to ask further questions. "Make sure you text me when Lucy gets there."

"Okay."

Ava heard voices in the background and then the noise became muffled, as if Matt put his hand over the phone. "Hey, I gotta go."

His announcement didn't come as a surprise. She wished she had a few more minutes with him, but she figured he gave her more than what he should have.

"When do you think I'll see you again?"

"My evenings are full but I should have a few holes in my schedule to swing by and see you. Maybe I could come and have lunch with you later in the week? Say, Thursday or Friday?"

It wasn't much, but she'd take it. "I'd love that. I have a field trip on Thursday, but Friday would work great. I'm sure the kids would like to see you, too." Her class adored Matt. When he was on medical leave at work he came often to the school to see her and started a bond with many of her students.

"I think I have a few leftover items from fairs this summer here at the station I could bring for them. Most of it says, 'Just Say No', but it's never too early to get the word out."

"It's a gift from you. They'd be happy with a lump of coal as long as it came from Sergeant Matt."

"Flattery will get you everywhere, sweetheart."

"Well, hopefully it will get me a lunch date with you."

"I'll call you later. I really have to go. Derek is giving me the evil eye." Ava could hear Derek's voice through the line but couldn't make out his words. Matt laughed.

Stalling would not make their goodbye any easier. "Okay. I love you."

"Love you, too."

Ava stood looking out the window for a few minutes after the line went dead, watching her neighbors enjoy the warm evening. Some kids played hopscotch on the front sidewalk. Miranda, the woman that lived on the first floor, ran along the front of the apartment complex ahead of a maroon car that crept along. Mr. Smith sat in his lawn chair reading a book. Ava shrugged her shoulders. Guess it was time to make the best of her evening. A night with Lucy would be fun. They hadn't had much time together lately and when they did, Lucy seemed distant. A sister-bonding night sounded more appealing by the second. Maybe Lucy would even give her more cooking pointers and critique her potato soup.

Ava jolted at the thought of her soup. "Oh, no!" she shouted as she raced back to the kitchen. She had never turned off the stove. She opened the lid and grabbed the spoon to stir. Brown charred pieces of potato lifted from the bottom and spread throughout the pot.

Frustration slithered through her teeth. A ruined meal for her ruined evening. It seemed fitting. She pulled open her junk drawer and rifled through the contents. She lifted out the pizza menu and placed the order. If only pizza could fix all of life's problems.

CHAPTER NINE

THE KINDERGARTEN FIELD TRIP TO THE PUMPKIN FARM COULDN'T have been going any smoother. All week the weather forecast had threatened storms for today, but this morning the sun shined and the temperature continued to climb. High 60's on a mid-October day would get no complaints from her.

Ava called her class together and began her counting game to make sure each child was present. Once every child was accounted for she gave instructions. "All right class, I need your attention." She waited until a hush fell across the group and she obtained everyone's eyes on her. "We have been having such a great day and I'm so proud of each of you and your good behavior. So far we have gone through the corn maze, picked gourds and pumpkins, and went through the haystack maze."

Ava did everything with the kids, and the haystack maze had been her least favorite activity. The dark, smelly tunnel did nothing for her and the straw that decorated her hair afterwards didn't help boost her opinion.

"Next on the schedule we have a hayride, and afterwards we'll eat lunch and finish our day by each decorating the pumpkin we chose before heading back to school. Please stay with your group leader at all times."

Ava gave out a few more instructions to the chaperones and then led her group up the ladder to find seats for the ride.

As she watched the groups file into the wagon she caught sight of the parking lot and couldn't help noticing a person leaning against a car watching them.

She narrowed her eyes to focus the distance in sharper to make out whether it was a man or woman. She eased her stance once it became clear she wouldn't be able to tell because of the person's baseball cap, sunglasses and heavy winter coat.

Her skin prickled with unease. Why on such a warm day would someone wear such bulky clothes? Ugh, Matt's paranoia was rubbing off on her. It wasn't a crime to wear a winter coat on a pleasant and sunny day. A fashion crime, yes, but that was beside the point. What bothered her most was the fact that the person's attention was focused directly on them.

Ava stood and used her palm to shade her eyes from the sun to get a better look at their admirer. No matter how hard she strained it seemed impossible to get a decent look at the face. The figure stood tall and large, not that the coat helped with her calculation on a weight. A man would have to be her best guess.

The man uncrossed his arms and stood straight but didn't move or look away. Ava swallowed hard. She hated being on edge. Taking a deep breath, she mentally shook off the fear that tried to push itself through her thoughts. Sitting back down she turned her head away from the parking lot, putting her attention back on the kids, vowing to not let her nerves get the best of her.

CHAPTER TEN

"**A**VA, ARE YOU GOING TO WATCH SOMETHING OR JUST FLIP channels all night long?" Jules asked, while looking up from the book she was reading at the opposite end of the couch.

"You can always leave if you are annoyed with my evening entertainment," Ava huffed. She took a deep breath, reminding herself that taking her bad mood out on Jules wouldn't be fair. "I'm sorry. I didn't mean it."

Ava wrapped her hand around the back of her neck, attempting to rub out the tension that had been building for the last two and a half weeks. Two long, miserable, uneasy weeks. Seventeen grueling days of being under lock and key. Matt had been going to extremes to protect her. She should feel appreciative and touched that he cared, but irritation had been seeping throughout her untamed thoughts the last few days. Now she was just plain aggravated.

"It's okay, Ava."

"No, it's not."

Only a few beats of silence hung between them. "Want to watch a movie?" Jules asked, setting her book down on the coffee table, obviously trying to distract her.

Ava checked the time to see it was shortly after seven o'clock. Jules would stay until Ava went to bed. The protocol that everyone kept in common.

"How about a walk?" Ava suggested.

"And have Matt find out? No, thank you."

A smile tweaked the corner of Ava's mouth. "Wimp."

"Sticks and stones, Ava. Sticks and stones."

"Fine. Let's watch a movie."

"Ava, you know this is just temporary."

"I know, but it doesn't change the fact that everyone's lives have been turned upside down because some guy threatened me out of anger."

Chad Taylor had yet to be found. He'd disappeared off the radar as quickly as he'd come. He had made no further contact, nothing suspicious in these past two weeks. For all they knew, the man left the city that night. However, Matt would not take any chances on that scenario.

Ava sucked in a deep breath to ward off the claustrophobia. Her apartment was small in the first place, but tonight the walls started to close in. Guilt nagged at her that everyone had to change their schedules to come and babysit her. At least Valerie understood her pain. Josh had encouraged her to move in with their parents for a time and she'd done so. Although, lucky for Valerie, she had finally persuaded Josh into allowing her to move back to her own place yesterday with the agreement to install a high-tech security system. Matt needed to catch on that her life needed to move forward again, too.

Plus, on top of everything else, Matt had returned to active duty last week. Over the last month she noticed his gradual pull back into work mode. He had become more intense and focused than in the past. Their usual strong connection was morphing into sloppy and watered down.

When his proclaimed plan came about, she jumped on board, thinking this would give them more time together. Instead, it turned into more time apart. He always had a reason why he couldn't make it to her place and more times than not, the cause was work-related. Last week's cancelled dinner plans with her and his proposed lunch that he backed out of had just been the beginning of a downward spiral of her feeling isolated and ignored. She needed to be more understanding as he worked through the adjustment back to his schedule, but this time his work focus seemed different.

Jules arose. "You pick the movie while I make us some coff---." A knock at the door made both women jump. They both shook their heads back and forth, answering the silent question if either one was expecting someone.

A second knock broke the eerie silence. "Hey, it's Matt."

Jules let out a deep breath and took five swift steps to reach the door, unlocking the dead bolt and letting Matt in.

"Hi, Matt." She closed the door once he crossed over the threshold. "I was just going to go make us some coffee, would you like some?"

Matt shrugged off his lightweight coat, draping it over the couch. A cold front had gone through last night, bringing the first bitter cold of the fall. He observed Ava as his smile crinkled the skin around his warm brown eyes. Ava stayed seated as all her defenses crumbled, trying to remind herself why she was in this bad mood.

Their moment ceased when Matt turned his attention back onto Jules. "Actually, Jules, if you don't mind, I was hoping I could relieve you of your duties."

Jules nodded. "Sure. I need to run to the market to pick up a few things anyway." She walked over to the counter that split the kitchen and living room to claim her purse and jacket.

Ava picked up Jules' book and brought it to her, placing the romance novel into her oversized green purse. "Thanks for coming over, Jules." Ava leaned toward her friend, wrapping her slender shoulders in her arms.

"Anytime." Jules stayed in her embrace, putting her mouth closer to Ava's ear. "Don't stay mad at him for long. He loves you." Her low, whispered reprimand came across loud and clear.

"Okay." The friends released. "See you Saturday?"

"Of course. I can't wait." Jules stopped to hug Matt before she left, announcing she'd let herself out.

As the door closed, all the air seemed to suck out of the room with Jules. Ava didn't like the awkward tension between her and Matt. Ignoring the problem wouldn't make it go away, but she wasn't ready for the conversation that they probably needed to have. A lump formed in her throat as the memories of her past came creeping back. Her chest tightened with the reminder of how distant Tim had become as their wedding approached and then the outcome it had produced.

"What's on Saturday?" Matt's question speared through her thoughts, grateful for the distraction.

She brushed off the melancholy, hopeful this subject would lighten the mood. "Dress shopping for the wedding." She thought she had told him about it, but they hadn't talked much lately. It shouldn't surprise her that it hadn't come up. Or that he forgot.

"Ava, I'm not sure that's a good idea."

Her eyes widened in fear of what his words implied. When Tim had time away from her during their engagement, he drifted towards another woman and his feelings changed. Had these past two weeks set them up for the beginning stage of their relationship crumbling? Was this the set up before he broke her heart?

Matt continued without noticing her reaction. "I guess if you are with a group, it should be okay." He grabbed his phone from his belt, punching in some information. "Let's sit down and go over the week, figure out who is coming when and if I need to fill an open day."

He stood lost in his technology world while tears spilled down onto Ava's flushed cheeks. Her life seemed to be spiraling out of control. She took a step back, needing space and a better outlook on their situation.

Her movement caused Matt to look up. "Ava, what's wrong?"

Everything. Where do I begin? "I actually thought you came over to spend time with me, not plan my security for the week."

Before he could answer she sulked off to the kitchen to claim some composure. Fidgeting with the coffee maker served as a good cover to hide her shaking hands. She would need a pot of coffee for the long night ahead. She'd make sure Matt didn't leave until they got things settled, determined that she would not walk down that road again.

She caught sight of him leaning against the post at the kitchen entry with his hands in his pockets, studying her. Leaning back against the counter she crossed her arms tightly across her chest, letting her stubbornness win while remorse at her rigidness got pushed aside.

Matt took a moment before speaking, assessing her out-of-character burst. "I know you are upset about my protection detail, but it seems like there is something more. What's going on, Ava?"

"I don't even know where to start."

He stepped into the kitchen, leaning against the opposite counter. His biceps bulged as he crossed his arms against his chest, overlapping his legs at the ankles while never breaking eye contact. "Okay. Then I'll go first. Are you mad at me because I wasn't at Valerie's house that night?"

Matt had yet to broach the subject about not being at the house. He had apologized and she left it at that. But maybe it went deeper than she thought. Maybe she did hold that against him, allowing everything to stack onto that sour foundation.

"No...maybe?" She covered her face with her hands, frustrated over not forming the words that needed to be said. "I do know that there is more that factors into what is wrong than the fact that I was alone when Chad came to the house."

"All right, then what is it, Ava? We can't work things out if I don't know what the problem is."

Ava hadn't felt this vulnerable since she made known her feelings of love toward him. Would this conversation end well? She couldn't imagine her life without Matt, but she learned the hard way two years ago that life didn't always go as planned.

She took a deep breath, ready for the truth whether she wanted to hear it or not. "Do you still want to marry me?" The words tasted like sulfur as they disgorged.

Matt rocked backwards as if her words literally slapped him. "What?"

"It's just that you've been so distant lately, and when we are together it's all business. You've been killing yourself at work and I'm being made to feel like you are using it as an excuse to be away from me. The night at Valerie's is just one of those instances. I've already dealt with a fiancé that pushed me away and I can't do it again. Tell me the truth, Matthew. Are you getting cold feet?"

His answer didn't come in words, but action. He crossed the tiny kitchen in two long strides, taking her tear-stained face in his gentle hands and kissing her. Hard. Ava unlaced her crossed arms and pulled his sculpted body tighter against hers.

It had been weeks since Matt had passionately kissed her with such desire. By the time he finally pulled back and rested his forehead against hers, her legs felt like Jell-O.

"I am so sorry, Ava. I've let fear rule my life, and yours, these past few weeks and instead of protecting you, I've been hurting you."

"Please don't shut me out. Talk to me," Ava pleaded.

"I fear a crazy man is going to hunt you down and hurt you. I'm working extra hours to track down leads. I can't sleep well knowing he can get to you. Doing a pathetic job at trying to keep my concerns of your safety to myself so that burden is not placed on you, but instead I just ended up pushing you away." He looked defeated in every sense of the word.

Ava traced her fingers along the buttons of his cotton shirt, trying to focus on his words and not his closeness that she had been craving for days. "I appreciate your concern for me, but it's slowly suffocating me."

His hand delicately stroked the side of her face. "I know. My human efforts have backfired." He stepped back, pinching the bridge of his nose. "I need to remember that God can take better care of you than I can."

She should have known that he would beat himself up. He wasn't there when Ray had attacked her and he wasn't there when Chad threatened her. Matt was trying to make up for where he felt he failed her. No matter what she did or said, she could never convince him that she didn't blame him.

"I can't live my life in fear, Matt. I walked that harsh road for too long to allow myself to dwell in its untruths again. I have to trust that God will protect me ... and so do you."

"I know. But putting you in a bubble sounds so much easier."

"Hey." Her fingers curved around his chin, forcing him to look at her. "I'm going to be fine. This Chad Taylor guy couldn't care less about me. He was angry, that's all. He moved on and so should we."

He shrugged. "I hope you're right, but I can't get rid of this dread in the pit of my stomach. Something doesn't feel right, Ava."

She tilted her head, considering his uneasiness about the situation. "If I promise to stay alert and keep you in the loop, can my life go back to normal?" Ava ignored the guilt that laced her mind as she kept her uneasiness about the field trip to herself. She couldn't bring herself to tell him, not when they were finally making progress.

He sighed a defeated breath. "Yes."

A smile flickered across her face. "So does this mean you still want to marry me?"

His rich laughter soothed her soul. The way she'd allowed herself to get worked up enough to believe an off-the-wall idea that Matt didn't want her could only be the work of the devil.

If she had brought up her concerns earlier, it wouldn't have gotten so strained between them. Usually they had good communication, that is, until her stubbornness became a factor. More than ever, she realized her tendency to stuff her feelings and concerns, and what a stronghold it would create in their marriage if she didn't work on making the changes that were needed.

"Yes." His voice rang deep and thick. "With every hope and dream inside me, I can't wait to make you my wife."

"I was hoping you'd say that." She clutched his shirt with her fingers, pulling him within inches of her face. Her eyes burned with fervor as their breathing accelerated simultaneously.

"If you're not careful I might cave and let you convince me to elope," he whispered.

"Thanks for the ammunition." She lightly kissed his lips, teasing him with her closeness, daring him to respond.

He didn't disappoint.

If Ava had her choice, they would run away to a tropical island to exchange their vows, barefoot in the sand. When she'd brought up the idea, she could sense Matt's desire to be married in a church with family and friends surrounding them. She had a choice to agree with him or argue her point of view, but all it boiled down to was becoming his wife. It didn't really matter where for her, just that she become his. And right now, nothing else mattered. No work schedule. No crazy guy

on the loose. No shopping for the perfect dress. Nothing mattered but the feel of Matt's arms around her, melting away all
the cares of the world.

CHAPTER ELEVEN

DEREK SHUFFLED HIS WAY THROUGH THE CROWDED PRODUCE section of the market. The store was busy for a Tuesday night and he took a deep breath to keep his patience in check. It wasn't like he had huge plans tonight and was in a hurry – just another normal night of being home alone. He had already been home from work and had a very unsatisfying frozen meatloaf dinner when he remembered he was almost out of dog food. He decided to make a trip to the market for a few other items, too. Why not? It was better than sitting in his recliner watching television.

Max was his faithful Golden Retriever – man's best friend. Derek got him when he purchased his house two years ago. At first he hesitated at having a dog because of his job requirements on the force and SWAT team. The hours were sometimes brutal and he wasn't sure if it would be fair for a dog. However, his next-door neighbors to the east attended his church and when they heard he was considering a dog, they offered to help out with feeding and taking care of it when he was gone.

He jumped on their offer and headed to the pound that evening. It was a decision he had never regretted. Especially on lonely nights like these.

Derek pushed his cart toward the fruit section. Fresh fruit sounded appealing to have on hand for quick snacks during the week. He loaded a plastic bag with apples. As he rounded the banana display he stopped short.

Jules? The woman in front of him had the same slender, tall frame with auburn hair pulled back in a ponytail. He rubbed his hand down his face. He was seeing things. That's what he got for allowing her to invade his thoughts profusely in the last month and a half. He side-stepped to the left to get a better view of her profile.

A smile spread across his lips. It was Jules. Her smooth porcelain skin held a hint of color on her cheekbones. She wasn't wearing much make-up. She didn't need it. Why cover up perfection? He took a moment to appreciate her skinny jeans tucked into her tall boots. Her golden sweater peaked out from underneath her light jacket, accenting the flaxen strands highlighted through her hair.

She stood in front of the pineapples, squeezing the pointy fruits in quest for the perfect one. Pineapple. He could eat pineapple. Once he figured out how to cut it open. He advanced toward her. The flutter of nervousness flickered in his stomach.

"Any tips on how to pick the perfect pineapple?" He hoped she didn't hear the slight tremor in his voice.

She looked up at him and he couldn't quite read the reaction that spread across her face. Surprise? Caution? He hoped not disappointment.

After their first encounter he thought she'd written him off completely. He would have understood if she had. He deserved it. Pursuing her before he had officially ended things with Chelsea was disrespectful and out of character for him. His only excuse, and a bad one at that, was his irrational thinking when his heart pounded with such force. He had not expected the red-headed beauty to make such an impact.

Thankfully when they met up again at Ava's apartment after the bank robbery she had not let his rushing hormones and unacceptable behavior ruin the chance of a friendship. Her demeanor had been polite but guarded, staying consistent on keeping her distance.

A smile worked its way to erase the frown, and her face and neck flushed lightly with a rosy pink color. "I wish I could. I have no clue. Glad to know it looks as if I do."

She shifted her purse higher onto her shoulder while admitting the truth, appearing uneasy and uncomfortable. Derek hated the fact he made her feel that way. Would he ever be able to fix what he had ruined? She had to have felt the connection between them while they were nestled beside each other at the campfire. How could he get them back to that moment?

Start slow. Keep the conversation light, Brown. "No Ava duty tonight?" He thought he remembered Matt saying it was Jules's night to keep Ava company and usually when Jules's name was spoken, he listened.

"Not anymore. Matt showed up to relieve me."

"I've never seen him as intense as he has been over this Chad Taylor guy."

"Yeah, it's sweet how concerned he is for Ava, but he is driving her crazy. For her sanity, I hope he loosens the reins a bit."

"I know Matt has great instincts, so if he's worried, he's got good reason. Matt's a smart guy. I'm sure he and Ava will work things out."

The conversation died down and he was afraid the silence between them would push her to excuse herself and leave, but she glanced down into his cart. "You have a dog."

"Yes. He is an old golden retriever that is young in heart. His name is Max."

She smiled, but a hint of sadness attached itself to the outskirts of her eyes. "I had a golden retriever named Molly while growing up. She was my best friend up until I was in second grade when we had to give her away."

He cocked his head to the side, deciding whether he should push the subject. He was already in the dog house with her, no pun intended, so why not make a bed and get comfortable? "How come you had to give her away?"

Jules didn't hide her hesitancy. She unashamedly made it known she wasn't sure she wanted to share her history with him. *Come on Jules, work with me. Baby steps.*

She bit her lower lip and took a deep breath. "My little sister became very sick and to help her condition my parents felt getting rid of the dog would be best."

"What was she sick with?" His additional question took her off guard and she stepped back slightly. *So much for keeping the conversation light*, he razzed himself.

"Oh, um, she had a rare lung disorder called Children's Interstitial Lung Disease."

Derek had never heard of it before, but it didn't sound good. He caught onto the word "had" and hoped it didn't mean what he thought it did. "Did she beat it?"

He noticed her emerald eyes gloss over from the tears that pooled in the corners. He knew the answer before she had to say anything.

"No. She came down with a bad cold that turned into pneumonia. There wasn't much the doctors could do for her. She lost her fight the day before her fourth birthday."

Derek started connecting the dots. Jules's sister died as a young toddler and she had become a pediatric nurse. That could be a coincidence, but he didn't think so. He assumed the tragic loss pushed her into becoming who she was today.

He tried not to stare, but he was in awe of this incredible woman that kindly put up with him and these personal questions when what he really deserved was a cold shoulder. "I'm sorry to hear that."

She lifted a shoulder. "It is what it is, but thank you."

He was sorry for a lot of things. Derek needed to finally sit down with her and apologize. Maybe now that she opened up to him about her life, she would be willing to finally let him explain his actions at the engagement party.

Jules's phone went off announcing a text. "Excuse me. I need to make sure this isn't work-related."

"Oh sure, I understand. Story of my life."

She reached inside her purse and pulled out her phone, smiling while reading the message. "Sounds like Matt and Ava worked things out." A slight giggle emphasized her words.

"Good for them." Now he and Jules needed to work things out. He cleared his throat and tried to push down his apprehension. He had never been so nervous around a woman before. She easily snuffed out his usual calm and collective stance. Julia Anderson made nothing easy for him. He liked it. And her. "If you are free the rest of the evening, would you like to go get some coffee with me?"

Her eyes slightly narrowed. He felt the need to straighten his posture as she weighed her options. Derek was tempted to retreat and give her an easy out, but then he saw her features lighten and decided to wait her out. He once waited on top of a ledge for six hours on a SWAT mission just to get a better view of a victim. He could wait five minutes for an answer.

Jules glanced down into her cart. "Well, I guess my food should hold for an hour or two before it needs to be refrigerated. Sure. Coffee sounds great."

Derek blinked. Did she just say yes? "Okay, well, I'll go check out and how about I meet you at the Starbucks on the corner?"

"I'm just finishing up. I'll be there soon." Derek turned to leave but Jules reached out her arm to stop him. "Didn't you want a pineapple?"

"Oh right, a pineapple."

❧ ❧ ❧ ❧

JULES FOUND DEREK AT A CORNER TABLE NESTLED UP AGAINST THE wall of windows exposing the dense traffic on the other side of the tinted glass. She tried to ignore his crystal blue eyes that peeked out from underneath his baseball cap.

He stood and pulled out her seat. "I hope it's okay, but I already ordered you a drink. You like skinny vanilla lattes, right?"

Jules sat down in front of her drink, swiveling to hang her purse on the back of her chair. "Yes. It's my favorite. How did you know?"

"That's a secret."

"Matt or Ava?"

"Ah, a cop never reveals his sources."

She playfully eyed him, enjoying the smug grin that he boasted. "I can see that I won't be breaking your defenses." She picked up her cup as a silent cheer toward him. "So I'll surrender with a 'thank you.'"

His cup met hers halfway. "You're welcome."

Jules' usual ability to keep herself at arm's length from Derek's charm was losing ground with each laugh. She checked her watch, surprised that an hour had already gone by. This moment could have been the mirror image of how she had felt at the engagement party while snuggled up next to him. As if all sense of time had diminished.

Derek had picked up their earlier conversation about her family. She had shared how her parents had divorced shortly after her sister Jenna's death. She knew their problems were not her fault, but as a nine-year-old, it sure felt like it – especially when her father walked out, rarely returning to see her. Now that she was older and mature enough to analyze her father's rejection, she could understand the pain her father dealt with and the pain it caused to see her while dealing with the loss of Jenna. It wasn't right what he did, but she could at least come to terms that it wasn't her fault.

It was her baggage. The past didn't define who she was, it just helped to create the person who she is today. She became a pediatric nurse because she had a desire to help sick kids. She loved being a nurse. Putting a smile on a sick child's face or making them comfortable in a very scary and unknown place was worth the long hours and days that sometimes took more from her than what she had to give. But in the last few months she had been struggling with an inner battle of feeling confident that she was hearing God's voice.

Jules was being harassed by her thoughts of discontentment. Was God calling her into a different field of nursing? Was this God's will for her life or did she allow her past to cover God's voice when she made decisions?

This frustration of interpreting God's voice also trickled into her romantic interests. Every relationship she'd had so far had crashed and burned. Deep down, she just wanted someone to love her, which didn't come as a shock after being rejected by her father. Thankfully, she had a good head on her shoulders that helped her to refrain from throwing herself at men to fill that void. She did yearn to find the man that God made for her. Was that so hard to ask? She thought all that had changed when she met Scott. Jules thought for sure this was the long-term relationship God had called her to, only to be sadly disappointed by the devastating outcome.

Scott had pursued her relentlessly for months and began hinting at making the big commitments that came alongside of marriage. When a fellow co-worker informed her that Scott was also seeing another nurse on a different floor, her emotions went on a wild journey. Surprise was followed by denial, which prompted anger, then ended in devastation. Her trampled self-esteem caused her to become flooded with the disappointment of her inability to hear God's direction.

Jules didn't mind Derek's questions about her family. He seemed sincere, but that was the problem. She liked him but she couldn't handle him caring for her as more than just a friend right now.

The conversation needed to steer away from her past. "So tell me about your family?" Not the safest move to learn more about him, but better than dredging up more of her past.

"There really isn't much to tell. I grew up over in Galena with my parents and two younger sisters."

"I have never been to that area of the state, but I hear it's beautiful with the rolling hills. Do you see your family often?"

"No. My family and I don't see eye to eye on some things. I still visit, but only a couple times a year and a quick visit is all I can muster."

His answer intrigued Jules. She needed to stop and not ask any more personal questions. She should get up, thank him for the evening, and leave. That would be safe.

Instead she leaned back against her chair to get more comfortable. "What kind of things?"

Derek took a moment to answer, obviously thinking through what he wanted to share. "My family owns a horse ranch. Along with raising trail riders, they also breed race horses. It's been in the family for generations, so the money runs deep. My family is absorbed with their wealth. Money is all that matters to them. Plus, they're not happy that I left the family business to become an underpaid, underclass cop. Their words, not mine."

A cowboy. Of course. She could picture him in a cowboy hat, boots and chaps … and now she needed to stop.

"I'm sorry to hear that. I'm sure if they took a moment to see what an excellent cop you are and the difference you make in people's lives, they would be very proud of you."

A soft smile crept along his lips that drew his cheekbones up. His freckle that dotted a single spot on the outside of his right eye became hidden from the wrinkles. "Thank you. It never hurts to hope."

"How did you know you wanted to be a cop?"

"I grew up engrossed with myself and the high class living. When I found Jesus, I realized I was called to help people and serve others. I still have my trust funds and stocks in the business, but I try and live as if the money isn't there. I guess I just wanted to prove I could do it on my own."

He quietly chuckle to himself. "I cannot believe I just told you all of that. It's a part of my life that I don't share with many people. Actually, I can add you to the lonely list with Matt and a few college buddies. You just have this way of drawing information out of me."

This was the Derek Brown she remembered around the campfire. The man that Matt and Ava spoke so highly of, the believer who walked daily in pursuit of righteousness, a cop who lived his life to serve and protect others. Jules's breath caught in her throat while she and Derek shared a moment of comfortable silence as their eyes locked. This mutual attraction was dangerously rising again.

She cleared her throat. "Well, your secrets are safe with me, as long as you don't judge this information I'm about to give you."

Derek crossed his arms on top of the table, leaning forward on his elbows. "I'm listening. Please dig me out of this hole."

She waited a few beats to make him sweat and said, "I've never ridden a horse before. I don't think I've really even seen one up close. I mean, show me a horse and cow together and I might just go over the edge."

His strong laugh warmed her heart and eased her slight embarrassment. "Well, that can be arranged, you know. You should come with me some weekend to the ranch. We could go riding."

Jules couldn't hide the shocked gasp of inward air through her open mouth. Being alone with him for an extended period of time was not a good idea for her thoughts or her heart. She could see them trotting off into the sunset, laughing and enjoying each other's company while he broke down the few defenses that she had left. She didn't want to hurt his feelings, but she had to remind herself of the reason she needed to keep him at arm's length.

"I don't think that is a very good idea Derek."

He didn't stand down. "Listen Jules, I'm sorry if I made things awkward for you with my offer. I've been meaning to talk to you about the engagement party for awhile. It shouldn't have taken me this long."

"Really, it's fine. Ava explained it to me."

"No, it's not fine, because I need to apologize. I'm so sorry that I pursued you while technically still with Chelsea. It was wrong of me and not the gentlemanly thing to do. However, I do want to set the record straight. First, I was planning to break up with Chelsea even before I met you. And second, I am not sorry for pursuing you, only for my insensitive timing."

Jules's body tingled from his second declaration. Everything in her wanted to share that she was glad he pursued her. That he was the type of man she would feel honored to be pursued by. That starting a relationship with him was what she wanted.

But she couldn't bring herself to say it.

"Apology accepted. I'm sorry I was too bull-headed to listen to it at the engagement party. Guess it comes with the red hair."

"I'd take the red hair with the stubbornness, if you'd let me."

He was asking for something she was unable to give right now. She needed time to mend her broken heart from Scott.

She needed insight into God's direction for her and sort out her feelings. Most importantly she needed Derek as a friend. She hoped her response wouldn't push him away.

"I feel as though I need to tell you something."

"Anything."

"A month before I met you I had been in a relationship that ended badly. I was getting very serious with a doctor I worked with and then it came to my attention that he was also seeing another nurse behind my back."

Derek rubbed his hand down his face. "And then you met me and I pursued you while still with someone. Way to go, Brown." He closed his eyes and shook his head. When his eyes found hers again, pools of regret shadowed the usual brightness.

Jules reached across the table and placed her hand on his lean, firm forearm that lacked even an ounce of body fat. "It's okay. It's not that I don't trust you, I just don't trust me. I need to work some things out with my mind and heart right now. I like you, Derek, but all I can offer right now is friendship."

Waiting for his response, Jules surveyed the depletion of customers as the coffee shop's closing time approached. For the first time she heard the soft blues music playing in the background, helping to keep private their conversation that didn't need an audience.

Derek covered her hand with his. She savored the warmth that saturated her cool skin. "Jules, I'm just glad that you want to keep me in your life. If a friendship is what you want, then a friend is what you will get." He leaned in toward her, invading her space by placing their faces a mere foot length apart, his voice reaching just above a whisper. "And did you know that friends can go horseback riding together?"

Now it was her turn to laugh. "Well played, Brown, well played." Her cheeks flushed with heat from his attention. "I see you are going to make this difficult."

"Persuasion is a gift of mine."

Jules bit her lower lip, debating. It would be fun. Probably an excellent way to make a giant fool of herself. How would she respond to being that close to a horse, let alone ride one? It was an intimidating animal, beautiful, but really big. It would be nice to get out of the city for awhile. She did have some vacation time saved up if she needed it.

On the other hand, to spend that much alone time with him ... it was easily almost a two hour drive there and then back. Plus all the time they would be together riding. It wouldn't be the brightest of ideas.

Before she could answer, he spoke up. "How about I sweeten the deal? Let's see if Matt and Ava would like to join us. Not as a double date, just friends hanging out. Plus, we could go when my family is gone. My youngest sister mentioned in an e-mail that in two weekends they are going to Kentucky for some horse show." He lifted his eyebrows. "So what do you think?"

It didn't take long for her to respond. She would have said yes even before he added this new scenario, which she liked even better.

"Okay, it does sound fun. You think Matt and Ava would be willing to go?"

"Oh, don't worry about Matt and Ava. He is forever indebted to me for all the extra hours I put in helping him search for Chad Taylor. He owes me big time. They will come, just leave that up to me."

They didn't stay much longer after they made tentative plans for the second weekend in November to go riding. Jules needed to get her groceries home before her freezer items defrosted. She wished she could call Ava and tell her all about the evening, but since hearing that she and Matt were working things out, she didn't want to interrupt.

Plus, she figured she'd be getting a call from her once

Derek got the chance to invite them to go horseback riding. It was probably for the best to have some quiet time to mull over what just happened. Ava would be overly excited and Jules was excited enough as it was. She didn't need a cheering section.

Chapter Twelve

Where is Chad Taylor? Those four words had captured Matt's usual level-headedness, turning him into a focused monster. It had been less than a week since he'd released Ava from her protection detail, and it had been the right decision. There was nothing more he could do. Every lead came to a dead end. He couldn't spare anymore of his free time tracking down a ghost. It wasn't healthy for his mental capacity or his relationship with Ava. In all honesty, trying to control the situation was driving him nuts. When he was finally able to give it to God, he felt a rush of freedom.

"Matthew." He jolted his attention up at the call of his name. He was so lost in thought he hadn't seen his dad enter the restaurant. As a cop he had an innate sense of his surroundings, but today his keen awareness felt muddy from his exhaustion of being back on full duty and not being able to sleep well.

"Hey Dad, thanks for coming." Matt stood up from his chair and reached across the table to hug his dad, Peter, as he approached.

"I'm glad you called. Your mom started talking about re-wallpapering the entryway today. I wasn't too disappointed to inform her that would be a job she would have to start on her own."

"I don't blame you. Mom loves her projects."

Matt's mom, Anna, was known for spur of the moment work projects around the house. One weekend when he came home from college she thought it would be a great idea to build a deck off their sliding glass doors that entered into the family room. After two long days, countless splinters, five excursions to the lumber yard and a trip to the ER for a smashed thumb, Matt, his dad and brother had *her* project done.

The men settled in their seats. Nursing his coffee until his dad arrived, Matt lifted the cup toward the waitress, silently suggesting he needed a refill. She smiled and headed their way with coffee pot in hand.

Matt was enjoying his Saturday morning off immensely. Being back on active duty after having so much time off was exhausting. He had been looking forward to a quiet breakfast with his dad and an afternoon of watching football.

This diner he had chosen held so much history for them. While growing up his dad would often take him and his brother, Gabe, out for breakfast here. It was their special time to talk about life while inhaling stacks of the diner's specialty, all-you-can-eat pancakes. Matt was sure that between the three guys' appetites, the restaurant had lost money over their many visits.

The young waitress arrived and filled his coffee to the brim. His dad turned over his coffee cup. "I'll also take a cup of coffee, please."

"Sure thing." She filled his cup and placed down the menus for them. "I'll be right back to get your order." The waitress with the nametag "Leah" spun around and headed to the nearby table that had acquired new customers.

Matt didn't really need to look at the menu; over the years he had been able to memorize it. He always tried to eat healthy, but breakfast was usually his weakness. That, and Ava's love for ice cream. It was hard for him to resist when she sat next to him with a huge bowl of it.

The waitress returned and his dad ordered the biscuits and gravy while Matt settled on scrambled eggs, toast and bacon.

"Gabe called this morning. He and Shelly are talking about coming for Thanksgiving," his dad revealed while taking his first sip of coffee.

"It's about time. I haven't seen them since the engagement party. I miss the kids." Matt's older brother lived in Chicago and finding time to come home proved to be difficult. Their three kids were young – the newest addition was just shy of a year old. Traveling still wasn't high on their priorities. Matt needed to try and make more of an effort to go and visit them.

"Did your sister call you last night?"

"Yes. That is great news about her promotion at work. When Sara puts her mind to something, there is no stopping her." Sara was the new and upcoming lawyer at her firm. She had been offered a slice of the partnership, a huge achievement considering her young age.

"I could say that about all my children."

Matt laughed. "True. We are quite the career-driven bunch."

When Matt began training for the SWAT team, he was in a zone. Every spare minute he had was devoted to the shooting range, working out or studying. Failure was not an option. His high test scores affirmed his dedication and sacrifice. His desire to excel was at times a blessing and a curse. He felt his inner battle raging since he had returned to work. Now that he had been released for active duty he needed to find a balance. And he needed his dad to help him find that balance.

"How was desk duty with the narcotics department?"

"Interesting and eye-opening. The city is really struggling with an outburst of meth, along with the increased crime that we believe are linked together."

Meth, being a highly addictive drug, brought along with its destruction, a wave of crime because its addicts needed

84

money for their habit. Property, car and identification theft were at the top of the crime list the police department was battling.

Another problem with meth was that it could be made with household products. It was hard to stop a drug that could be created by anyone, anywhere. Laws were beginning to be enforced to help stifle the uprising of home labs. The federal government had been working hard in previous years to get the DEA regulations to touch the pharmaceutical side of things since two main ingredients in cooking meth were ephedrine and pseudoephedrine. The companies had initially tried to change up the additives in the medicine to make the cooking process more difficult for meth producers, but subsequent studies showed the body had a harder time absorbing the decongestant for their legitimate customers and so work in that area had ended.

In an effort to help, many states had passed legislation that in some ways restricted the sale of products that contained ephedrine or pseudoephedrine by placing them behind the register, placing limits on the amount that was purchased, and some even went more aggressive where a prescription from a doctor was needed.

"Now that I'm older, I must say, I don't miss my job as Chief of Police as much as I thought I would," his dad confessed.

"It definitely has its pros and cons."

"Do you have any new leads on Chad Taylor?"

"No. Until something new surfaces, the case is dead."

Matt welcomed the interruption when the waitress brought their breakfast and refilled their empty coffee mugs. He didn't want this subject opened up today, for he was in too good of a mood.

His dad seemed to sense his discomfort and mercifully changed the subject. "I hear Ava is wedding dress shopping."

The thought of Ava twirling around on a platform, in search of the perfect dress, brought a smile to his face. She had shared with him last night how unsettled she was about shopping for a wedding dress again. She claimed it felt wrong, weird. She also struggled with guilt that her parents were paying for another dress, refusing her best efforts to pay for it herself.

He stopped by her apartment on the way to the restaurant to remind her to have a good time.

"Everything okay with you two?" his dad asked.

Matt finished off his eggs and leaned back against his chair. "It's good now. We had a rough couple weeks when we had to work out a few things with my job schedule. Sometimes I feel as though I can't keep my head above water."

"Matt, God has created and equipped you to be a cop and now soon to be a husband. You can do neither well without Him."

"How did you do it, Dad?" Matt recalled the years his dad served the city as an officer. He filled the role with dignity and honor and promoted with action just how important his family was every step of the way. He never ever felt neglected by his dad while growing up. That's mostly why he had invited him out for breakfast today, in hopes that his wise father would pass along a nugget of truth that would help him in his quest to become the husband that Ava deserved.

"I prayed for wisdom. When I was at work, I gave everything to the department. When I was home, your mom and you kids had all my attention."

"Being on SWAT makes that scenario so difficult for me. I'm continually being pulled in so many directions. Ava hasn't said much, but I can tell it's hard on her." The abruptness of him having to leave was never easy. She was always supportive and understanding when he left or had to cancel plans. He could sense her fear for his safety by the worry that wrinkled her brow, but she kept her comments to herself.

He easily scolded himself that this last episode had nothing to do with SWAT, but had everything to do with keeping her at arm's length while in desperate search of Chad Taylor.

He still couldn't believe that she would come up with a crazy idea that he didn't want to marry her. Then again, if he put himself in her shoes with the past she had and the distance that he kept from her, it really shouldn't have surprised him.

"Ava's a good woman, Matt. You have found your perfect match. Find comfort in that. Ava respects you and the job you serve. Of course it will be hard on her. Your mom struggled the first few years we were married. Missing me, scared I would get hurt. She survived and so will Ava."

"I don't want her to just survive. I want her to flourish and thrive."

"There is no secret potion, son."

"You made it look so easy."

"It's not easy at all, just necessary."

Matt took a moment to reflect on the words his father had just spoken. When he had taken on the job as Sergeant and joined the SWAT team he was younger and single. The job was all he had at the time. With his father's guidance and wisdom, he was just realizing for the first time that the problem maybe wasn't his job at all. He just needed to change his expectations for himself from unrealistic to realistic.

"Thanks, Dad."

"Anytime. Did you see that the Bears play Green Bay tomorrow? You and Ava want to come and have dinner with us and watch the big game?"

Before he could answer, his phone started vibrating on the table. He swiped it up, a surge of energy coursing throughout his body. The SWAT emergency code flashed across the screen. So much for his relaxing day off.

"I gotta go, Dad. It's SWAT."

"Go. I got the check."

"Thanks, I'll get it next time. I'll talk to Ava about tomorrow and let you know. She has been salivating all week about this game. I hope your neighbors don't mind some loud cheering." He stood up and retrieved his jacket from the back of the chair, slipping it on in one fluid motion.

"Sounds like a good time to me."

"Great. I'll call you later. I'm looking forward to seeing the new wallpaper." He patted his dad on the shoulder, enjoying the grimace that worked its way through his aging features.

"Don't remind me. Be safe."

"Always," he replied, grabbing his last piece of toast for the road and running toward the exit.

CHAPTER THIRTEEN

SWAT Lieutenant Keith Rogers stood in front of the white dry erase board, black marker in hand, finalizing those last few details of the mission that lay ahead. The team that consisted of twenty officers crowded the small room they called the "Bullpen." Matt rubbed his shoulder, not from pain, but discomfort in being in his head-to-toe black uniform that seemed tighter than he remembered two months ago. This marked his first mission since returning to active duty.

Matt checked his watch, wondering how much longer the meeting would last. Time was of the essence. The mission was clear and one that didn't come as a shock to him or his fellow officers.

A call had come in from a local motel just outside the city reporting suspicious activity going on in one of their rooms. New guests had taken an adjoining room and noticed a strong odor coming from the room on the opposite side of the wall. After the manager was approached with the complaint, he checked his records, noticing that the room had not been cleaned in over a week because of the request of the guest.

When he knocked on the door, the occupants refused to open the door, telling him to leave and stating the room was just fine. That's when the manager called the police. In light of the situation sounding drug-related, the Deputy Chief of Investigative Services decided to send in the SWAT team as a precautionary.

Lieutenant Rogers put up a picture of the motel room's indoor and outdoor blueprints, assigning each unit to their particular assignment and position. "Our scouts have sent word that all other guests have been evacuated from the motel. They are unable to get a look into the room yet, but at this point we are estimating at least four to five bodies in the room.

"Remember team, if this is drug-related like we believe it is, the users will most likely be high. Individuals are frequently violent, bizarre acting, excessively anxious and confused – just a few of the side effects we'll have to keep in account. Enter with caution.

"If meth is in the process of being cooked, we need to keep forced entry at a minimum because of the highly volatile hazardous chemicals within the closed room."

The Lieutenant snapped the lid back on the marker, emphasizing his speech had come to an end. "We're finished here. Let's load up."

Matt tried to hide his disappointment. The Lieutenant had forewarned him that Derek would be continuing the role of Team Leader today for their unit. Being Matt's first mission since a bullet ripped through his shoulder, he wanted Matt to have a few missions under his belt before placing him back in that high level of leadership – but that didn't mean he had to like it. Derek excelled at his job and would lead the team well. He deserved his time to be in charge.

The SWAT truck parked on the opposite side of the motel, making sure they kept a low profile from any view of the room. The motel showed signs of being open for years with dingy siding that needed a good power washing. All the outside room doors needed a fresh coat of paint. This motel sat on the rougher side of the city and came as a surprise to Matt that it remained in business. The room sat on the first floor at the end of the row. Outside stairs stood diagonal from the room that led to the second floor of rooms.

To their advantage, the room had only one exit, and that exit opened up to the parking lot, not a shallow hallway that had rooms surrounding it or the added stress of having to work on a second level. It did increase the probability, though, that the persons of interest would feel cornered and desperate.

Thanks to a video feed propelled through the air vent, the scouts were able to confirm that five persons were inside and travel stoves had been set up by the mini kitchenette to cook what looked like meth.

The plan consisted of two women officers to knock on the door, working undercover as the cleaning crew, hoping the door would be opened by the occupants and not by force.

Derek signaled two officers from the unit to stand alongside the door on the left side of the cart while he and Matt took the right side under the window. Matt's thighs burned as they stayed crouched under the window. He needed to work on his squat exercises during his next workout.

The undercover cops, Swartz and Miller, stepped up to the door and awaited their signal from Derek. Once everyone was in place he gave the go-ahead.

Officer Swartz's knock was met by commotion inside. "Who's there?"

"Cleaning services. We have fresh towels and soap."

"We already told someone we weren't interested. Go away."

Officer Swartz looked down at Derek, looking for confirmation of what to do next. Derek motioned with his hand for her to keep talking.

"Please just let me drop them off with you so I don't get in trouble with my boss." Matt smiled from her persuasive speech.

The request was met by a few grueling beats of silence. "Hang on."

Derek lifted his hand to speak into the microphone attached to his cuff. "Be ready."

As the chain lock started to jiggle a crash sounded inside the room and shouting erupted. The voices rattled frantically. The words were muffled but Matt could make out a few swear words that penetrated through the glass window.

Matt wasn't comfortable with the commotion inside and he could tell by Derek's sudden rigid stance that he shared the same trepidation. Derek brought his hand back up to his mouth. "Stand down."

Derek's correct assessment had the team backing off. They needed time to regroup after hearing the frenzy going on inside the room. They couldn't raid the room in the middle of meth cooking. The undercover cops turned on their heels, pushing the cleaning cart back down the sidewalk. The officers on the other side of the door repositioned by stepping back, following the rolling cart. Derek tapped Matt's shoulder, motioning for him to follow.

Moving along the outside wall while keeping their crouched positions, Matt heard the sound of glass exploding before he felt the wall give way, slamming against him.

CHAPTER FOURTEEN

MATT FELT EVERY INCH OF THE UNYIELDING PAVEMENT THAT scraped the skin exposed through his ripped clothing. His face touched the nip of heat as he shielded it from the splinters of glass propelling with anger toward him. Finally, coming to a cessation of movement, Matt rested his head back against the cold ground, allowing himself a moment to thank God he remained alive. With a reduced amount of strength he pushed a broken piece of wall off his frame, surprised he wasn't buried under rubble. His ears rang with such intensity that he couldn't make out the commotion that surrounded him.

Finding his equilibrium, he slowly pulled his body up, perching on his elbows. The rest of the units stormed full force toward the motel room that had a ten to twelve foot hole, he guessed, in the middle. A small fire slowly escalated while bodies stretched across the room floor. One victim lay across the opening of the hole. The bottom half of his body was stuck inside the room, while the upper half draped, covering the partial wall. The smell of burning flesh pushed his gag reflex into high gear. He turned his face away, hoping to cut off the scent.

Matt's blood pushed with force throughout his body as he scanned the parking lot for Derek. On his second sweep he discovered him a few yards behind him rolling to his side.

Matt tried to stand up to go check on him, but his legs gave out from under him. Checking his man card against his pride, he crawled instead.

"Derek." Matt coughed hard from the inadequate amount of energy he needed to reach Derek. "Are you injured?"

Derek finished rolling up to a sitting position, sliding his helmet off. "I'm fine, I think. You?"

"I'm good. Nothing that a few bandages and cold packs can't fix."

"Does your face hurt?"

Matt noticed his partner's red skin that in all probability mirrored his own. "Probably as bad as yours. You look as if you've just been on vacation in the tropics for a week and forgot to take your sunscreen." Matt didn't know much about degree of burns, but he was guessing by the look of Derek's face that they had first-degree.

"I've been wanting to get a good tan." He began to loosen his vest.

"Trust me. Bronzed is not the look you're sporting right now. I'd say a plump tomato is more of a resemblance."

Derek nodded toward the building that now swarmed with officers and medical personnel. The fire had almost been put out and stretchers had started to make their way into the room to load up victims and take them to the hospital. The whole scene seemed like it moved in slow motion for Matt. He wanted to go help, but he was still too weak to stand with much conviction on his feet. Better to stay back and let the others help. At this point he would just be more of a burden.

"Not quite the way I wanted to execute this mission as team leader."

"There was nothing more you could have done. I would have done everything exactly the way you did and I will make sure the Lieutenant knows that, too."

"Thanks."

Two EMTs made their way over to them. "You guys okay?"

Derek waved them off. "We're fine, thanks. Go make sure the more seriously injured are helped first."

"We will. The last ambulance is yours. Make sure you're on it."

Matt had no desire to go to the hospital, but it was mandatory. He could try and talk the Lieutenant out of it, but it would be wasted breath. He scrunched his face, realizing how quickly the tightness from the burn had set in. Maybe it wouldn't be all that bad to end up in the ER for a couple hours for a check-up. The hospital was sure to have better ointment than the over-the-counter stuff he could pick up at the pharmacy on the way home.

"You know Ava is going to panic when she hears about this?"

Matt's gaze slowly crept over to Derek. "Thanks for reminding me."

"Glad to help."

"Maybe she won't notice."

Derek looked up at his beet red face and laughed. "Good luck with that."

&*&*&*&*

THE ER WAS FULL DUE TO THE EXPLOSION AND A FIVE-CAR PILEUP on the freeway. Matt and Derek volunteered to share a room to help with the progress. They had been checked out an hour after they arrived and were now waiting for their release papers and prescriptions for the antibiotics and ointments for their burns.

Once their shock wore off, they both began to feel the beating their muscles had endured in the explosion. Derek had some road rash along his side and shoulder. Matt's right side of his face bore the visual scars between him and the window. The tiny cuts would heal. No stitches were needed. Both had flash burns on their face and bruises that would claim their territory in the next day or two. Thankfully, nothing was broken and Matt's shoulder had been spared any brutal contact from being thrown twenty feet.

A knock at the door stopped their conversation. The Lieutenant stepped into the room. "Thompson. Brown. I've been told you are just waiting on release papers."

"Yes, Sir," Matt answered for the both of them.

"I will also need your statements before you leave. An officer will be in shortly to handle that."

Both men nodded their acceptance of the protocol. Matt had no desire to spend any extra time here. What he really wanted was his bed. At least Matt wouldn't have to be the one to file the paperwork this time.

Lieutenant Rogers pulled a chair over and sat down, lifting one leg up, ankle on top of knee. "We have a problem on our hands. After going through the video feed and what was left of the room, there is an abundance of ingredients to make meth – more than five poor college dropouts should be able to acquire."

Matt perked up. "You think they have a supplier?"

"Yes."

Derek's inquiry came next. "Have any of the cookers spoken up?"

"Out of the five, only two are conscious. They are not giving any names or information. But we are just starting. The DEA and our narcotics unit have been trying to confirm for the last month that a super lab has started in our city and is branching out into the community. Not only do we think they're selling the units to users, but we believe they're also training up groups that are willing to start home labs. Unfortunately, we believe this is just the tip of the sword."

Chad Taylor? The thought caught Matt by surprise, but it made sense. He had appeared in the city almost a month ago, and that's just when he'd come to their attention through his appearance at Valerie's house. He could have been here much longer. Valerie had said that while they were in Arizona he had been a pharmaceutical supplier to a small scale drug lord. He knew how to get his hands on ingredients. Could he be the mastermind behind a super lab? Or maybe just the puppet someone used to get their dirty work done? Either way, it was just a hunch and not one he wanted to suggest on a whim.

"Do we know who rented the motel room? Was it one of the five in the room or someone different?"

"We are not sure yet, but the investigation is turning toward an additional person. We do know for a fact that whoever first acquired the room paid for it with cash for the entire month. The manager gave us the tapes of the security feed from the day the room was rented until today. We were unable to see his face. He's smart and kept his face down and away from the camera. The height and build doesn't match any of our cookers. We are working toward finding this man as a key player."

Matt wanted to keep in the loop of this search. "Sir, with your permission, I would like to help in any way I can in this investigation."

The Lieutenant didn't hide his confusion, "That isn't your department, Thompson."

"I know. But I did work with Narcotics for a few weeks and I sat behind a computer looking through mug shots of criminals for hours on end. I'd like to help if I can."

"Good point. I'll have Detective Bennett get in contact with you." He stood up, smoothing out his uniform pants with a quick slide of his hands. "I suggest you two take the rest of the day off and go home and rest. I don't want to see you again until Monday and that's an order."

With that, Lieutenant Rogers left.

Once the door closed Derek turned to him. "What was that all about?"

"Chad Taylor." Derek knew as much about the dead-end case as Matt did. He had even tracked down a few leads for Matt during operation 'Keep Ava Safe.'

"You think he could be the mastermind behind a super lab?"

"I don't know, but it wouldn't hurt to stay in the loop."

A knock at the door broke off their discussion. Matt expected the officer for their statement, but Jules' auburn hair came as a surprise. Matt noticed Derek's posture change and the genuine smile he tried to hide. Oh yeah, he was smitten.

Derek stepped a little closer, his voice uncommonly shaky. "Hey, Jules."

"Hi, guys. Sorry to intrude. I was getting ready to start my shift when I heard you were here. Thought I'd come down and see how you are doing."

"Thanks. Did Ava call you?" Matt did not like having to make that call. He tried to get a hold of her before she heard about it on the news, but he wasn't quick enough. The media was out to make his life more difficult. It must be a conspiracy. She had heard that SWAT officers were injured, but that was the extent the news was allowed to share until the department was able to give a full press release. At least he had a chance to soften the blow that he was on the injured list, but okay.

"Yes. And she should be here any minute. She was looking for a parking spot when she called." She stepped closer to the men and examined them. "No offense, but you guys look horrible."

Derek laughed. "Do you always speak to patients with such encouragement?"

"Well, seeing that my typical patients are usually at the mental capacity of learning their alphabet, I'm much more

98

kind to them. I thought you guys could use some truth. If it would make you feel better, I can always give you lollipops." She reached in the front pocket of her Mickey Mouse scrubs and pulled out two suckers.

Derek leaned forward and grabbed the red one. "You're forgiven."

She turned to Matt, waving the orange one. "Matt?"

"No, thanks. Unless that is coated in pain killers, putting anything in my mouth right now doesn't sound appealing." His jaw ached from the road rash, burns and glass cuts. He could, however, push pain aside for a little comfort kiss from Ava.

As if hearing his mental cue, Ava walked into the room. She stopped in her tracks, gasping while covering her mouth with her hand.

Matt cringed.

Derek laughed again. "You girls are going to give us a complex."

Ava ignored him as she rushed over to Matt. "Are you okay? You didn't say much on the phone. Now I can see why."

She touched his arms and chest with ease and went for his face but pulled back. It looked as if she was afraid to touch him and yet needed the assurance that he was okay. Even though his muscles screamed, he pulled her closer, positioning her beside him on the bed with his arm around her waist.

"I'm fine. A little sore. Nothing a little time can't heal."

She traced his face with widened eyes. "How bad does your face hurt?"

"Not much." He only lied a little.

Derek cleared his throat. "I'm feeling fine, Ava. Thanks for asking."

Ava teased back, "Hey, wait your turn. Don't you see that my fiancé's face is red and will clash with our wedding colors? I can only handle one crisis at a time."

Pain erupted through Matt's chest as he laughed, but he didn't care. He was so proud of Ava and the way she was handling the situation. He had expected her to come in upset, panicked, eyes full of tears. She proved him wrong. And it felt good. He relaxed in the encouragement that not only would Ava survive as a cop's wife, but she *would* flourish and thrive, just as his dad had predicted.

Chapter Fifteen

THE PLAYGROUND ROARED WITH CHILDREN'S VOICES AND LAUGH-ter, giddy in their few minutes of free time. Ava watched as a few girls pushed each other on the swings, giggling with each added foot of height. A long line of eager kids stood waiting for the slides. She called out a warning to be careful not to push. The last thing she needed was an injured kid on her watch.

Ava turned back to her conversation with Kate but kept the children in her line of sight. She wrapped her jacket snugly around her midsection as the breeze picked up force, a disappointing reminder that the cool fall weather had crept upon them.

"Are you excited about the carnival tonight?" Kate inquired while mimicking Ava's movements with her own jacket.

Tonight the elementary school hosted its annual fundraiser carnival tonight to boost their funds for the rest of the year. Ava had joined the committee this year as a teacher representative. She was in charge of setting up and overseeing that everything ran smoothly. It was a tall order, but she was up for the challenge.

"Yes, I'm looking forward to it but will also be glad when it's over. I hope we have a good turnout." The countless hours she had spent working on the carnival were more than she expected. It would be nice to have this finally off her plate.

Kate nodded her head. "I'm sure it will be a huge success. With you on board this year, the advertising has doubled. Plus your idea of having a silent auction on the side is brilliant."

"I just hope we bring in enough to reach our goal."

The school worked hard all year with many fundraisers to reach their revenue goal to help support the kids throughout the year. So many parents had no idea how much work went in to help lighten the financial burden for them. In today's economy it was hard for parents to budget in all the activities the school did with the children. The school stepped up and covered most of the cost for field trips. They purchased books and many of the classroom's activities had been covered by these fundraisers.

Ava looked forward to this fundraiser because it promoted a night of family fun. It warmed her heart to hear her students' excitement about coming to the carnival with their families.

"Did you find enough volunteers?"

"I think so. It would be nice to have a few more, but I think we'll manage. I appreciate you and Kyle helping out."

"No problem."

"I even got Matt and Derek to agree to come and work security."

"Good idea. See, you were meant for this job."

Ava smiled, tipping her head a slight degree to the side, letting the praises settle. "Thanks."

"How are Matt and Derek doing since the explosion?"

"Better. They still have a red tint to their faces, but the cuts have already healed."

"I'll have Kyle give Matt a hard time about it tonight."

"You should. And have him poke fun at how Matt needs to remember to use sunscreen when outside. He's only heard that line about a million times."

They laughed together until Kate stepped forward to check on a little girl that had fallen in the stones. She seemed okay, just a few minor scraps on her hands.

Ava scanned the playground once more, making sure all remained calm. A group of boys were playing a game of basketball. It looked to be more for fun then competitive.

She took a moment to focus on the football game, fifty yards away out in the grass, which seemed to be more tackling than two-hand touch. There would be dozens of grass-stained pants when it was all said and done.

As her eyes swept the remainder of the grassland, a car parked outside the fence caught her eye. Trying to get a better view of the car, she side-stepped to the right a few feet. She moved a piece of hair that caught in her eyelashes from the wind. The car looked to be a maroon color, small, boxy. As the sun came out from behind the clouds, the shadows shifted, revealing that someone was sitting inside the car.

The pit of her stomach tightened as she realized she had seen this car before. It had been here earlier in the week, too. And if she really thought about it, she vaguely remembered seeing it in the parking lot during the kindergarten field trip. She had been so focused on the person, she didn't think to get details on the car.

Ava did her best not to overreact. It could be a parent watching their child enjoy recess. It could be as simple as a coincidence. Maybe she got the color and shape of the car wrong from the other days.

But the uneasy feeling had merit. On Monday Josh and Valerie stopped by to share the news that Chad had made contact again. This time, instead of barging into her home, he called her on the phone by ways of making it untraceable. He wanted to meet Aaron, but Valerie refused. Before Chad hung up on her, he vowed that it was far from being over. They were where they started a month ago with finding him, but at least now they had a pretty good idea that he had stayed in the city.

Ava had believed this problem with Chad was behind them, not a set-up for round two. She thought for sure Matt would put her back under lock and key again, but he surprised her with his calm approach. Things would stay as they were, but she needed to remain cautious.

That has to be it, she assured herself. *I'm just being paranoid.* Just as she worked up the courage to approach the car's occupant that currently added to her stress level for the day, the bell rang. She stopped short but kept her eyes on the car. The person inside must have caught on to being watched. The car started up and sped off, too far away for her to make out a license plate number.

"Ava. You okay?" Kate's question brought her direction back.

"Oh yeah, sorry. Just daydreaming. I'll meet you in the gym after school to finalize set up."

"Yep, see you then." Kate disappeared through the doorway, herding the kids back to their classrooms.

Ava followed behind, holding up the rear. *It's nothing, Ava. Just let it go,* she demanded of herself as the heavy door closed behind her.

❧ ❧ ❧ ❧

Ava breathed in a breath of sweet relief. The carnival was over and it had been a huge success. Everything had gone off without a problem. Judging by the attendance and a quick look at the silent auction itemized sheet, they had even gone over their projected monetary goal.

Walking around the gym, she surveyed the volunteers cleaning up each designated station. Grabbing an empty box, she headed to the entrance to join Jules to collect the decorations of pumpkins, gourds and straw bales.

Out of the corner of her eye she spotted Matt and Derek

helping tear down the dunk tank. A small giggle escaped at the memory of the guys doing their best to be good sports throughout the evening.

The children had clung to them, wanting their attention. A few girls from the fifth grade class had begged Matt to come to their face painting station. Little did Matt know, Derek had bribed them with extra tickets to do it if they would paint something girly on Matt's face.

Poor Matt had walked around the gym for almost fifteen minutes before someone had mentioned they liked his butterfly and heart face paint.

Ava could have intervened at one point to lessen his embarrassment, but she had learned long ago to leave Matt and Derek alone when they were pulling pranks on each other.

True to his competitive spirit, Matt did not cave or walk away defeated. Instead, when Derek agreed to be in the dunk tank Matt put his sinister plan into action. While Derek changed clothes, he added freezing cold water to the previously-filled lukewarm water. Then to make it worse, he passed out more tickets to the kids to ensure that Derek would be dunked more often.

Matt also bought a few tickets for himself.

Derek's lips had turned blue by the end of his half-hour slot. By the look in his eyes, Matt had just dug his own grave. They were not even, not by a long shot. Ava hoped she wasn't around when his payback came due in full force.

"The guys seem to have made amends," Jules pointed out as they both looked across the gym at the two men in uniform.

"For now." She could only imagine what Derek had up his sleeve. They saw the guys laughing together as if nothing had happened.

"Are they always like this?" Jules asked, placing the smaller pumpkins in the box.

"They usually go in spurts. It's like there is this hidden

line neither will cross, but sometimes I wonder how close they get." She sat down on her knees to collect the gourds in a pile. "You and Derek seemed to enjoy each other's company."

Jules stopped working and caught Ava's attention by her sudden abrupt stop. "We are just friends."

"I'm just stating a fact. That's all."

"Well, you can keep your facts to yourself. Please. I don't want Derek getting the wrong idea."

Jules had been working extra hard these last few weeks to keep Derek at arm's length, enforcing the idea that she wasn't interested. But Ava knew better. "Okay. Okay," she put her hands up in surrender. "But when you're ready to admit that you have feelings for Derek, you know where to find me."

Ava dodged out of the way of Jules' friendly push. Glancing over at the guys, she put a hand up to stop Jules from her rebuttal. Matt was on the phone and his face looked grim. Derek leaned closer in attempts to hear the conversation easier.

Matt ended the call, spoke to the volunteers, and headed toward them with Derek on his heels.

A lump grew in Ava's throat as she played through all the scenarios it could be.

"Matt, what's wrong?" she asked before he fully reached them.

Concern grew between his brows. "That was Josh. Aaron is missing."

CHAPTER SIXTEEN

THE FOURSOME MADE THEIR WAY TO THE HOUSE WHERE AARON stayed for childcare and where he had turned up missing. Matt led in his car, the girls followed in Ava's car, and Derek brought up the rear.

Matt's conversation with Josh had been brief without a lot of details. He didn't take time to debrief the group, figuring they'd all get the full story together when they arrived.

Matt wished he could be with Ava, hold her hand, be her rock. However, he wasn't sure how much he could reassure her that everything would be okay. He wasn't sure himself. Missing children didn't happen often, but when they did, the results often didn't end happily.

His car filled with prayers for Aaron. That God would go before them and give wisdom to find the little boy who had found his way into each of their hearts.

Police cars surrounding a yellow house helped identify their destination. Josh ran out to them as soon as they stepped out of their vehicles. Fear tore through his eyes.

"A detective is here. An Amber Alert has been put out. A search party is forming. They say that's all they can do for now." Josh ran his fingers through his blond hair, his words tumbling over each other.

Matt reached up and put his hand on his shoulder, squeezing to show his support. "We will do all we can, Josh. We won't give up until we find him."

Ava joined them, encircling Josh in a hug. "What happened?"

Josh looked back toward the house. "Valerie is so upset. I don't know how to help her." His eyes dropped to the ground, defeated.

Ava's calming voice took control as she placed her hands on both his shoulders, demanding his attention. "Josh, tell us what happened."

Josh pinched the bridge of his nose, trying to restrain his emotions. Josh would want to be strong for Valerie, but Matt sensed this would be his time to unload, to decompress without Valerie watching. "Yeah, okay. Um … Valerie had to work late tonight. She had an evening appointment with a client. The babysitter was outside in the yard playing with Aaron when the phone rang inside. The phone call was an unknown man calling about her childcare rates. When she made it back outside, Aaron was gone."

Matt stepped forward, taking charge of the situation the best way he knew how. "All right, let's go join the search party. We can't help Aaron by standing around here."

*& *& *& *&*

THE DUSK TO DAWN LAMPS LINING THE STREET BEGAN BLINKING their confusion over what time of day it was. Darkness crept in, a subtle reminder that their time of finding Aaron during daylight was coming to a close.

They had rounded up thirty-five volunteers, along with police, to make up their present search party. Until they had more information on where Aaron went or a probability of who took him, the plan remained to canvass the neighborhood.

It didn't take a genius to guess that if he was taken by force, all fingers pointed to Chad Taylor. When theories had been discussed, his name was brought up. Along with the small chance a stranger saw him alone outside and took hold of the opportunity to snatch him, and the possibility that Aaron took off by himself and got lost. They had no leads in his whereabouts, so they worked every angle.

"Aaron!" During the last fifteen minutes, that was the only word spoken between Ava, Matt, Derek and Jules. They stayed together as a group, covering the south end of the babysitter's neighborhood.

Ava cupped her mouth to push her voice further. "Aaron!" Tears stung the corner of her eyes. *Where would he be*?

She couldn't bring herself to go back to Valerie without Aaron. Watching her fall apart earlier was devastating enough. Valerie had thrown up twice while hyperventilating. There was talk about sedating her, but Josh calmed her down enough that the idea had been pushed to the side, for now.

Besides death, a missing child was every mother's greatest fear. The unknown, the loss, the hope – they were strangled together in a web of misery.

Ava passed an elementary boy out on his bike and waved him over. She produced a picture of Aaron, with hopes the youngster had maybe seen something – anything that would lead them to finding him. Her heart sank when he showed no recollection of Aaron or knowledge of his whereabouts.

Whistling to get the group's attention, Matt flagged everyone over. Ava noticed Derek give Jules a side hug of encouragement as they approached. "What's up, Matt?" Derek queried as they made a circle.

"We are coming to the end of our part of the neighborhood search." He took out the map to show what they had already covered and what still needed their attention. "It looks like we still have this block of houses," he pointed to the area of interest, "and the neighborhood playground to search."

"You think if we split up we can cover more ground faster?" Derek probed Matt's thoughts.

"Yes. We are running out of daylight. Maybe five minutes left at most. Derek, you and Jules cover the playground while Ava and I go knocking on the doors of the remaining houses."

Derek nodded his agreement. "Let's meet back here---"

"Stop!" Jules's abrupt cry silenced Derek. Her frame jerked straight. "Do you hear that?"

The group paused and listened. Jules put her hand up to keep them silent a few moments longer. And then they heard it, a small cry. So muffled Ava couldn't believe Jules had heard it over their conversation.

"Where is it coming from?" Ava's question fell silent against no response as they listened for the soft cry again.

When they heard it again, Matt took off running. "It's coming from the playground, I think. Let's go!"

"Aaron!" They each shouted as they sprinted toward the playground. Splitting up to cover more ground, the cry became more defined for Ava as she reached the plastic tubes that sat under the wooden stairs as a part of the steps that went up to the slide.

Falling to her knees, she pulled out her flashlight and clicked it on. Aaron's tear-stained face met her light. "I found him!" Ava yelled, then settled her attention back to Aaron. "Aaron. Hi, buddy. It's Ava." She crawled into the tube as he held his trembling arms out to her. Scooping him up, she tucked him against her. *Thank you, Jesus*. She ran her hand over his hair, trying to soothe him. The awkward position her body was in began to hurt, but she wasn't going to release him for anything.

His small toddler body shivered as his cry deepened. He had to be scared, cold and hungry. Ava heard commotion outside the tube. Matt ducked his head inside the cylinder, relief washing over his features. He waved his phone and then stepped out of view to make the call to Valerie.

Ava pressed her lips against the child's head, praising God again for His protection. "Are you okay, Aaron? We were so scared because we didn't know where you were."

Aaron would be four next month. He could hold a conversation and had a great stack of vocabulary words, but would he ever be able to tell them what really happened?

"I okay."

Matt reappeared, the timing perfect to have a witness for the question she needed to ask. "Can you tell me what happened?"

Aaron sat up in her lap, his head dusting the top of the tube. Wiping his eyes with the sleeve of his shirt, a shuddered breath escaped. "I was outside playing with Miss Carmen. She go inside. Then a man came to the fence. He said he was my daddy and wanted to take me to the playground. So I go."

Ava jerked her line of sight to Matt, her heartbeat quickening. "Then what happened, buddy?"

"He bring me here. We played. Then he said he had to go. I get scared because I not want to be alone. But daddy say that someone find me soon." Aaron leaned back into her arms again. "I so happy you found me, Miss Awa."

Ava wrapped him closer to her. "Me too, Aaron, me too."

An hour later the grueling night was wrapping up. Valerie and Josh met them at the playground. The sight of mother and son reuniting was beautiful. They had shown Aaron a picture of Chad to confirm who had taken him. Aaron appeared confused at first, but then informed them it was the same man and that he had hair on his face now.

Aaron answered as many questions as he could until he couldn't keep his eyes open any longer. Josh took the pair home and proposed that he camp out on Valerie's couch for the night. Tomorrow they would discuss in more detail what had happened and where to go from there.

Matt's hands came from behind to rest on Ava's shoulders. She leaned her weight back against his chest, soaking up his strength.

"This is far from over, isn't it?"

Matt took a deep breath, releasing it before he answered. "I don't think we've seen the last of Chad Taylor, if that's what you mean."

"That's what I was thinking. But what I can't understand is, if he wanted Aaron, why didn't he just take him? He had the chance but didn't take it."

Matt slid his hands down her arms and gathered her into an embrace and kissed her cheek so lightly it almost tickled. "I've been mulling that exact question around in my mind since we found Aaron. I think in Chad's own twisted way, he loves his son. All he has asked from the beginning is just to meet Aaron. When he was refused that request, his anger became ignited. I really don't think he wants to take Aaron away from Valerie. At this point, I think he just wants to scare her. Let her know he's in charge. It makes me also think that he's not finished with you either."

His declaration caused her to pull from his embrace and turn to face him. "What makes you think that?" Dread engulfed her.

Should she tell him about the car parked at school or the person in the parking lot during the field trip? They had finally gotten on the right track again. Would this piece of information tear them apart again? Weighing the possibilities against the outcomes, she decided to continue keeping it to herself. She didn't even know if the person in the car intended to be a threat to her. Ava didn't want to make more out of the situation than what it was. Yes, it would be best just to stay silent, for now.

"Don't worry." Matt pulled her tightly into his chest. "I'm not going to make you walk around in a bulletproof vest. I just want you to realize that Chad Taylor is capable of about anything. It seems like he is out for revenge, and I'm sure you made his list."

CHAPTER SEVENTEEN

THE CRISP MID-NOVEMBER WIND MADE ITS PRESENCE KNOWN AS Jules stood at the crest of the hill, overlooking the Brown estate. She figured it would be impressive and the property would be expansive, but she didn't expect this. Over fifteen hundred acres of rolling hills, mowed down trails for the horses, and a small creek running alongside the perimeter dotted by a white vinyl fence. There were also two large pole barns for hay and equipment storage and horse stables connected to a large barn used for training the horses.

The fact that three houses were spread out through the property put her over the edge. The entrance led up to the main house. The large home had a front façade built of rock, dated for the years it stood, but still beautiful in its age and character from the statues to the intricate ways the rock was cut out. Derek said that the interior had been remodeled to fit his mom's modern taste. The driveway continued down and curved to the right, leading to a second house that held an overly large pool in the backyard. It was smaller than the main house but had been built in the last twenty years and its newness showed. His parents used this house for their out of town guests.

The last was a log cabin tucked into the wooded area on the southern part of the property. Derek said people wouldn't know it was there unless they took the gravel drive and disappeared into the woods. It sounded very peaceful. Jules looked forward to seeing it during their ride.

They didn't take the time to tour the inside of the houses, though. They came to ride. With limited time due to a storm that was picking up pace over Iowa, they made riding their first priority.

Throughout their exploration of the grounds, Jules blamed the anticipated horse ride she was getting ready to endure for her fraying nerves. However, she was beginning to accept that it probably had to do more with the little glances Derek gave her when he thought she wasn't looking. He didn't hide his interest in her and she didn't know what to do about it. She liked where they stood, enjoying his friendship. He was easy to talk to, could make her laugh and didn't take life too seriously. She needed that.

They walked into the horse stall, stopping at the doorway. The cement aisle was lined by horses coming into view in response to the commotion of the foursome entering their domain. Wooden name plates hung outside each stall, introducing them by name.

"All right, it's time to pick out your horse," Derek announced, stepping further inside. "Captain is mine, but all the others are up for grabs. These first six stalls on the left are the older, gentler mares that will give you an easy ride." He pointed to his left and then moved to the other side of the aisle. "These are experienced mares and geldings, but they'll keep you on your toes. Down at the end are our new additions, I would suggest not picking one of those unless you enjoy getting thrown."

"Don't you have a pony or something? I've heard miniature donkeys are a good ride." The group laughed at Jules' question. She laughed with them, but deep down she was totally serious. The horses might be old, but they were still big.

She wasn't used to animals and farmland. Growing up in

the city didn't give her much of a chance to experience nature up close.

Derek came up and took her hand, pulling her with him toward the third stall. Her breath halted as he threaded their fingers together. "This is Gracie. She has been with us the longest and knows the trails without being led. She'll be good to you. I think you two will make a good pair."

"I think I'll go with Sasha," Ava said. "She's had her eye on me since we walked in."

"That makes two of us." Matt leaned over and caught her cheek in a kiss.

Red crept into Ava's cheeks. Jules watched the couple speak quietly to each other, a conversation only meant to be between them.

"Mr. Brown, it is good to see you." An older man approached the group. Derek dropped her hand to shake his.

"Hi, Henry. It's good to see you, too. And you know I prefer it when you call me Derek." Derek turned to the group. "Henry, these are my friends, Matt, Ava and Julia. Guys, this is our trusted and loyal ranch hand, Henry Shaw."

Introductions and handshakes made their way around the circle. "If you have chosen your horses, I will get them ready for you to ride." Henry walked to the wall covered with saddles and riding equipment.

"Thank you, Henry. We will take Gracie and Sasha." Derek turned to Matt. "Who did you choose?"

"You pick."

"Okay, let's go with Gunner and I will of course take Captain. We'll meet you outside Henry."

ↄↄↄↄ

JULIA'S NERVES SETTLED DOWN AS THE RIDE PROGRESSED. IT wasn't as scary as she thought it would be. Derek rode beside her while Matt and Ava followed. He talked a lot about what it was like to grow up here. The memories he shared of his childhood were touching. She tried to focus on his words and not his baby blues poking out from under his cowboy hat. The scenery wasn't the only breathtaking sight.

Derek pointed to a rock that overlooked the creek. "I asked God into my heart right there on that rock. I was eighteen."

"Who introduced you to God?"

"A friend of mine invited me on a camping trip with his youth group. There was this girl I was interested in who was going, so I agreed under the hidden pretense of spending time with her. One night around the campfire the youth pastor shared his testimony and then gave the salvation message. I listened and banked every word he said, but I was too proud to go forward and accept in front of my friends.

"When I got home I took a walk, trying to clear my head. God continued to speak to me, showed me my sin, but also reminded me that His unconditional love and grace covered it. I stopped on this rock and just started talking to Him. I felt silly, but I couldn't stop. All my reservations crumbled when I finally grasped that a life without God was no life at all."

"When did you know you wanted to be a cop?" Jules' question was quiet as she mulled over the words he shared.

"That summer, before I left for college. God just placed it on my heart. I knew he put that desire in me."

Jules kept her eyes forward, keeping focus on the trees that showed their last evidence of color change, anxious to now get off this subject. This was an area in her life she struggled with, hearing God's voice and direction. How did someone really know what God was telling them and where He was directing them to go?

"Where does that path lead?" She nodded with her head, too afraid to take her hands off the reins for even a moment.

If he noticed her change of subject, he let it pass without

dispute. "There is a small fishing pond down there. When I was in elementary school my grandfather would pick me up as the sun was rising and we would go down there and fish for hours. He didn't speak much, said it was good for a man to sit in silence for a few hours, but I always remember the time he took just to be with me."

Silence hung between them until Jules got up enough nerve to ask her question. "So how did you know God called you to be a cop?"

Derek didn't respond right away, taking his time to form his answer. "It wasn't like God came to me in a burning bush as He did with Moses. It was more subtle. The idea of protecting the innocent and serving others intrigued me. That idea began to foster in my mind and heart. I brought it before the Lord, prayed about it, dug into His Word and then waited for Him to answer. A sense of peace washed over me. That's the best I can describe it."

"Do you think God brings people into our lives to direct us? Or that a circumstance can mold our outcome?" She thought of her sister and how her death had been the pushing force in becoming a pediatric nurse. Maybe God had used that loss to show her where He wanted her to be. She had never really questioned her decision until this last year, when everything felt like it was falling apart and out of her control.

"Yes. Like your sister. Her death was life-altering for you. That loss was a part of what God used to direct you into who you are today. Your natural ability to take care of others, your compassion, your tender spirit – those gifts you were born with and God used them to mold you."

She nodded. He hit the nail on the head. Only Ava had been able to read her that well. How did he do that? Did she come across that transparent?

"Thanks. I need to think about that a little more."

They rode for another hour until Matt spoke up from behind them. "I don't know about the rest of you, but if I want to be able to walk normally tomorrow, we might want to head back."

They all came to a stop, some more natural at it than others. Derek's grin gave everything away. "I guess I should have told Henry not to put the brand new saddle on your horse. Oops, sorry. You might be walking bow-legged for a few hours."

Matt's face dropped. "Oh no, you didn't."

"You put freezing water in the dunk tank. You knew payback was coming."

Jules and Ava looked at each other, suppressing their laughter for Matt's sake. "Sleep with one eye open, Brown," Matt warned.

Derek's laughter broke their defense, and Ava and Jules joined in. "Come on, Matt, let's head back and I'll find you an ice pack."

"You guys head back. Jules and I will be there in a little bit." Ava's statement surprised Jules, but she liked her thinking. A few minutes alone with Ava would be nice. Her emotions were ready to explode.

Derek looked uneasy to leave them behind, but didn't argue. "Okay, stay on the trails. Come back before the weather hits. The horses may be experienced, but they hate thunderstorms. I'll check and see if the chef can have supper prepared for us before we head back."

The guys left on the trail that headed back to the stables while Ava and Jules turned, guiding their horses toward the creek that led them through the wooded area the cabin rested in and then into the pasture. They rode a few minutes in silence. Jules appreciated the time to collect her thoughts. The clouds rolled in, announcing their time would be limited.

"I'm going to say something and then I don't want to talk about it again unless I bring it up. You don't get to tell me 'I told you so.' I don't want your opinion unless I ask for it. I just need you to listen while I get something off my chest."

Ava nodded. "Okay."

Jules exhaled. "I like Derek … a lot. I know you already know this, but I think I've fully grasped the depth of my feelings. And I'm scared spitless over it. He cares about what I like, makes me feel important, gives me space before I even need to ask. He is solid in who he is, who he wants to be – and that intrigues me. My heart thumps wildly when he is around and I often catch myself wondering what it would be like to be in a relationship with him."

Jules glanced over at Ava, relieved she followed the rules by keeping quiet. She continued, "The thing is, I'm not ready for him yet. I need to understand how to hear from God and know this is what He wants. Scott messed with my mind and I want to know that I'm for sure making the right decision with Derek. I need more time, but what if Derek doesn't want to stick around and wait? What if I lose my chance with him because I dragged my feet?"

There was more she needed to reveal to Ava – and it had to do with more than just her feelings toward Derek. The sky turned a deep gray color. They needed to turn back. Jules pulled on the reins to slow Gracie down.

"Let's take this trail and head back. The sky isn't looking good." Jules looked to the west. They had come down this trail from the stables and she was sure it led them back to the guys. The horses began their matching stride as they headed back to the ranch. "All right, you can give me a quick overview of your opinion."

Ava smiled. "Are you sure? I'd hate to break the rules."

Jules relaxed. "I know you are going nuts to keep your advice to yourself. Spill it."

"I'm glad you're finally realizing how you feel about Derek. He's a great guy and he's good for you. That being said though, doesn't mean you should rush into anything if you're not ready. It's not fair to you or Derek. If you two are meant to be together, you will be. A few weeks or months shouldn't derail Derek's feelings for you. And if it does, then he doesn't deserve you."

Thunder rumbled over them as the first drops of rain began to fall. Gracie voiced her nervousness. Jules brushed her mane softly with her hand, hoping to calm her down. She became more jumpy by the second, feeling the storm that approached.

"Ava, we need to go."

"Do you feel comfortable picking up speed?"

"I'm going to have to."

A sharp crack of lightening brightened the sky. Thunder growled around them, snarling at them as a vicious reminder that their time had run out. Gracie shook her head, annoyed at Jules pulling on the reins. Her front legs jumped up as Jules leaned forward, wrapping her arms around her neck in a desperate attempt to hold on. Without the resistance of the reins, Gracie took off galloping in the reverse direction into the woods.

Jules screamed for Ava's help but couldn't hear her response as she and Gracie raced off further into the woods with Ava soon disappearing into the background.

CHAPTER EIGHTEEN

"WHERE ARE THEY, MATT? THEY SHOULD HAVE BEEN BACK by now." Derek checked his watch again. "I don't have a good feeling about this." The dark clouds had moved in faster than what he felt comfortable with. Did the girls not notice the storm approaching at rapid speed?

"I'm sure they got distracted talking about how wonderful we are. They should be back soon." Matt kept his head back against the chair, eyes closed, not willing to move.

Derek took a sip of his coffee. "I wish that is what Jules is saying about me, but I won't hold my breath. I feel like I haven't gained any ground with her."

Matt opened his eyes. "If I learned anything through my relationship with Ava, it's to give her time and space to sort out her feelings. Is she worth the wait?"

Derek didn't need a second to think about it. "Yes."

"Good. Then be patient."

Streaks of lightening brightened the sky, followed by a rumble of thunder that jolted them both from their chairs. Derek decided not to wait around anymore. The horses couldn't handle this weather. They would be spooked by now. He could only imagine what sort of reaction the girls encountered from the fierce storm that hovered over them.

"I'm going to grab Captain and go look for them. You stay here in case they come back. I've got my phone."

Matt agreed as Derek rushed into the barn to grab the reins

and saddle. His hands worked quickly with the equipment, like second nature, as if he had never left the ranch.

Captain followed him out, uneasy with the weather. Derek spoke calmly, stroking his nose. "It's okay, boy. I know you can do this. We need to find the girls."

"Derek, look!" He turned, looking into the direction Matt pointed.

Ava barreled down the trail, Sasha picking up speed as she approached the stalls. Derek ran out to meet her, helping to calm the horse to a stop. Ava's breathless words poured out. "Jules needs help. Gracie took off into the woods. I'm not experienced enough to go after her. Derek, help her, please!"

Derek sprinted back to Captain, mounting the horse in a flowing motion. "You were down this trail?" He pointed to where she came from.

"Yes, we were near the cabin when I lost sight of her."

"Stay here. Call me if she returns." He left as he heard their confirmation.

It felt good to be back on a horse, riding at full speed. He might not miss the drama that surrounded his family, but he did miss the wide open spaces and the feel of freedom and calmness that washed over him as he rode. Whenever life got the best of him when he lived here, he would take Captain out for a ride. It became his favorite time to talk to God, unload his burdens.

Every emotion worked itself over Derek except calmness. Ava told him what general area Jules had been in, but that was a long time ago. He would follow the trail for now and pray he ran into her sooner rather than later.

Rain began to pour down relentlessly. His hat helped to shield his face, but it was still hard to see what stood twenty feet in front of him.

"Jules!" Her name became lost over the thunder. He called out again.

He entered the woods that passed by the cabin. He called her name again in hopes she had been able to stop Gracie and find shelter. After no response he finished following the trail until it merged with the trail leading to the creek.

He made a quick decision to change course, hoping Jules knew enough to follow the creek back to the barns. Captain splashed down into the creek, holding his own as the water scattered in every direction. Coming out into a clearing, Derek took his first deep breath in minutes when he saw her red hair in the distance.

"Jules!"

She stopped, turned. He was too far away to read her facial expression, but close enough to notice her limping as she switched directions and walked toward him. He brought Captain to a halt and jumped down.

Jules looked vulnerable as she approached him wobbling, her hair matted down from the rain. She appeared sheepish, putting her head down to avoid his eye contact.

His raw emotions revved on overload. He didn't have enough time to mentally decide how to react to his feelings of wanting to protect her.

Reaching for her, he pulled her into his chest, enveloping her in his arms. She stiffened at first, but soon relaxed, laying her head on his shoulder. Her soft sobs had him drawing his hold tighter. He needed to get her out of this weather. She had to be chilled to the bone from her drenched coat and hair.

Pulling her back, he placed his hands on each side of her face. He was startled to see his desire reflected in her eyes. His heartbeat accelerated by her closeness, the fact that their lips were mere inches apart.

He cleared his throat. "Are you okay?"

Jules looked down, unwilling to continue looking him in the eyes. "Yes. Gracie threw me off near the creek. I thought it would be best to just follow it until I was found. I think my ankle is sprained, but nothing is broken except my pride."

Derek tipped her chin up, forcing her to look at him. "You scared me." His thick voice betrayed the emotions that teased his heart.

"I'm sorry. What about Gracie, will she be okay?"

"Yeah, she will find her way home."

The rain poured harder. The water trailed down her face, along her cheeks and over her lips. He leaned his forehead against hers, her breath slid down his neck. His hormones went into overdrive. He dropped the few inches it took to put their lips closer.

He settled with testing the waters by brushing his lips against her cheek. She shuddered beneath his grasp as a warning he needed to back off.

"Derek." His name came out barely a whisper.

"I know." He stepped back to give her the space she needed.

"I just need more time," she admitted, her lips forming into a thin line.

Not wanting to completely step back, he pushed a stray hair out of her face. "It's okay. I know you are not ready. I'm not going to push." He took a step back. "I know we are just friends and that's all it's going to be for now."

"I don't want to lose you."

"You won't."

"I just – I don't – I…"

"Jules, it's okay. Now isn't the time for this conversation anyway. Let's get you back to the house and check out your ankle." He started to lead her toward Captain.

"Wait a second. You want me to get on a horse again?"

He grinned. "It's either that or I carry you back."

She looked back and forth between him and the horse. "Fine. Help me up onto this death ride."

Chapter Nineteen

DEREK EASED JULES DOWN INTO HER OVERSIZED LEATHER CHAIR. He had dropped Matt and Ava off first and then brought her home to help get her settled for the night. He grabbed the ottoman that sat in front of her couch and pulled it over. "Here, prop your leg up on this to keep it elevated."

Jules obeyed out of pure pain that pulsed throughout her ankle. "You don't have to go to all this trouble, Derek. I'll be fine."

"Don't try and make me feel better."

"It's just a sprained ankle. I'll be up and around in no time. I've been wanting a few days off of work anyway. Plus, paying bills is totally overrated."

He stopped, adjusting her leg to see her teasing smile. "Well, I guess that's what you get for daydreaming about me as a storm approaches."

She couldn't believe how close his sarcastic comment touched the truth. The only comeback she had was to drench her feelings in what would appear to be returned sarcasm. She kept her voice at a monotone pace and rolled her eyes. "How did you know?" She closed her eyes and leaned her head back against the chair. She wanted to act bored in hopes he couldn't see the truth she tried to hide. "It must have been the smell of the horses that reminded me of you."

Derek's laughter rumbled from deep in his chest. He pulled

a blanket out of the basket and placed it under her ankle to give it more height. "I'll go get you some ice. Do you need anything else?"

"I'll take a Diet Coke. I'm hungry, too. How good are you with frozen dinners in the microwave?"

"Let's just say I might have missed my calling. I'm excellent at pushing buttons."

"That you are. You push mine all the time."

His mouth dropped open. He hit the left side of his chest with this fist, implying she put a knife through his chest.

She laughed. "Come on, you totally set yourself up for that one."

"True. Okay, I'll go check out your freezer. Anything else?"

"I'm sure I have a load of laundry that needs washed and the bathroom could use a deep cleaning. Seeing I'm handicapped and all," she batted her eyelashes and pouted. She looked around her living room. "I'm fresh out of bells, so I'll clap if I need you."

Derek took his fingers and delicately pushed a stand of hair behind her ear. She ignored the way her pulse doubled in speed from his touch. "Did you take an extra dose of your pain meds? I've never seen you this silly."

She did feel carefree. Today might have made her realize how real her feelings were for Derek, but after their talk in the rain as she stood injured and looking like a drowned rat – that was not her finest moment – there was a breakthrough with her relationship with Derek. Like the sun that poked out of the clouds after the storm.

They had an understanding. They were both interested, but now was not the time. They would just be friends, enjoy each other's company – and a little flirting never hurt. With the pressure off to make a decision, she could finally relax and be herself.

Now, to have a little more fun. "I only took the four pills."

His eyes widened. "What! Jules, you were only supposed to take two!"

She grinned. His reaction, priceless. She patted his arm. "I only took two. Please, this isn't my first rodeo."

"Woman, you are relentless."

She clapped her hands. "Diet Coke, please. Your tip is going down with each minute that passes."

"You are lucky my guilt is so thick because otherwise I might be tempted to step on your leg."

"We both know you'd hold no respect for me if I didn't give you a hard time."

He leaned over and stopped when their noses almost touched. His peppermint gum invaded her senses. "You can just keep your tip. I've got other plans for how you can pay me."

Saliva stuck in her throat as she attempted to swallow. "And what is that?"

"That can wait until after dinner. Her Highness is hungry." He handed her the television remote and vanished into the kitchen.

&c &c &c &c

DEREK STUCK HIS HEAD INTO THE FREEZER. IF HE COULDN'T TAKE a cold shower, he'd take option two – a frozen face. As if Jules didn't capture all his thoughts, she had to go and let loose and pull him in even more. Nothing was sexier to him than a woman that made him laugh and enjoyed life. He wouldn't be able to play off his desire to be with her much longer if she kept this up.

He had just seen a glimpse of the real Jules. She had finally allowed him to see her for what she was, carefree, funny, and loveable. Ugh. He was headed for a broken heart if he didn't pull back the reins around his heart. *Friends. We are just friends.*

He pushed around the contents that were stuffed in her freezer and found two chicken linguine meals in the back right corner. Following the instructions, he stuck the first meal in the microwave and punched in the time.

Leaning back against the counter, he took the few minutes he had to pull his thoughts and feelings together.

Jules had been different since the ranch. Their talk didn't last long, but he got the information that he needed. She didn't come right out and say she liked him and right now she only wanted his friendship. She wasn't ready. It wasn't what he had been praying and hoping for, but at least she didn't crush any chance they had of someday being together. He just needed to be patient and remind her daily how perfect they were for each other.

A tall order for his patience and his heart.

Lord, you know my desires. But I also know your timing is perfect. Guide my relationship with Jules and help me to keep my mind on You so I know where You are directing me to go.

His *Amen* blended in with the beeps from the microwave. He switched and put in the new meal. He set up two trays and cracked open a Diet Coke for Jules and filled a glass with water for himself.

He made his way back into the living room, relieved that Jules had her attention on the movie she had found.

They ate in comfortable silence. Or more so, he ate while she played with her food. "Are you going to eat? I think you've only taken a bite or two. I didn't slave away in the kitchen only to throw it away."

"I'm sure there were a lot of blood, sweat and tears. Sorry, I guess I'm not as hungry as I thought I was." She wiped her mouth with her napkin and finished off her drink.

"It must be your nerves from being in my presence."

"Don't flatter yourself."

"Wouldn't think of it."

"Do you want the rest of my meal?" She pushed her plate to the front of the tray. "I'm done."

"As much as I love this gourmet chicken, I think I'll pass."

"Hey, don't knock the free food."

"You're right. You should pay me to eat this." He took a swig of his water to wash down the bad after-taste.

"Add it to my tab."

Derek pumped himself up for what he was about to ask and cleared his throat. Why did this woman make him so nervous? He could always count on his smooth words and confidence through his years of dating. Now his stomach knotted and his hands sweat. He walked a fine line with Jules and it deflated all his best moves.

Preparing to throw a Hail Mary pass, he hoped he didn't get blind-sided by a sack. "I'll just collect now." He turned himself on the couch to face her head on. "I need a favor."

"No, I will not walk Max this week." A smile crept along her soft lips.

"You are so lazy." He took a deep breath. "What I need is a date for the department's Christmas party." He paused for only a moment to try and gauge her reaction. "Only as friends. I just don't want an evening of mingling by myself while all the wives try to set me up with one of their relatives or 'the perfect girl' they know for me."

She bit her lip. "I don't know ..."

"Trust me, it will be fun. Ava will be there to keep you company. Plus, I will be the perfect gentleman and will only make out with you afterwards if you ask." He gave her a sly wink.

The tip of her lips quirked up. "You sure do know how to make a girl's dreams come true."

"I aim to please."

She bit her nails as she contemplated his request. Sweat raced down his back. He felt the need to fan his shirt from his failed deodorant that couldn't keep up with his nerves.

"Okay. I'll go. It sounds like fun. But I do have a second cousin once removed that would look great as your sidekick."

His laughter filled her tiny room and his worry depleted. "As tempting as that sounds, I'll just stick with you."

CHAPTER TWENTY

THE CROWDED AND LOUD RESTAURANT DIDN'T SEEM TO DETER the group. A girl's night out was just what Ava's high stress level needed and by the relaxed stance of Jules, Valerie, Erica and Lucy, it was appreciated by all, no matter the surroundings. Everyone had been so high-strung since Aaron was taken, Valerie especially.

Valerie was nervous and still scared not to have him in her eyesight, and everyone understood. She had taken a leave of absence from work to decompress from what had happened and to look for a new daycare. She held no harsh feelings toward the last sitter, but Chad knew where Aaron stayed, so his childcare location had to change.

It had taken countless pep talks to convince Valerie to leave Aaron for the evening. It took Josh's plan of action to finally get her to be at peace with leaving him. Josh volunteered to stay and watch Aaron and invited Jake, Matt and Derek over for the evening of watching the big college game on ESPN. If Aaron wasn't safe in a house with four men, two being cops, there was no hope.

Ava caught Valerie check her phone. "I'm sure Aaron is fine, Valerie."

Her cheeks tinged pink from being caught. "I know, but an update doesn't hurt."

"How are you and Aaron doing?"

Valerie turned to Lucy's tentative question, taking a deep breath. "Okay. It's been almost three weeks and I still panic when Aaron isn't near me or I lose sight of him for a few seconds. Thankfully kids are so resilient. The first couple days he asked to sleep with me and he always wanted me to hold him, but now he seems to be back to his normal self.

"I don't know what I would do without Josh. He has been my rock through this whole nightmare. To be honest, I'm surprised it hasn't scared him off. I would understand if it did."

"Oh Val, do you not see the way he looks at you? He's not going anywhere," Ava encouraged.

A soft smile parted Valerie's lips at the mention of Josh.

"Have you figured out your daycare dilemma?" Lucy asked.

"Yes. There is a woman at my boss's church that I just hired to come to my house to watch him. I have upgraded my security system. Plus, it helps that she leads a woman's self-defense class a few nights a week. I start back to work on Monday from my leave of absence." She shrugged her shoulders. "I think I'm ready."

"That is great news. I'm sure you are so relieved."

"I am. Aaron met with her a few days ago and they really clicked."

"Are they any closer to finding Chad?" Erica asked.

"I don't think so. He's too smart to get caught." Valerie looked across the table at Ava. "Has Matt said anything?"

"No. It's a bit of a sore subject for us, so I don't bring it up often. I figure when he knows something he'll tell me or lock me in my apartment again."

"Yeah, how rough to have a handsome cop as your fiancé who goes out of his way to want to protect you," Lucy teased.

Ava playfully shoved her shoulder. "I know, but we each have our own cross to bear. Why me, God? Why me?" she teased back. "But seriously, I can't be under lock and key again. I'll go crazy."

"Having been in Ava's shoes, I can understand. It's nice that they care, but when your freedom is smothered, it can change your outlook.

The waiter brought out more refills and took up their empty plates. Once he left Erica cleared her throat. "Ava, I heard you picked out your wedding dress. What does it look like?"

Ava didn't mind talking about the wedding, but she couldn't help the embarrassment that festered from the fact this was her second wedding to plan. A second wedding dress to pick out. "It is strapless and simple, but still very elegant."

"She's being modest. Let's just say, Matt's jaw will drop," Jules inserted.

"And of course it was the first one she tried on." Lucy piped in. "She tried on others just to humor us, but we all knew that dress was made for Ava."

"Have you decided on colors yet?" Valerie asked.

"A deep purple and silver." She checked the time on her phone. "We better get the checks so we don't miss the movie."

"Ava, are you avoiding talking to us about your wedding plans?" Jules asked. It was just like her to read her mind.

"No." Stares of unbelief met her false answer. "Okay, I admit, I feel a little foolish planning another wedding. If I had my choice, we would just elope."

"Have you told Matt how you feel?" Erica asked while she placed her cup down and leaned forward to hear better over the growing noise around them.

"We talked about it right after we got engaged. Matt said he'd do whatever I wanted, but I knew he preferred a traditional wedding. From the beginning of our relationship he has always put me first. I want to do this for him. My thoughts are silly and I know that. Don't get me wrong. I am so excited to marry Matt and become his wife. It's just a very humbling experience. I guess I'm just a little on edge because the invitations go out tomorrow."

"Ava, you know there is no shame in what happened with Tim. Your marriage to Matt is a new beginning and we are all excited for you," Erica encouraged.

"Speaking of weddings," Ava turned the conversation back on Erica, "where are you and Jake at on the road to getting married?" She asked, happy to share the spotlight.

Erica released a nervous giggle and turned to get the waiter's attention. "Check, please."

❧ ❧ ❧ ❧

AFTER THE MOVIE THE GROUP SPLIT UP INTO THEIR DESIGNATED cars. Lucy took Erica and Valerie home while Ava and Jules left to return to her apartment for the rest of the night. They had plans to finish up addressing the invitations to send out in the mail tomorrow.

"You aren't limping as much. Does your ankle feel better?" Ava asked Jules as they rounded a car and headed down the aisle her car was parked in.

"It does. I can tell the days I spend too much time on my feet and I have to walk at a slower pace, but overall I think it's almost healed."

As they approached Ava's car, the car across the aisle grabbed her attention. It looked to be the same make and color as the one that had appeared in the school parking lot at random times.

"Jules, get in the car." Her words shouted out short and terse. Her frame became rigid as if a rod had been slipped down her spine. She grabbed hold of Jules' arm and pushed her toward the vehicle, hoping she didn't re-injure her ankle.

"Ava, what is wrong? You are freaking me out!"

"Just do it."

Jules obeyed and slid into the passenger side. The security

light overhead produced enough light for Ava to see inside the car. It looked as if it was empty. On a foolish impulse, she advanced the car to make sure. She peeked into the driver side window. Nothing seemed out of the ordinary, nothing to give her insight to the owner of this vehicle that had haunted her for weeks.

Ava fumbled inside her purse to find a pen and some sort of paper to write on. She found an old grocery receipt and walked around to the back of the car, jotting down the license plate number.

"What was that all about?" Jules asked once Ava had joined her in the car.

"Just my paranoia getting the best of me."

"I need a better explanation than that."

"I'll tell you all about it back at my place."

CHAPTER TWENTY-ONE

AVA HANDED THE MUG OF HOT TEA TO JULES WHO SURROUNDED herself with envelopes and stamps at her kitchen table.

"Thank you," Jules blew over the top to cool it down before she took her first sip.

"I would have made coffee, but between my nerves and the caffeine I would never get to sleep tonight."

She picked up her pen and finished the address she had started but had stopped when the tea kettle whistled. They had a fourth of the invitations left to do and it had already passed midnight. Ava didn't bring up what happened in the parking lot yet, and Jules hadn't pushed.

The conversation needed to happen but was not wanted by Ava. For weeks she had convinced herself it wasn't a big deal. That she was merely overreacting. But the fear that coursed through her body just at the sight of the familiar car made her realize that was not true.

"I think I'm being followed," Ava blurted the statement out. It felt good to get it off her chest. Hearing the words bounce around her kitchen also tightened her chest from the fact that her notion might be very quickly becoming a reality.

"What? Why do you think that?" Jules dropped her pen and leaned forward.

"Well, I have just noticed this same vehicle in our school

parking lot. There is usually someone inside, watching. I even saw it on the kindergarten field trip when we went to the pumpkin farm. The vehicle I saw tonight looked just like it." She covered her face with her hands and exhaled slowly. This nightmare would just not go away. Her stomach turned. "Matt is going to be furious when I tell him."

Julia's mouth dropped. "You haven't told him!"

She frowned. "No. He has been so stressed with work and it's a sore subject between us. I didn't want to say anything until I knew for sure." She scrunched her face. It sounded so much worse once she said it out loud. She bent over and lightly banged her head against the kitchen table in a repetitive pattern.

"I'm not going to sugar coat this for you, Ava. He is going to be really mad."

"I know." Her words came out muffled as she talked into the wood.

"You need to tell him soon." In her peripheral vision, she watched Jules lean back against her chair with a displeased frown setting upon her face.

Ava left her head rested on the table, too tired emotionally and physically to move it an inch. "We are looking at houses tomorrow. I will tell him afterwards." There was no reason to dampen their time searching for their perfect starter home. Plus she needed time to figure out how to tell him.

She sat up. "You could tell him for me. He wouldn't yell at you."

"I could have Derek do it. He still owes me."

"For what?"

"Oh, I agreed to go to the department's Christmas party with him."

Now it was Ava's turn to be surprised. "What does this mean?"

"Nothing has changed. I'm just doing him a favor."

"Sure you are. Just keep telling yourself that. Whatever helps you sleep better at night." Jules hadn't mentioned much more about Derek since their trip to the ranch and she didn't want to push. Now it made sense.

"And that's not the half of it. As if it's not complicated enough, guess who called me last night, begging to have me back?"

"Doctor Jerk himself? Please tell me you hung up on him."

Jules shrugged, "His apology seemed really sincere."

Ava tried not to roll her eyes. She and Jules stared at each other. Ava broke first. She could no longer hold her tongue. "Julia Marie Anderson, there is only room for one idiot woman at this table and I am holding the award right now. You can't take him back."

"I didn't say I was going to take him back. I just listened. I thought with our history he deserved that."

A hush fell over the room except for Ava's ragged breathing. "No. What that man needs is a good kick in the pants and to watch your backside walk away."

"Ava, don't you think you are being a little dramatic?"

"Dramatic would be if I threw this tea cup across the room. Don't tempt me." She did give herself a pep talk about the need to calm down and help Jules talk this out rationally. Jules had been her anchor during the most difficult time in her life. She needed to take a turn and step up to the plate. Jules had been struggling with hearing from God lately and confused about a lot of things, especially with her love life. She put her hands up in surrender. "Okay. I admit I didn't handle this new update as well as I should have. I'm sorry. I just don't want to see you hurt again."

Jules' face softened from her apology. "I'm trying to take control of my life, Ava."

"Isn't that God's job?"

Jules' eyebrows slammed together as she frowned. "Yes,

but it would be of great assistance if He helped me out and told me what to do. My life feels like a mess and I don't know which way is up to dig myself out of this hole. I like Derek but I can't commit because I want to know for absolute certainty that I'm supposed to be with him. Then Scott re-enters my life and I have to wonder if I stalled with Derek because I am meant to take him back." Jules didn't even try to lower her voice. Frustration leaked out with every word. She let out a cry, "Maybe I should just become a nun."

Ava reached across the table and squeezed her hand. "As stellar of an idea as that is, before I take you to the convent and sign you up, let's talk this out. What did Scott say?"

A sigh escaped. "He said that he misses me and that he is so sorry that he hurt me. That he was in a really bad place, knows he messed up and wants to work things out."

Ava needed a barf bag.

"Okay. So we know for sure you have feelings for Derek. Do you have feelings for Scott still?" She could barely choke the words out.

"It was nice to hear his voice. I was in love with him, Ava. You just can't turn that off." Jules pushed to her feet and paced Ava's small kitchen. "All right, let me put it in perspective for you. Let's say when Tim showed up at your apartment a couple months after your wedding, he instead came to tell you he was wrong and wanted you back." Jules turned a questioning eye toward her. "What would you have done?"

Ouch. Perspective hurt. Putting herself in Jules' shoes made her look at the situation a little differently. Her calloused opinion against Scott wasn't going to help Jules. The realization of how she would have handled the situation made her understand the confusion Jules suffered.

"I would have heard him out. Gave him a chance to explain, to understand why he did what he did."

Jules sat back down at the table and ran a hand through her

hair. The look in her eyes put Ava on edge. "Don't be mad, but Scott asked me out … and I agreed."

Ava blinked twice. She might not agree with the steps Jules had taken, but she was a big girl and needed to find out for herself where God was calling her. What Jules needed was a supportive friend, no matter what.

Maybe she should have made coffee. It had turned into that kind of night. "Jules, if you feel you need to see Scott, then do it. But can I give a friendly suggestion?" Jules nodded so she continued. "I think you need to tell Derek."

"Why? We are just friends."

"Fine, I'm too tired to argue. You are just friends. Blah-Blah-Blah. But whether you want to deny it or not, you both have feelings for each other. He deserves to know what is going on. You'd want the same respect, wouldn't you?"

"You're right." Jules' serious demeanor broke and she started to giggle.

"What?" she asked, wondering if Jules had officially lost it.

"I'll tell Matt, if you tell Derek. We could do each other's dirty work."

Ava joined in on her deliriously tired laugh. They were a sad pair. The time had come for her to own up to her mistake and she needed to tell him herself. *Ready or not, Matt, you are getting the truth tomorrow.*

CHAPTER TWENTY-TWO

Matt's jeep held an unbearable silence as they followed behind the realtor to the final house showing. Disappointment sat at bay as their hope diminished with each house they toured.

They had gone into their house hunting journey with high hopes of finding a house today. Their realtor, Wendy had a list of five houses – and none of them came close to what they wanted or the price range they could afford.

Ava and Matt wanted a move-in ready house with three bedrooms that had a big back yard in a good neighborhood. Ava didn't think they were asking for much, but the market just didn't hold what they wanted. They weren't necessarily pressed to find and buy a house right away since they could always live in one of their apartments until they found something, but Matt continued to voice his desire on wanting to find something before the wedding.

As they checked out the last house on the list, Wendy got word that a new house had just been put on the market. She didn't know much about it, but Ava and Matt decided it would be worth a look. What would it hurt at this point? After a few calls, Wendy had it all set for them to go see it right then.

Ava stared out the window, watching the houses they passed as her stomach twisted with the realization that their day wouldn't be getting much better. Later this afternoon when they returned to her apartment, she intended to come clean with Matt about the suspicious incidents that had been happening. It was probably nothing, but she had purposefully kept from him the one thing he'd asked of her. Scum ranked high on the list of vocabulary words that described how she viewed herself right now.

Matt reached forward and turned down the radio. As if on cue he grabbed hold of her folded hands and merged his hand in between. "You've been really quiet today."

She turned her head to give him her full attention and pressed a smile upon her face. "Sorry. Just nervous about how things are going to work out." The truth came out two-fold, even though Matt didn't know that yet.

He squeezed her hand. "I know, I thought today would be different and we would really like one of those houses. It will all work out. We just need to be patient."

"Ah, yes, my best attribute. I've always been known for my patient spirit."

Matt laughed at her thick sarcasm. "I guess there are a few other characteristics that rank higher." Ava raised her eyebrows. "Hey, you said it."

"Oh, there is so much for you to learn. Like nodding while saying, 'yes honey, whatever you say, dear'. And let's not forget the most important one, 'you're right.'"

"Has anyone told you how hilarious you are?" His sarcasm matched hers. He flipped on the turn signal and maneuvered the Jeep as they turned right onto a new street.

"Yes, and I believe that would be one of those characteristics of mine that you put before being patient."

A slow smirk dissolved his lips as he nodded, "Yes honey, whatever you say, dear. You're right."

Ava patted his forearm, "Aren't you the quick learner?" She leaned her head over and rested it on his shoulder. A sigh escaped. "What if we don't like this house either?"

Matt lightly kissed her hair. "Then we keep searching until we find the right one. I want to find a house just as much as you do, if not more, but it doesn't have to be today. God knows our desires and He has already gone before us and will prepare the way for us. If we rush God, we could miss out on all the goodness He has in store for us. We will find our house in His perfect timing."

Ava sat up and let his words of wisdom wash over her as she soaked in the peace of the truth he spoke. "You're right."

"Wait, what did you say? I must have misunderstood you. I thought you said, 'you're right.' Isn't that my line?"

Ava couldn't help but giggle. "I didn't realize I was marrying a comedian."

Before he could serve up a rebuttal, the realtor turned into a driveway. They parked in front of a two-story gray house with white trim and a red door. Ava's breath caught in her throat as hope spiked. It was adorable. Landscaping of bushes and flowers decorated the front walk and merged into a front porch that stretched from both sides of the front door.

She quickly looked over at Matt to read his reaction. It mirrored her own.

CHAPTER TWENTY-THREE

"**M**ATT, JUST PUT THE BAGS ON THE COUNTER AND I'LL GRAB us a couple drinks and plates," Ava said over her shoulder as she entered the kitchen.

"Okay. Is it alright if we eat in the living room while we watch football?" Matt already guessed what her answer would be but asked anyway as he placed the to-go bags from the local Mexican restaurant on the counter.

"Do you even need to ask?" He smiled from knowing her so well. "Grab us a couple trays from the hall closet. It will be easier to eat off of those than the ottoman."

Matt found the trays and had them set up and the game turned on before she came back in the room. He caught himself reminiscing over how their day had worked out. They had found a great house – *the* house. When they had pulled up they were both hopeful and a tour of the home sealed the deal. The house came in older and square footage smaller than they had originally wanted, but they both agreed it would be a perfect starter home for them.

With every room they went through, Matt could envision his life with Ava in it. Nights in front of the fire, family and laughter surrounding their dining room table, the spare bedroom full of baby items once they were ready for children. Each room brought a new excitement over their future.

They left the realtor with their offer and were told they

should hear a response by Monday.

The only aspect of the day that concerned him came from Ava's quiet demeanor. It wasn't like her. To most people she would have appeared fine, but he could tell something was off.

Sure, she asked questions and dreamed alongside with him through each room, but her smile didn't have its normal sparkle.

Matt stood up to help as Ava entered the living room with the plates teetered carefully over her arm and hands. "You'd make a cute waitress," he said as he took his plate and drink from her.

"No thanks, I think I'll just stick with eating the food. However, I should back off a bit. I do have a wedding dress to fit into."

Those were the comments that made a man sweat. Talking to a woman about weight set men up with a booby-trap question that never had the right answer.

He kept it safe and simply kissed her forehead. "So, still no hints on what your dress looks like?" he asked as they sat down.

"I wouldn't want to take away your joy of anticipation."

"I've got plenty to anticipate over." He winked at her as her cheeks flushed a light pink color. To help push down his desires, he safely changed the subject. "Did you get the invitations sent out?" he asked as he opened his drink and poured the liquid into the glass filled with ice.

Ava finished her bite and cleared her throat. "Not yet. Jules and I finished them up late last night. I'll send them out on Monday."

They had decided on a small wedding with only family and close friends. Everyone invited already knew the date so there wasn't a rush to get the invitations out early. "Why don't I send them out? That's something easy I can do to help out."

Ava sat her drink down. "Sure. Thanks."

The rest of the meal they ate in silence except for a few cheers throughout the game. At halftime Ava stood, gathered the plates, and went to clean up and make a fresh pot of coffee.

Matt tried to push down his discomfort over her sudden bout of quietness. He replayed the day to make sure he hadn't said something to upset her, but he came up empty.

After putting the trays away he picked out a soft blanket from the pile Ava stashed by her reading chair and sank deep into the couch. Ava returned minutes later with two steaming mugs of coffee.

Matt gestured for her to join him. He arranged the coasters and took the mugs from her to sit them down. He pulled Ava down beside him and wrapped the blanket around them.

Ava dug her face into his shoulder. "Ava, is everything okay?" If she wasn't going to say anything he would just have to push the subject. She only shook her head. When she didn't answer, he poked further. "Are you having second thoughts about the house? We can always keep looking."

Ava sat up quickly and locked her eyes on his. "I love the house. I will never forget how special this day was as we walked through the house dreaming over our future." Confusion pushed his eyebrows together. He slipped a strand of hair behind her ear that was too short to fit in her ponytail.

He searched her blue eyes, hoping he had overreacted about her quiet stance, but the cloud of uncertainty that reflected back swallowed up his hope. Matt lifted up her chin, "What's going on, Ava? I'm starting to worry."

Ava reached across him and picked up her mug, wrapping her slender fingers around it as she took a careful first sip. She glanced back up at him. His breath caught as she exhaled what seemed to be a defeated breath.

"I think I'm being followed."

Every muscle in his body tensed. Her declaration didn't even touch his radar of ideas he had compiled about what might be wrong.

His words tumbled over each other in a lousy attempt to make a full sentence. "What? When did? Where?" He took a deep breath to give his mind and lips a chance to work at the same speed. "Why do you think you are being followed?"

"I've noticed a vehicle appearing at school and a few other places where I have been. At first I thought it was just a coincidence, but after last night I'm not so sure."

Matt raked his fingers through his hair as he absorbed this new information. He scooted to the edge of the couch and leaned his elbows onto his knees. "What happened last night?"

Ava's eyes never reached his as she explained. "Last night after the movie a car was parked near mine that looked very similar to the car that I've been noticing for awhile, and I just got an unsettled feeling about it. I think with everything combined, it just put me over the edge."

Matt tried to rationalize her statement and pull out the details he needed. "Have you seen someone? Can you identify the person you think is following you?" *Could this be the work of Chad Taylor? Or a stalker created from seeing Ava so much in the news? Maybe it is all just a coincidence?* Matt's mind raced over the possibilities.

She shook her head. "No. Each time the person stayed far enough away or wore too many clothes for me to get a good look at the face."

"Could you tell whether it was a man or a woman?"

"My best guess is a man, but only because he had so many clothes on and usually a hat and sunglasses."

Dread squeezed Matt's heart. He stood and went into Ava's kitchen to retrieve paper and a pen. He didn't want to forget anything she mentioned. He found what he needed in the front of her junk drawer and headed back to the living room. He sat across from her on the ottoman.

"All right, it might be nothing or it could be something. Let's get a timeline set up. Start at the beginning and don't leave anything out. Each detail is important, no matter how insignificant you may think it is."

Ava nodded and took another sip of her coffee before placing it back on the coaster. She folded her hands together and closed her eyes, he assumed to gather her thoughts.

"Okay, it all started the day of my kindergarten field trip to the pumpkin farm. I was sitting on the hay wagon waiting for the ride to start when I noticed someone watching us from the parking lot, dressed for a blizzard."

"Can you remember the clothes?"

"Yes, only because I thought it was so strange to be wearing that kind of clothing on such a pleasant day." She used her hands to work through the outfit. She started by touching her head. "The person wore a baseball cap."

His questions tumbled out. "Did it have anything written on it? Can you give me at least a color?"

"Um, I'm pretty sure it was navy with the Chicago Bears C in orange on the front."

"Good. Okay, what else?"

"An oversized winter coat. Black, maybe? Jeans and white tennis shoes."

Matt kept up with her as she gave the details until he realized the gap in time. "Wait a second. Your field trip was back in October." He looked up at her. "Ava, that was over a month ago."

She looked down at her gathered hands. "I know."

A kick in the gut couldn't compare to the words that just knocked the wind out of his reality over the situation. He'd first assumed that all of this had just happened over the last day or two, but instead it was a whole month ago. He tried to mask the disappointment in his voice. "In fact, that means this happened before the night we worked things out and you promised you would let me know if anything happened."

Ava leaned forward, placing her hands on his knees. "I am so sorry, Matt. I truly thought I was just being paranoid."

He could understand one incident but it sounded like there had been a few piled on top of this one. How could she go this long without telling him? Before getting too upset, he decided to get all the details first in case he had been assuming the worst. "Okay, what happened next?"

Matt continued writing as Ava unfolded about the last month of seeing the same type of car at the school's parking lot different times, seeing the car parked outside her apartment building one night, and then finished off with the scare last night.

Frustration brewed with each date he jotted down. It offended him that he had been working to the point of exhaustion to protect her – only to find out she had been holding what could be vital information from him.

The television volume increased from a commercial. Matt grabbed the remote, shutting it off. Looking over the timeline a date stuck out and his pulse quickened.

"Ava, one of the days you saw the car in the parking lot was the same day that Aaron went missing. You knew that something didn't seem right and yet you kept this information to yourself. That whole time we searched for Aaron, you said nothing." He drew a closed fist to his mouth before he said something he would regret.

She bit her lower lip and nodded. "I know it sounds bad, but I really thought it wasn't a big deal."

"Don't you think that was a decision we should have made together?"

Ava grabbed his empty hand and squeezed. "Please understand I didn't keep this from you to hurt you. It's just …" she cleared her throat, "it's just that we had finally worked things out and I knew you were so stressed. I didn't want to add to that over something so little."

He could read between the lines. "You mean you didn't want to have to be under protection again."

She rubbed her hands over her face. "Yes, that probably played a small role in keeping it quiet."

Matt needed space. He stood and walked over to the window and peered down to the half-empty parking lot. This discussion blind-sided him and he had yet to gain balance. But he knew where to find it. *Lord, help me to handle this your way. Guide my words and give me the discernment to know which direction to go with this new information. Give me wisdom and the grace to love and respect Ava, even though I don't feel like it at this moment.*

Composed and ready to further their conversation, he turned around to find Ava watching him, regret pooling in the depths of her glassy blue eyes. He could tell she had remorse, but it didn't change the fact that she had deliberately kept things from him.

"Matthew, I …"

He cut her off as he put a hand up to stop her. He took a couple steps toward her. "Listen, I'm not going to pretend that you hiding this from me doesn't hurt. How can I lead you within our marriage if you can't trust me? I thought when we worked out our issues that you believed I would give you the space you needed. After Aaron went missing, I respected you and honored your desire to not be under heavy protection."

Ava stood and shortened the distance between them. "You're right. You gave me the space I asked for and I appreciate it. It kills me that you think I don't trust you. I do, Matt. If I'm really being honest about it, I think I kept it a secret because as long as I ignored it, I thought maybe the uneasiness would just go away."

Matt shut his eyes, willing himself to keep a tight hold on

his words. How could he make her understand? "Ava, this is so much bigger than you want to believe it is. Maybe Chad couldn't care less about you, but why risk it? Your face was all over the news from the bank robbery. Then our engagement announcement went in the paper, exposing you further. Against my wishes, I might add."

He rubbed his temples in hopes that the massage would lessen his growing headache. "Plus, this isn't just about you. Aaron and Valerie are at risk, too. Chad has already shown he will go to extremes when it comes to his son. For just a second, pause and look at it from my perspective. Let's say that was Chad in the car watching you. Had you said something the first time we could have easily gotten him the next time and this nightmare would be over. Or maybe it was just a parent watching their kid at recess, but I guess we'll never know. This could easily be all one big coincidence or maybe not. But I can't pursue these leads if I don't know about them."

Ava's face crumbled before him. "I guess I never thought of it that way. You know I would never mean to put Aaron and Valerie in harm's way."

Matt tilted his head to the side, watching her finally grasp the severity of the situation. "I know you wouldn't." He walked back to the ottoman and picked up his paper and pen. "Let's finish the timeline." He reviewed her statement again. "Why don't you go over what happened last night."

Ava sat back down and went into depth, recapping her night from dinner to the movie to finally finding the maroon car parked by hers. Matt's hope peaked when she mentioned that she took down the license plate.

"Can I see it?" he asked, salivating over maybe having a break in their search. If they had the license number of the vehicle he drove around in, it would make finding him so much easier.

"Sure." She jumped up and found the number at the bottom of her purse.

Matt refrained from kissing the paper in hopes of a slight victory. "Thanks. I'll go make a call."

&·&·&·&

A VA TRIED TO KEEP BUSY WHILE MATT MADE HIS CALL IN THE spare bedroom. She tidied up the living room, washed and put away the dishes from the last few days, and refilled their mugs with fresh coffee.

Matt's words continued to echo through her mind. He didn't hide his disappointment in her and she didn't blame him. She sat down at the kitchen table to wait for his return. Her mug was half-empty when he stepped into the kitchen.

She stood quickly. "What did you find out?"

Ava noticed how he kept his distance from her. "The license plate number is a match to an elderly couple that lives on the Northeast side of the city."

Hope drained away with his answer. "Oh. So what does that mean?"

Matt shrugged his shoulders. "I don't know. I called Derek and gave him a quick rundown of what is going on. He is going to meet me at the station. Our first step is going to see if this couple has any connections to your school."

He turned, retrieved his coat from the counter and slipped it on. Panic set in with the realization of him leaving. She followed after him as he made his way to the door. "Matt, wait. Please."

Matt stopped and rotated around to face her. He stared at her, waiting for her to continue, but she couldn't. How could she make things right between them? Every attempt she made to say something didn't seem to be enough. The tears began to burn behind her eyes. She refused to emotionally break down and have a pity party in front of him when she was the sole reason for the tension between them.

"Matt, I really am sorry. I wish I could go back and change it, but I can't. I know this may sound meaningless since I have already failed you, but I am being completely sincere when I tell you, I promise I will keep you informed from now on. I also know that it may take awhile for you to regain your trust in me. I accept that." She stepped forward, yearning to touch him, but held off, wanting him to make that prompting. "Please forgive me."

Vulnerability picked at her while she stood there waiting for his response. Matt unfolded his arms and stepped forward. "Ava, I forgive you." He reached and took her hands into his. "These circumstances we have had to deal with are not common and it's hard to know how to handle them correctly. Just please remember, we are in this together, we're a team."

"Thank you. I will. By the end of this, you will be sick of hearing all the details." Ava stretched up on her tip-toes and wrapped her arms around his neck, pulling him closer. He reciprocated her touch by tightening his hold.

Matt's phone started ringing. He loosened his grip and pulled his phone out of his pocket. "I'm on my way, Derek." Matt's frame stiffened. "Really. Okay, I'll be there in fifteen minutes. Thanks."

Ava tensed. "Is everything okay?"

Matt pulled his keys from his jacket pocket. "Derek said they had an arrest come in that looks to be in connection with the drug bust we had at that motel a few weeks back."

"Do you think it has anything to do with Chad Taylor?" She hated bringing that man up in conversation between the two of them. So far he had only caused them heartache.

"That's what I'm about to find out."

CHAPTER TWENTY-FOUR

MATT STOOD BEHIND THE ONE-WAY MIRROR WATCHING Detective Sean Bennett work his magic. The suspect, Jason Walters, sat in a chair with his hands folded on the table. His shaved head made his features sharper as his darkened eyes betrayed the evil from within. A snake tattoo worked its way down his neck into the crease of his shirt. The man was only twenty-seven, but drug abuse had aged him another decade.

Bennett walked around the table like a tiger ready to pounce, stopping when he stood across from the suspect. He perched his hands down on the table and leaned down to make eye contact.

"Mr. Walters, things aren't looking good for you right now. You are being charged with multiple charges." He jabbed the folder lying on the table with his finger. "We have you on possession with intent to deliver over 35 pounds of methamphetamine, possession of drug paraphernalia, and resisting an officer. It would be in your best interest to work with us and give us the information we need."

"I don't have to tell you nothing."

Bennett stood straight and crossed his arms. "We don't take these charges lightly. We found your house stocked with illegal drug supplies and equipment. You had quite the operation going on and it's one I don't think you could have pulled off by yourself. And if that is the fact, we will be adding racketeering to your charges. You are looking at many years behind bars, unless you can give me some names. Help me and I can help you."

Walters began to fidget as his calm disposition quickly unraveled. His eyes darted around the room as he shifted his frame back and forth. "Can I get a cigarette?"

"Not right now, but I can get you a soda or something."

He rubbed a hand down his face. "Fine. I'll take a Pepsi."

Bennett opened the door and relayed the message. A minute later Walters had his drink. Bennett sat down in the chair across from him. He eased back, working to make the criminal more comfortable with him. "Jason, I know you don't want to rat out your contacts, but do you really want to take the fall for them?"

"I'm not a squealer."

"Listen," Bennett opened a file and turned it around to face him. "This is the list of crimes I can bury you with. Grab hold of this opportunity I'm giving you before it's too late. I'll give you ten minutes to think about it and then the offer is off the table."

Interrogating a suspect worked on a fine line of using details that surrounded the case and psychological manipulation to get a confession, or in their current circumstance, needed information. Bennett had a way of intimidating a person of interest, only to turn and play it cool until the hammer came down.

Bennett left the room and joined Matt, Derek and a few other officers in the observation room. Derek patted Bennett on the shoulder, "You are a master of art, my friend."

Matt had to agree. There were two detectives that Matt would always want in his corner during an interrogation, Sean Bennett and up-and-coming Detective Trevor Hudson.

Bennett smiled from the compliment causing the wrinkles

around his eyes to gather and his teeth to gleam against his dark skin. "This kid won't know what hit him." He looked between Matt and Derek. "What are you two doing here anyway? This isn't your case. You have to have better things to spend your Saturday afternoon on than watch an interrogation."

Matt stepped closer to the window, giving Walters a stare-down, wishing he could read minds. "Let's call it a conflict of interest."

"Okay, I'll bite. What do you have?"

"Remember at the beginning of October when my fiancé had a run-in with a guy by the name of Chad Taylor?" Bennett nodded, so he continued. "I know our trail has gone cold for him and it's just a hunch of mine, but I think he could be the mastermind behind our outbreak with the meth labs." He pointed toward the room where Walters sat. "You even said yourself that his operation was big – big enough that we *know* someone is helping him."

Bennett crossed his arms over his chest. "Are you sure this isn't just some ghost chase to find the man that threatened your girl?"

Matt stood up straighter, offended by the remark. "No, now just give me a chance to explain and show you what a real possibility this could be."

Derek cleared his throat, "It makes sense, Sean. Just hear him out." Matt relaxed his stance in part because his partner had just proven that he would take his side, and also because he realized this could be the lead they had been long waiting for.

Bennett tightened his lips, "All right. Make it fast."

"Over the last few months we have been working on the possibility that a super lab has formed and that there is a supplier working with many of the new labs starting around our community. So look at it from this angle. First, the equipment at the motel bust is the same equipment found in Walters' home. Second, the motel's video surveillance showed the man that came in to pay cash for the room is the same height and build of Chad Taylor. Third, Taylor has a history of working for a small scale drug lord. He has been groomed for this exact position and we know that he can get his hands on the ingredients – and a lot of it."

Adrenaline surged through his body as he fought for what he believed. This was the break they needed and probably his only chance for his voice and reasoning to be heard. Bennett stood like stone through his entire argument. He had no idea if he had gotten through or not.

"Okay. Get me a picture of Chad Taylor. I'll see what I can do."

Matt watched Bennett saunter back into the interrogation room five minutes later. He wanted to be in that room, not stuck behind a mirror.

Bennett's voice rumbled over the sound system set up in the room. "Jason, time is up." He joined him at the table. "Let's review. You can either go to prison for these charges here," he patted the file, "or you can give me some names of your accomplices and we can lighten that load of charges in court."

Walters smoothed his hands over his bald head. Even from a distance Matt could see sweat beads bubbling across his brow. He was breaking.

Bennett noticed too and pushed in further. "Come on, Jason. Don't let these guys get away with it and pin it all on you."

"I don't know, man. I don't know." His right leg bounced up and down nervously, the top of his thigh hitting the bottom of the table with greater force by the repetition. Bennett had him right where he wanted him.

"I'll tell you what I think. I think you are a good guy that

158

just got caught up in something that got out of your control too fast. I think you were struggling for money and saw an easy out."

Jason looked up. "I just needed to get my back rent paid up."

"It's a problem that feels impossible to solve sometimes. I get it. We all have financial problems at some point or another. So what did you do? Try meth a couple times, get hooked, and decide you could sell and use? Who got you started?"

"A friend."

"Some friend. He must be a good one if you are willing to take all the heat."

Jason grunted. "His name is Ben. Ben Kline."

Bennett scribbled on his notepad. "Okay, now we are getting somewhere, Jason. Did Ben help you start selling, too?"

"Ben got connected with this guy that got us the ingredients and equipment. We just cooked it and got it ready to sell."

Matt and Derek turned to each other. Matt took a deep breath to deflate the combustion ready to explode in his chest.

"Do you have a name for this guy?" Bennett asked.

"No. Ben worked with him. I only got a look at him a couple of times during the transfers. Listen, I've given you all the information I can. I want out of here."

Bennett opened the new file he had carried in. He pulled out a picture and turned it to face Jason. The picture was Chad Taylor's driver's license picture taken in Arizona a few years ago. Ava testified after the break-in that it looked similar to what he looked like now. "Is this the man you worked with?"

Bingo. Jason's startled eyes told them all they needed to know. "How did you?" Jason cursed. "I'm not saying anything more."

And he didn't. Bennett tried for fifteen minutes to break him but he held tight to his word. It was obvious that Chad Taylor held an authority that no one wanted to mess with.

Next up would be Ben Kline, in hopes they would be able to break him.

They knew what Chad Taylor was capable of … now they just had to find him.

CHAPTER TWENTY-FIVE

AVA RELAXED INTO THE OVER-SIZED CHAIR IN THE CORNER OF her parent's living room and let the Thanksgiving turkey settle as she watched the scenes play out before her. She had so much to be thankful for, especially her family that surrounded her now with love and the laughter that filled the room.

The guys lined up on the couches, talking smack about their fantasy football teams while the Bears were beating the Lions by a large margin in the fourth quarter. She eyed her dad nodding off while trying to keep attention to the conversations around him. Valerie and Erica sat on the floor playing Uno with Aaron, letting him win. Lucy and her mom sat at the dining room table, deep in discussion over Lucy's new painting.

She stole a look over at Matt and caught him watching her. They shared a smile until he turned his attention back on her brothers. Her heart squeezed with thankfulness for the love of this good man that she would be marrying in a few short weeks.

Despite the chaos that encircled and threatened to tear them apart, they were more grounded than ever. The wedding plans had come together and their offer on the house had been accepted – the closing date set for the Wednesday before their wedding.

She and Matt continued to work on their communication and sort out how each other felt over the circumstances that had risen up with Chad Taylor. Matt had replayed what he could share from the interviews of the two men in cohorts together with Chad. Neither would give him up, so now the police just had to work off the tips they got and hope they could track him down.

Ava followed up on her promise to stay open with him; however, there wasn't much to go on. She had yet to see the car again or have the feeling of being watched.

Her mood started to dampen. To push off the cloud of gloom she got up and joined her mom and Lucy at the table. Lucy dripped of talent. Everything she touched became a masterpiece – whether an entrée she made at the restaurant or a painting she created in her spare time. It was a known fact among Ava's siblings that she had not been blessed with the creative gene that Lucy possessed.

Lucy had in process a painting of a vase with flowers, explaining to their mom the techniques she used. "So you see, here in the background I used transparent paint to give it the receding look," she shifted her hand, "and then used opaque paint to help the vase and flowers advance."

Ava sat next to their mom as she scanned the painting. "Oh yes, I see." Their mom said, rubbing Lucy's arm. "You are so talented, my dear."

Lucy peered down, studying her work. "Thanks. Painting has become my passion. It started as a hobby, but now I'm thinking of maybe pursuing it full time."

Lucy wanting a career change didn't come as a surprise to Ava, but the thought of her giving up cooking did. "I didn't know you wanted to give up being a chef. Why?"

"It's not so much that I want to give up cooking altogether, but my job has been stressful lately. Painting relaxes me. Dillon thinks my last few paintings have been good enough to get them displayed at the Rockford Art Studio."

Ava's head spun from the notion that she didn't really know what was going on with Lucy. "Who is Dillon?" She looked over at their mom but received a blank stare in return.

"He is the co-owner of the Rockford Art Studio. He has been making appearances over the last month at my art class." Lucy's explanation held a defensive tone.

Ava turned in her chair and leaned around their mom to look her sister straight in the eyes. "I didn't mean to upset you, Lucy. I'm just surprised, that's all."

Lucy's didn't back down from her earlier rigid stance, "It's fine, I already knew you all would give me grief about it."

"Lucy," their mom intervened, "we only want you to be happy."

A timer went off in the kitchen and Lucy stood up, "I have to go check the pies." She abruptly walked out of the room, leaving Ava and their mom sharing a confused look between each other.

"What was that all about?" her mom asked.

Ava had the same question as her mom just voiced. She gave her a quick hug and assured her, "Don't worry about it. Let me go talk to her."

These were the moments that having a sister with a completely opposite personality and mind-set made life interesting. She didn't understand the lifestyle Lucy lived, jumping from one thing to another, living life on a whim. Lucy discussed art with finesse, using words Ava had no clue what they meant. Like opaque. What the heck was opaque paint? All Ava cared about was if the Crayola markers in class were washable.

But maybe that was the point. Maybe she hadn't tried hard enough to understand Lucy and the things she loved.

The scent of pumpkin pie filled the hallway leading into the kitchen. The oven door slammed shut as she entered the kitchen.

Ava waited to speak until Lucy had the pies arranged for the cooling process. "Hey Lucy, I really am sorry if I upset you."

"It's fine."

"I can tell it's not fine. What's going on?" She stepped up to the butcher block island that separated them.

Lucy let out an exhausted sigh. She walked around the island to join Ava. Bracing her arms on the counter, she jumped up and back to take a seat. "I'm sorry. I'm just having a pity party and trying to bring everyone down with me."

Ava followed suit and jumped up on the island, taking the spot beside her. "What is Thanksgiving day without a little drama? And how dare you throw a party without me! I'm offended." Lucy's smirk gave Ava the confidence to continue. "Seriously though, it's me, Luce. You can tell me anything."

Lucy tethered her fingers together and placed them on her lap. "I'm just …" she tilted her head back and closed her eyes. Ava waited her out. A few more seconds ticked away until she began again. "I'm jealous. I'm the only one without someone. I'm the only one who has no idea what they want to do with their life. And the realization has begun to hit that you are getting married and things won't be the same anymore."

Ava wrapped her arm around Lucy and pulled her closer. She wanted to kick herself for not seeing this sooner. "Lucy, you have so much going for you. You are so talented and just because you haven't figured out what you want to do, that doesn't mean you won't. You have the world at your fingertips. Don't look at this as a setback, but rather for the excitement that lies ahead." She slid her hand up and began to play with a strand of her hair. "You know, I have always been envious of your carefree take on life."

Lucy tilted her head to the side. "Really?"

"Really. It's what makes you, you. Nobody wants to

change that. And for the subject of you not having someone – just be patient. I can understand how lonely it may be watching your siblings in relationships, but your time will come." Lucy's eyes welled up with tears, calling for a little comic relief. "And that man will be a good one because you, little sister, are a lot to handle."

Lucy laughed as she buried her face into her hands and then used the tips of her fingers to brush away the tears. "I know, right?"

"Hey Ava, we need to …" Matt stopped short at the doorway when he saw them sitting together up on the butcher block island, crying and laughing. "Oops, sorry."

Lucy waved him in. "You can come in."

"I don't want to interrupt, but …" he stepped into the room, "Ava we need to leave soon to get to my parents."

Ava checked the clock on the stove. "Oh, you're right. Can you give me another ten minutes?"

He looked between the two of them. "Sure." He leaned forward and kissed Ava on the cheek. He stopped in front of Lucy and kissed her on the top of the head. "Only if we can take one of Lucy's amazing pumpkin pies with us?"

Lucy's smile beamed. "Deal." Once Matt left, Lucy turned her attention back to Ava. "I guess it's not the end of the world if you marry him."

Ava laughed and then turned serious. "I'm sorry if I haven't been spending enough time with you lately. With planning the wedding, school, and dealing with all the chaos, I haven't really made you a priority."

"It's okay. I haven't really given you a chance with my carefree lifestyle and all."

Ava pushed Lucy's shoulder from the teasing. "Look who has her spunk back." Ava jumped down from the island and went to the cupboard to get a container to take a pie with them. "I know I don't understand your artist lingo, but I really do love your work. In fact," she dropped her voice level down, "I was hoping you could help me out with something."

Lucy slipped down from the island and joined her, keeping with her quiet demeanor. "Thanks. What can I do for you?"

"I have been trying to figure out what to give Matt for a wedding present and I came up with an idea. When he first told me he loved me, we were at a secluded spot that overlooked Pierce Lake. I thought it would be sweet to have a painting of that spot to remember it by."

Ava didn't expect the hug but gladly accepted it.

"Yes! I would love to do that for you." Lucy exclaimed quietly.

"Great. Do you need to go see the spot or would a picture of it be okay? I took one with my camera before we left."

"A picture would work fine. The season is different now. This way I can envision how you experienced it."

Ava left her parent's house with one more item to add to her thankful list: Lucy, the carefree, every-day-is-different sister that she didn't fully understand but loved with all her heart.

CHAPTER TWENTY-SIX

JULES STOOD IN FRONT OF THE MIRROR, TURNING FROM SIDE TO side to catch all angles of outfit number fifteen she had tried on for the Police Department's Christmas party. Her nerves had gotten the best of her and overflowed into her appearance.

She hadn't seen Derek since he dropped her off after spending the day at his family's ranch. Although, he had called her twice since then. Once to check up on her ankle and then another a few days ago to make sure they were still on for tonight.

Talking to him came easy. Derek had a way of making conversation effortless by knowing just when to ask questions and when to give input. He could be funny one minute and the next, serious.

She smoothed down her dress and tightened her belt one more notch. Maybe if she changed her shoes? Checking the time she moved quickly back into her closet and slipped on her knee high boots.

Last would be the finishing touches with jewelry. If she didn't pick up her pace, she wouldn't be ready before Derek arrived. She chose a pair of dangly earrings and a necklace to match.

Her forehead exposed a thin line of sweat beading at her hairline. She fanned herself with her hands. What was her problem? She was just doing Derek a favor, that's all! They were only friends.

She had been rehearsing that line in her head for the past couple weeks. Not that it had done her any good as she prepared to spend the evening with him, on his arm, meeting his friends. Or could the tightening of her stomach be because she had to tell Derek that she had plans to go out with Scott the following weekend?

What a mess she had made of things.

The doorbell rang.

She jumped. Maybe just one more layer of deodorant …

&&&&

THE CHRISTMAS PARTY BUZZED WITH VOICES AND LAUGHTER. THE banquet room had Christmas trees outlining the perimeter, each decorated with a different theme. A pianist sat in the corner at a baby grand piano, playing Christmas music softly as people mingled and shared stories about their kids, discussed which football teams would make the play-offs, and which side they stood on politics.

Jules hadn't expected the comradeship between the officers, but what really surprised her was the reason why they came together. It wasn't a party dedicated to them, per se. In fact, she learned that they had to pay a good amount per plate, with all proceeds going to the Boys and Girls club downtown. Not only did these officers daily give their lives to protect the community, but they went above and beyond to support it, too.

Derek returned to their table with drinks in hand. "I hope punch is okay."

"Yes." She took her drink. "Thank you." Her heartbeat escalated when their fingers brushed against each other's. She thought she had her emotions somewhat under control until she had opened the door to find him standing on her front porch, unashamedly handsome in his dress pants, a bright blue shirt and skinny tie. How dare he.

He leaned in closer, inches away from her ear, to be heard over the growing noise. "Are you having a good time?"

"I am." And she was – probably too good of a time. "Thanks for inviting me."

Derek looked up, groaning. He took a sip of his punch, closing his eyes.

"What's wrong?" she asked, leaning in closer.

He plastered a smile on his face and talked through his tight lips, "My boss's wife is heading our way. Prepare yourself. I don't know whether to apologize now or later …"

"Derek! Oh my, don't you look handsome tonight." A middle-aged woman approached with a dash of gray hair and too much make-up.

"Hi Mrs. Rogers, it's nice to see you." He shook her hand and turned to Jules. "Mrs. Rogers, this is my friend, Julia Anderson.

Derek had made sure all evening to make her as comfortable as possible. He never let on to anyone during introductions that they were anything other than friends. She appreciated his gesture, but couldn't help wondering how it would feel to be introduced as his girlfriend – the woman of his choice.

Jules smiled and shared introductions with her. Mrs. Rogers lightly grabbed a strand of Jules' hair. "You have beautiful hair. I've tried to go with your auburn color for years but couldn't find the right shade for my skin color. You'll have to tell me what color and brand you use."

"Oh, um, it's natural." She looked over to see Derek trying to hide his grin.

"Well, you should be thankful. Women spend good money to try and get that color." She stepped back and looked between her and Derek. "So you are just friends, huh?"

Derek interceded promptly. "Yes, we are just friends."

"Hmmm." She looked back and forth between them again. "That's too bad, you make a cute couple." She opened her purse and fished through it. "But if that's the case then you might still be interested in my niece, Monica. Oh, here it is." She handed him a card. "This is her business card if you want to give her a call sometime."

Derek took it from her and slipped it into his shirt pocket, "Thanks, I'll keep that in mind."

Mrs. Rogers glided back into the crowd. Derek lifted up his hands while giving her an 'I told you so' look.

"You weren't kidding."

"And the night is still young," Derek added.

Matt and Ava returned to the table after making their social rounds. "Bummer, I see we just missed Mrs. Rogers," Matt said with a sarcastic tone.

Jules couldn't help but tease, "Matt, it's good to see you walking normally again."

Derek's eyes widened as he gave her the 'cut it off' motion with his hand crossing over his neck.

Matt patted Derek on the shoulder. "Oh yeah, thanks for reminding me, Jules, I haven't had a chance to return the favor to Derek yet."

Derek didn't even try to hide his menacing smile. "You know, I've been thinking maybe now is a good time to call a truce."

Matt took a good long drink of his punch. "I'll consider it."

Jules enjoyed watching them banter back and forth. However, she was incredibly aware of Derek at this moment. His laughter that turned quiet when he thought something was really funny, the way he used his hand to smooth over his hair, and how when he laid his arms upon the table his shirt tightened from his muscles underneath.

She dropped her gaze when he caught her staring. Maybe coming here with Derek had been a mistake. It became harder to keep her distance from him the more she spent time with him. Was she really confused about her feelings for him or was it just an excuse to keep her from getting hurt?

"Good evening." A man stood up at the podium giving the crowd a moment to settle down before he continued. Derek leaned over and whispered to her that it was the Chief of Police. "Thank you all for taking the time and opening your wallets for this great cause of supporting our Boys and Girls club. We all desire for our community to improve, and what better way than to reach into the lives of our young generation and teach them how to work hard, give, love, and train them to be leaders.

"Please enjoy yourselves and from the bottom of my heart, I wish you all a very Merry Christmas." The crowd applauded. "As a special treat for you tonight while we wait for our food to be served, we have someone who will be singing a song for us. Please, everyone join me in welcoming our very own Sergeant Derek Brown."

The room erupted in applause as Derek shot a sharp look in Matt's direction. Matt smiled. "Our truce can begin *now*."

Chapter Twenty-seven

Derek walked Jules up to her door. She fumbled with her keys to find the correct one. Once she had the door unlocked and pushed open she turned back around to face him.

"Would you mind coming in for a bit? I could make us a pot of coffee."

Jules's request came as a surprise. Her mood had changed since they left the party and he couldn't read what had caused it. "Sure."

They stepped inside and he helped as she took her coat off. He hung it up on the hook for her and placed his alongside it. He followed her into the kitchen and took a seat at the table.

Jules started the coffee and grabbed two mugs out of the cupboard. "So, you never told me you could sing. You are really good."

Derek still couldn't believe Matt did that to him. He took their pranking to a whole new level. Over his dead body would they have a truce at this point. "Thanks." He loosened his tie as he explained, "Back in college I was in a band that did a few gigs around campus. Now I just randomly stand in on the worship team. Matt knew I had been working on a song for the Christmas Eve service." Matt even had his guitar there waiting for him when he got on stage. The man had put a lot of effort into this plan. But Matt hadn't seen anything yet.

Jules opened the fridge and scrunched up her face. "I'm not much of a hostess. I'm all out of creamer."

"Black is fine. It makes me feel manlier."

She laughed. "As if that is a problem."

He caught a hint of pink highlighting her cheeks from the comment. He decided instead of teasing her about the remark, he would just change the subject. He pointed at the fridge door. "That looks like a new picture since I was here last."

Jules stared at it for a moment before answering. "It is. My mom surprised me and came up from Florida to visit me over Thanksgiving."

From what little Jules shared about her relationship with her mom, he gathered that they were not very close. "Was it a good visit?"

She joined him at the table. "Yes. It was a short visit, but I know she is trying to make an effort to repair the distance between us."

He debated whether to push the conversation further. She had given him the back story of her family history at the coffeehouse but other than that she stayed very tight-lipped regarding her family. His gut told him to continue. "Did something happen to cause the strain in your relationship?"

Jules let out a soft breath as she broke eye contact with him and put her sight on the picture. "My mom did a great job as a single mom and I always knew she loved me and would take care of me. Once I started college my mom decided to move to Florida. I think she just needed to get away from here and leave her broken past behind her."

She turned back to him. "She wanted a fresh start. I know I was an adult at that point, but I still had to work through more abandonment issues. I'm glad she pursued a new life for herself, it just hurt that she wanted it without me. During the summers I would live in Florida with her, but after graduation I got a job here in the city and my own place, and we drifted further apart. She got wrapped up in her new life and I did in mine."

Derek listened intently but couldn't shake the impression that Jules deliberately kept a barrier around herself. She was tired of being hurt and he couldn't blame her, but how much longer could she keep up with this façade without falling apart? He slowly began to make sense of why she continued to keep him at arm's length. He was just one more person she had to protect herself against.

The coffee finished and she stood to fill their mugs. He watched her walk away from him. All night he had been yearning to embrace her as his own. He wouldn't be able to hold up just playing the role as her friend for long, but that was exactly what she needed tonight.

He slipped out from his chair. "Julia."

She turned and his heart tightened from the tears that filled her emerald eyes. His long legs only took two strides to cross her small kitchen. He pulled her into his chest and wrapped his arms around her. He bent his head down to whisper into her ear, "You don't have to act so strong for me."

As he held her, soft sniffles exposed her sadness, but her rigid body displayed her unwillingness to let him in. She leaned her forehead against his chest and used her hands to wipe away the tears. "Stop being so nice to me, I don't deserve it." She broke free and took a step back. "Derek, I need to talk to you about something."

"Okay." He wished that this was the moment he had been waiting for. The moment where she finally voiced that she had feelings deeper than friendship for him – but the look in her eyes sucked the air out of his lungs.

"My ex, Scott, called me and wants me back. I agreed to go out with him next weekend and hear him out. I know you and I have been doing this balancing act for awhile and I'm sorry if I have been giving you mixed signals. I really don't know what I want and I'm confused about a lot of things. Like my feelings for you, for Scott, hearing from God, knowing what His will is for my life."

Jules could have punched him in the stomach and it wouldn't have touched the pain that her words caused. He had been a fool. He wanted to get mad and blame her, but the realization crept in that the blame fully fell at his feet. He let his heart fall for a woman that was never his to begin with.

Her confession about Scott came as a surprise, but not her confusion over her relationship with God. He had seen her struggle with life decisions and direction. For weeks Jules had been attempting to over-compensate this weakness by trying to put everything in her control.

He wanted to put all his pride behind him and beg her to choose him. To show her how good they would be together, but Jules needed to figure that out for herself. From the beginning she had asked him to be her friend and give her time to sort out her feelings, and he had only manipulated her along the way. He had ulterior motives in inviting her to the Christmas party tonight with the hope she would change her mind and want him as more than a friend.

"Please say something." Her words sliced through his thoughts. She leaned back against the sink, her arms crossed tightly around her midsection. Uncertainty clouded her eyes.

"Why do you want to go out with Scott?" He kept his voice calm while his insides crumbled.

"I'm confused about a lot of things right now and my life feels out of control. I need to do something about it. I was in love with him, Derek. I need to see if there is still something there or not."

"And what part of getting your life back together involves God?"

"Don't preach at me, Derek." She closed her eyes and her face softened when she opened them. "I'm sorry. I didn't mean it."

He looked at her for a very long time, weighing his next move. "Wait here. I'll be right back."

Derek ran out to his truck and grabbed his Bible. What Jules needed right now was a friend and a word of encouragement. He cared for Jules enough to want the very best for her, whether that included him or not.

He found her sitting at the kitchen table drinking her coffee. He laid his Bible in front of her. "I promised you that I would be your friend, and that's what I'm going to do." He sat down across from her. "We all want to understand our future and learn God's purpose for our lives. It's not going to come all packaged up in a neat little box with a bow on it. God's will is revealed gradually as our relationship deepens with Him and we experience His working through all the events in our lives.

"There are ways to hear God's direction and voice in your life, Jules." He tapped the Bible with his finger. "One of my favorite verses is Psalm 119:105 that says '*Your word is a lamp to my feet and a light for my path.*' God can't lead you, Jules, if you don't seek after Him. You could talk to someone you trust that could be a mentor. God can bring people into our lives to help guide us and bestow wisdom. Pray. Your relationship with God can't grow if you don't talk to Him." He took a deep breath. "Can I show you something?"

She nodded.

"I found this verse when I was trying to figure out if I wanted to join the SWAT team or pursue something different." He flipped through the pages until he came to the verse he mentioned. "This is from Isaiah 42:16, '*I will lead the blind by ways they have not known, along unfamiliar paths I will guide them; I will turn the darkness into light before them and make the rough places smooth. These are the things I will do; I will not forsake them.*'"

176

Derek searched her face, hoping she grasped the truth he shared. "Let God make your rough places smooth, Jules. Take the time and find the peace you've been searching for."

He took his thumb and wiped off the tears that trailed down her cheeks. There wasn't much more he could say.

He stood to leave. She reached out and grabbed his hand. "Thank you."

His smile covered the tight lump forming in his throat. He squeezed her hand. "That's what friends are for." He leaned over and gently kissed her on the head. "Call me once you get things figured out."

Derek turned and left, leaving his heart sitting at the kitchen table.

CHAPTER TWENTY-EIGHT

AVA FINISHED UP THE MATH LESSON AS FAST AS SHE COULD. HER audience that consisted of twenty students had quickly lost their ability to pay attention. Although at this moment, she was probably having a harder time staying focused than they were. She had been explaining how adding two squares with two squares equaled four, but in the back of her mind she had been adding up the number of days until her wedding.

"All right, good job, everyone. Go ahead and finish the last two problems on your paper by yourself." She walked around the room checking their work and helping those who needed it.

"Miss Williams."

Ava smiled as her student Ethan flapped his hand in the air to get her attention. She made her way over to him. She crouched down to meet him at eye level. "What do you need, Ethan?"

"Is it okay if I count with my fingers?"

Her smile broadened by the sweet question that came with his nervous look. "Yes, if that helps you, but try and do it in your head first."

He let out a sigh of relief. "Oh good, because this is hard stuff for a six-year-old, you know."

She ruffled his hair as she stood back up. Not everyone could handle teaching this age group. They took a lot of work and patience, but she loved every minute of it, most days. To see their little minds at work soaking in the knowledge she shared continued to spark her passion for teaching. And it didn't hurt that they were adorable.

Most had finished by the time they needed to move on to the next activity. "Clean up your desk by putting your pencils away and your paper in your backpack to take home. Don't forget to grab your backpack, coat, and anything else that needs to go home, and then line up at the door to go to art class." The kids obeyed and stayed on task for the most part. On Mondays the kids had Art at the end of the day and left to go home from there. She would just return shortly before the bell to assist and help the kids get to where they needed to go.

As Ava headed back to class after dropping her kids off in the art room, she passed the office. She caught eye of the secretary flagging her down. Sticking her head inside the door she asked, "Hey Trina, what do you need?"

Trina stood up and lifted a long rectangle box with purple and silver ribbons around it. "You just got a delivery."

Ava clapped her hands as she made her way into the office. She took the white box from her, noticing a card attached. "Thanks. I'll take it back to my room." Ava stopped and turned at the door way. "Who dropped it off?" She'd know soon enough but would be disappointed if she had missed Matt.

Trina looked up from her computer. "The floral shop just delivered it."

Ava tried not to run as she walked briskly back to her room. She couldn't contain her excitement. Next Wednesday they'd close on their new house and after the honeymoon they would start moving in. That coming Friday night they would be married. They had decided on a candle-lit evening wedding to replay his proposal.

As much as she had been uncomfortable planning another wedding and working through the embarrassment of not getting it right the first time, she couldn't deny the excitement that bubbled beneath the apprehension. In just a few short days she would be united with Matt – as his wife.

Ava untied the ribbon, removing the card from its hold. She opened the envelope and pulled out the message. She froze. The note simply said, *Ava~ I haven't forgotten about you ... keep watching your back.*

She flipped open the lid to find a half-dozen black roses.

❧ ❧ ❧ ❧

A VA SAT IN THE CONFERENCE ROOM, STARING AT HER HANDS clutched tightly in her lap. Just when everything had seemed perfect, in an instant it came crashing down around her. The last fifteen minutes had been a blur. She called Matt immediately from her room. He gave her instructions not to touch the box any further and to not leave the school under any circumstances until he arrived.

Out of pure willpower she had managed to hold it together as she made her way back to the office to inform them what had happened and to make sure someone could replace her with helping the kids after school.

Principal Hunt guided her into the conference room to wait and told her he would secure her room to make sure no one entered to disturb the evidence. School would be out shortly and believing that the threat was only geared toward Ava, they decided to keep the children in classes but heighten security.

Trina had brought her a cup of coffee, but she hadn't touched it yet. Her stomach churned enough that she didn't know if she would be able to keep it down.

The door jerked open as Matt raced into the room. She barely had enough time to get into a standing position before he pulled her up the rest of the way and buried her in his embrace. Being in his arms broke down her defenses. She covered her face in his shoulder, the tears she'd held back earlier engaging in full force.

He stroked her hair, giving her time to calm down. A chill worked its way up her neck from the fact that she had no idea what would happen from here on out. She took a deep breath and forced herself to pull it together. There was no point fighting the inevitable.

She loosened her grip and leaned back. Matt's eyes betrayed the fear she struggled against. He took his fingers and pulled back the hair that had matted against her cheeks from the tears.

"Ava, I'm so sorry. Are you okay?"

She nodded, not sure she could form words yet. She eased back down in the chair. He pulled out the chair next to hers and sat down. "Can you tell me what happened?" She didn't have much time to explain on the phone. Just the mention of her thinking that Chad Taylor sent her the flowers had put him on immediate high alert and she didn't need to finish.

She wiped a tear that escaped down her cheek and cleared her throat. "Yeah, um, I got a delivery from the flower shop that I thought was from you. I took it back to my room to open it. I read the card and realized it wasn't. I opened the box and found half a dozen black roses."

Matt ran a hand down his face. "What did the note say?"

"It said, 'Ava, I haven't forgotten about you … keep watching your back.' I left it all on my desk like you asked."

He reached over and held her hand. "Good. I know this is scary, but we have to cover everything. Has anything happened lately that you haven't told me about?"

Ava didn't blame him for asking the question. She deserved his uncertainty over whether she had been hiding precious information from him again.

She shook her head, "No, nothing. I promise. The movie theatre parking lot was the last time I felt something wasn't right. When the delivery came I didn't suspect anything was wrong since …" She stopped, her eyes focused on the table, thinking back to the box. She gasped, her eyes widening as the realization hit her.

"Ava, what is it?"

"The ribbons on the box," she looked over at him, "they were purple and silver." She waited a beat before adding, "our wedding colors."

CHAPTER TWENTY-NINE

A BELL RANG ABOVE THE DOOR AS MATT ENTERED THE FLORAL shop. Cold air rushed in behind him before the door completely closed. He scanned the small room stuffed with arrangements and the overwhelming scent of roses. He approached the counter, not finding anyone standing behind it.

Matt hated leaving Ava so soon after his worse fear appeared to be coming true. It didn't take a genius to figure out that Chad was behind the package. They needed proof to add to his charges when they finally found and arrested him. He didn't know what worried him more, the fact that Chad had made contact or the fact that he knew their wedding colors. How did he get close enough to them to know something so specific without them even noticing?

A woman appeared from the hallway. "Hello officer, sorry to keep you waiting, how can I help you?"

"No problem. I need your help with information on an order. Earlier this afternoon you delivered a box of black roses to a Miss Ava Williams at Rockford Elementary School. I need to know who purchased that order."

"Okay, let me see what I can do for you." She walked around back of the counter and began typing on her computer. "I remember the order, only because it came across as strange. It's not often someone wants black roses ordered." She used her finger to slide down the screen. "Yep, right here. Huh, well, it looks like the order came in over a week ago. I remember it was a man, but I don't have a name. He paid in cash."

Was this guy ever going to run out of cash? Frustration over another dead end made his bad mood worse. "Can you tell me, did you choose the ribbon or did he specifically ask for it?"

"He requested it."

"Do you remember anything else? Did you happen to see what vehicle he was driving or did he mention anything about himself?" Matt was grasping at straws.

The one thing that continued to bother him about this situation was "why." Why would Chad risk being caught just to scare Ava? For weeks he had kept a low profile only to surface over a flower delivery. It didn't make sense. Did the cocky punk just consider himself untouchable, or had the waiting game become too much for him?

The woman tipped her head to the side, looking lost in thought. "I'm sorry, I mostly remembered the order. I think he wore a hat and had a beard."

He pointed up to the camera mounted in the corner. "Do you by chance have any security tapes?"

She cringed. "No, this is just a live feed. With my work area in the back, I like to have the front of the store under surveillance so I can see up front while I work on the orders."

He gave her a smile, not wanting her to feel bad about not having the answers that he needed. She had just been doing her job. How could she have known what trouble a simple delivery had caused? "Thanks for your help. I appreciate it. Can I leave my number with you in case you remember anything? No detail is too small."

"Sure." She grabbed a note pad and pen and had him write down his information. "I'm sorry I couldn't be of more help. I'll call if I think of anything else."

He shook her hand. "Thanks. Have a good day, ma'am."

Matt walked out to his squad car, not sure what his next move should be. He checked the time. He would run to the station and fill out a report and then pick up dinner to go, on his way to Ava's apartment. He had called Jake before he left the school to come and escort her home, but he would feel better if he had his eyes on her himself. Whether Ava liked it or not, she had just been handed a very tight security.

CHAPTER THIRTY

JULES SETTLED INTO THE CHAIR BY THE WINDOW TO KEEP AN EYE out for Scott. He would be picking her up any minute for their "date." It had been a long wait since he had called and asked her out so they could talk, but this had been the first day that both their schedules were free at the same time.

Sure, they had seen each other at the hospital, but he respected the space she had asked for and kept their conversations strictly business-related. Despite her confusion over her feelings, she had been looking forward to tonight.

She had taken Derek's unexpected but truthful advice, digging into her Bible more in the last week than she probably had in the last year. Time after time she'd found herself on her knees talking and praying to God. When Ava had started to date Matt and wasn't sure whether she should pursue a relationship with him or not, Jules remembered all the times she had encouraged her to pray and talk to God about what to do. Why hadn't she taken that advice seriously for herself until now?

On Wednesday she had met with Ava's mom, Grace. Derek had encouraged her to find a mentor, someone to speak truth and wisdom into her life. Grace had been like a second mom to her growing up and Jules respected her opinion and the life she lived. It took all of about two seconds to know that she needed to contact her.

As always, Grace had made her comfortable and held no judgment in her voice with the questions she asked and the advice she gave, and they continually ended up back in the Word. They discussed Derek and Scott, but more of the conversation had been directed toward the healing that needed to take place within her first – starting with the death of her sister and the relationship with her parents, to the understanding that God had never left her but had just been waiting on her to pursue Him.

Repairing relationships and dealing with the past didn't come easy. Jules needed to extend grace to her parents and make an effort to offer forgiveness and reconciliation. She hadn't even talked to her dad in probably two or three years. Offering forgiveness was difficult, especially when the person didn't ask for it or deserve it. But then again, she didn't deserve God's forgiveness either. Through talking with Grace she began to realize that if she couldn't forgive others, how could she fully understand how deeply she needed the Lord's forgiveness?

Tonight with Scott she wanted to put the old hurts behind her, listen to what he wanted to say, and forgive. She had been caught up in a holding pattern in her life and she needed to break free. As to whether or not they had a future, forgiving Scott was a great first step.

Seeing the hurt in Derek's eyes when she told him about Scott had crushed her. She needed to make things right between them but couldn't do that until she dealt with Scott. One relationship at a time had become her new motto.

Confidence had been built in the fact that she could make decisions and not feel alone in making them anymore. She didn't know how tonight would end, but she had assurance that peace would come as long as she pursed God.

Scott's BMW pulled up into her driveway. She stood and gathered her coat and purse and walked out the door with her head held high.

❧❧❧❧

THE EVENING HAD GONE SMOOTHLY SO FAR. SCOTT HAD TAKEN
her to a restaurant downtown and they decided to get
their desserts to go. Jules walked out of her kitchen and into
the living room with forks in hand. She handed Scott's to him
and took a seat at the opposite end of the couch.

Scott leaned forward, taking a peek at her dessert. "What
was it again that you got?"

"Chocolate Tofu Mousse."

"Does that even constitute a dessert?"

She pointed her fork at him. "Hey, don't knock it until you
try it."

He scrunched up his nose. "I'll pass. I'm not really in the
mood to taste cardboard." He then took an enormous bite of
his peanut butter chocolate cheesecake that probably held a
thousand calories in one slice.

She giggled, happy to see that the friendship they'd originally started with a couple years ago hadn't left.

He wiped his mouth with the napkin she gave him and
took a sip of his coffee. The amusement faded from his face.
"Julia, I'm really sorry about what happened between us and
for how I hurt you."

She finished her bite and swallowed, almost choking from
the sudden shift in conversation. "You did hurt me, Scott. I
thought I was going to marry you and then I found out you
were seeing someone else behind my back. I never figured
you as a cheater."

"I'm not." He cleared his throat. "I wasn't, but then I started going through some really hard stuff, getting mixed up in
bad decisions that ultimately rolled over into my relationship
with you."

"Why didn't you tell me you were going through a hard time?"

"I don't know. It seemed easier to keep my darkness hidden. But I want to change." He ran a hand through his wavy brown hair and readjusted his glasses. "I am really trying to get my life back together and one of those aspects is you."

Jules understood where he was coming from. She, too, had a life that needed mending. How could she have been with him so long and not know the struggles he had been dealing with? Maybe they hadn't been as close as she had originally thought. "I don't know, Scott." She was enjoying herself tonight, but that didn't necessarily mean that she should pursue a relationship with him. "I'm not sure if there is anything left to repair."

He looked at her for a very long time. "Remember our first date to the movie theatre where we were the only ones there and spent most of the time laughing and talking and making fun of the horrible acting?"

She smiled. "Yes."

"What about the day we spent hiking at that campground in Southwestern Wisconsin? Or the nights we snuggled on the couch, not caring what we watched as long as we were together? Remember after your birthday party we walked along the river and I told you that I loved you? And don't forget how we stayed up all night working side by side on a diagnosis for a patient." Laugh lines pinched the corners of his eyes as he smiled. "Julia, we are good together."

He placed his Styrofoam to-go box down on the floor and scooted closer to her on the couch. "I know I hurt you, Julia, and I wish so badly I could go back and change the past, but I can't. But I promise you, if you give me a second chance, I will prove to be the man you deserve."

She dropped her gaze as he reached out and took her hand. He tightened his grip as her hand trembled. "Scott," her voice betrayed her inner conflict. She shook her head as she tried to continue, "I just don't think ..."

"Wait." Scott rubbed his hand over the back of his neck. "Just think about it, please. You don't have to decide now, just think about it."

She couldn't make sense of what to do under his weighty stare. She nodded. "Okay, I'll think about it."

He brushed her chin with the back of his knuckles. "Thank you." He pushed to his feet, drawing himself tall. "I'll go so you can think about it." He grabbed hold of her hands and pulled her up off the couch. "Walk me out?"

She gave him a nod, "Of course."

Saying goodbye out on the porch, she wrapped her arms tightly around herself to create warmth from the chilly night air. Scott faced her, rubbing his hands up and down her arms, a gesture he had done often when they were together and she was cold.

His eyes fastened on hers as he stepped in closer. "I had a really good time with you tonight."

"Me, too." She couldn't deny that she enjoyed his friendship, but the whole time he spoke about their memories she began to see that's all they were to her, just memories. Good ones, but memories nonetheless. The question that faced her now was, did she have any desire to make new ones with him?

Scott leaned in, invading her space. His lips lightly brushed against hers. For a moment she let herself kiss him back, allowing him to deepen the passion as their lips found their familiar dance.

Vehicle tires screeched in acceleration as a truck passed by, jolting her into realizing what she was doing.

Not once during the entire night did she have any peace about getting back with Scott. He had asked her to think about it, but all along she knew what her answer should probably be. And yet here she stood tucked in his arms, giving affection to the man she didn't want to be with, becoming enlightened by the thought of the man she did.

Derek.

She pushed Scott back. "Stop."

His chest rose from his heavy breathing. "What's wrong?"

Jules took a half step back. "I'm so sorry, Scott, but I can't do this."

"I shouldn't have kissed you, I'm sorry."

"No, this," she pointed back and forth between them, "I can't do us again. I know I told you I would think about it, but I don't need any more time. Thank you for your apology. I forgive you and hold no bad feelings toward you, but I don't want to get back together with you."

Hurt flashed across his eyes. "Oh, I see."

She wanted to reach out and touch his arm, console him from the sadness her rejection caused, but she didn't want to give him any further mixed messages. Allowing him to kiss her had been a huge mistake and damage enough.

"You're a great guy, Scott, and some woman is going to be lucky to have you. You're just not the great guy for me."

His eyebrows narrowed as he frowned. "Is there someone else?"

She wished she could say yes, but only time would tell whether she had burned that bridge or not. "No."

Scott looked at her for a very long time. "Okay. You know where to find me if you change your mind." He turned and walked down the steps, following the sidewalk out to his car. He turned, "Friends?"

She smiled, thankful that the old hurts, the past, and their mistakes hadn't derailed their friendship. "Friends."

❧ ❧ ❧ ❧

DEREK SLAMMED HIS HAND AGAINST THE STEERING WHEEL OF HIS truck. What had he been thinking?

He had heard through the grapevine – Ava, to Matt, to his ears – that Jules' date with Dr. Scott was tonight. After Jules told him about her plans to go out with Scott, he pretty much gave up. Why hadn't he fought harder for her?

So instead he sat at home, mulling over the idea of Jules with Scott. By nine o'clock he had finally convinced himself to go past her house. If she was alone, he'd decide then whether to knock on her door and plead his case for them to be together and share how much he really cared about her.

When he approached her house he slowed down to turn into the driveway, only to find Jules out on the front porch kissing Scott. He accelerated, wanting to get out of sight before she caught sight of his truck.

Now he sat in an empty parking lot, sulking. Here he had encouraged Jules to seek God's direction, and he had just failed miserably trying to make everything happen in his own timing and power. He'd allowed his feelings for Jules to cloud his judgment and his emotions to rule over his decisions. Watching her kiss Scott was just what he deserved.

His phone rang. Jules' number showed up in the display screen. He shut off his phone, turned on the ignition and headed home.

CHAPTER THIRTY-ONE

DEREK PUSHED THE BAR UP ON HIS FINAL REP, GRUNTING FROM the pain. "Ten." He and Matt had finished off their shift with a trip to the gym.

Matt spotted him from behind and helped ease the bar back into place. "You seem to be pushing pretty hard today. Everything okay?"

"I'm fine." Derek sat up on the bench, wiping the sweat from his face into the towel. "Add another ten pounds to each side, will you?"

"You've been going awhile, maybe you should take a break." Matt handed him his water bottle.

Derek took a long swig. "No, I'm in the zone. I want to keep going. One more set with the added weight and I'll be done."

Matt unscrewed the safety clamps and added ten more pounds to each side. "Ripping your arm muscles to shreds isn't going to fix your problem."

Derek threw down his towel and leaned back against the bench, "And what problem is that?"

"Jules."

"I don't want to talk about her." Derek lifted up the bar and began his set, pushing harder with each rep.

"I can see that."

He made it to eight and had to stop. It was by far the most

weight he'd ever lifted. Maybe Matt had a good point. "I'm done." He placed the bar back, stood up and stretched.

"Derek, I don't really want to do this, but I'm under strict orders from my bride-to-be that I'm supposed to ask you what is going on between you and Jules." Matt lifted his hands up in surrender from Derek's glare.

What could he say? She chose the other guy. It was Tuesday evening and Jules had left him a message every day since Friday night. He couldn't bring himself to talk to her and hear what he already knew.

"There is nothing going on between us." He swung his towel over his shoulder.

"Ava mentioned that Jules has been trying to contact you for almost a week. Listen, I won't tell her anything. I'm just concerned. I haven't seen you this tense before."

Derek scratched the scruff on his face from the few days of not shaving. Sooner or later Matt would find out the details anyway. "You know how Jules went out with Scott Friday night?"

Matt nodded, "Right."

"Well, I decided to go to her house, see if I could talk to her. Instead I drove past and became the audience for them kissing on her front porch."

Matt grimaced. "Ouch."

"Tell me about it."

Matt slapped him on the arm, his muscles vibrating from the impact. If he was already this sore from the workout he hated to think what pain tomorrow would bring. "Derek, you need to call her."

"Why should I? I know what she is going to say!" The days had not diminished his frustration. Quite the opposite, they had fueled the fire. Granted, he had told her to call once she got things figured out. He still just couldn't believe this would be the outcome. He needed to call her, and he would, but not until he could do so without losing his temper and saying things he would later regret. Until then, he would continue to ignore her calls.

"I know you are upset. I would be, too. But you need to talk to her whether you want to or not."

Derek shook his head. "No. What I need is a shower."

He walked away before Matt could offer up a rebuttal. He also needed to get his mind off of Jules. He grinned. A good prank could just make that happen.

CHAPTER THIRTY-TWO

AVA SET THE TABLE, MAKING SURE EVERYTHING LOOKED PERFECT before Matt arrived. She had chili simmering in the crock pot, cornbread in the oven, and had picked up an apple pie and ice cream for dessert. Her cooking had improved and she didn't panic as much while preparing the meals. Lucy continually told her she would improve once she had more confidence in herself. She had actually been enjoying her time cooking lately – not that she was ready to announce that to anyone yet.

She wanted tonight to be special, just a time for them to be together before the whirlwind of activities started. Today had been her last day at school until after Christmas break. She had planned personal days to cover the rest of the week so she could get everything done.

Tomorrow morning they would close on the house and officially become homeowners, Thursday they would decorate the church and Friday night was the wedding. She had been under tight security ever since last Monday when the ominous purple-and-silver-ribboned flowers had been delivered at school. This time she gave no resistance to her protection detail. She took advantage of the down time to finish last-minute wedding preparations.

Last night Lucy had brought over the finished painting that Ava planned to give Matt as a wedding gift. Lucy had captured the scene perfectly. They had decided not to pack and move into the new house until they returned from their honeymoon, so Ava stashed the painting in the back of her closet, knowing that Matt wouldn't look there.

Matt made true on his promise not to shut her out during this round of tightened security. There were only a couple nights he hadn't been able to come keep her company, but of course made sure that if he wasn't with her, someone else joined her. Over the last week the police had a few leads to go on, but the way the search seemed to drag out, they probably wouldn't find Chad until after they were married.

Matt knocked on the door, calling her name. She smiled when she opened the door to find him standing there with a small Christmas tree in hand. "What is this?" she asked as he made his way into her living room.

"A little Christmas cheer." He sat the two-foot tree on the table in the corner. "I know it was hard for you to give up decorating for Christmas this year with all the stuff going on. It's not much, but I thought it would help." He leaned down and plugged the lights into the wall. A soft glow illuminated.

It still surprised her at times how well he knew her. "It's perfect. Thank you."

"Not as perfect as you are for me." He shortened the distance between them. Her heartbeat thumped so wildly it pulsed in her ears. He placed his hands on both sides of her head and his eyes slowly traced down her face, stopping at her lips. He leaned in, pausing to smile before he kissed her.

His soft lips melted into hers until he leaned back to catch his breath. She threaded her fingers behind his neck to make sure he didn't back away too far. "I love you." Those words didn't even begin to describe the emotions that she held for this man. To think, eight months ago she had almost turned him down when he asked her out, to now knowing that she couldn't – or didn't want to – live without him.

He smiled. "I love you, too. Hard to believe we are buying a house tomorrow and getting married in three days."

"Closing is at ten in the morning, right?" she asked.

"Yes. Oh, and I know we originally planned for me to come pick you up, but I really need to finish up some paperwork at the station beforehand since I will be off until after the honeymoon. Do you think you could find someone to drop you off?"

"Sure. I'll see if Mom or Jules is available. It shouldn't be a problem." She smiled. "Speaking of the honeymoon, I need to start packing. Can't you give me a little clue about where we are going?" Matt wanted to give her a surprise honeymoon and cover all the details. She found it romantic.

"Let's just say you won't need very many clothes."

"Matthew."

"Hey, a groom can dream." His kiss covered her flushed cheek. "Dress for warm weather, but that's all I'm telling you."

"The warm sun and my man next to me sound like paradise."

He turned his head in the direction of the kitchen. "Do I smell chili?"

Her eyes widened. "Yes, and hopefully not burnt cornbread." She scrambled to the kitchen and opened the oven door, thankful that no smoke billowed out. A light brown color coated the top – perfect timing. She might be getting this cooking thing figured out. Now she had to remember to work on setting a timer.

Matt stopped at the counter and picked up the newspaper. "Since when do you get the paper?"

Her heart sank. She had hoped this subject wouldn't come up until after they ate. "My neighbor gave it to me." She stepped up to the counter and took the paper from him, flipping through the pages. "You know how the paper has been doing a feature a couple times a week in December about the great events that have happened in the city during the last year?"

"Yeah," he drew the word out slow, his eyes narrowed.

She found the page and turned it to him. "Well, an officer saving his fiancée during a bank robbery made their list. We were the story featured today."

Grabbing the paper from her, Matt sat at the stool and began reading. She left him to read while she filled their bowls for dinner. She did a quick taste test of the chili and coughed, reaching for fluids as she realized her earlier mistake of adding too much chili powder held consequences. She was in the middle of guzzling down a glass of water when he finished.

"I'm impressed. It's a good article with the correct facts. Someone did their homework. Not to mention a pretty hot woman is in the picture."

Her mouth hung open from the shock. She thought for sure he would be upset over the public attention. "You aren't upset about this?"

He laid the paper down and came into the kitchen, wrapping her up in a hug. "Chad Taylor already knows who you are and how to find you. You being in the public eye doesn't matter as much anymore. Plus, I'm tired of that man stealing so much from us these last couple months. I'm not going to let the thought of him ruin a very nice evening and dinner that the love of my life has prepared."

She raked her fingers through his hair. "I'm glad to hear it. However, I think that I can ruin a dinner all by myself." She twisted out of his arms and opened the lid to the crock pot. "I hope you like it spicy. I guess there is a difference between one *teaspoon* and one *tablespoon* of chili powder."

CHAPTER THIRTY-THREE

MATT GROANED AS THE SOUND BROUGHT HIM OUT OF A DEEP sleep. He turned over in bed to read the clock. 6:55 a.m. Who would be pounding on his door this early on a Wednesday morning? He swung his legs over the side of the bed and sat up, rubbing his eyes.

Last night after he left Ava's house he had been called in for a SWAT emergency, only for them to show up onsite and not be needed. He didn't mind that the situation had been handled well without their help, but the four hours of sleep last night just wasn't enough. He had hoped to sleep in a little more before heading to the station.

The knock persisted. He slipped on sweatpants and a t-shirt, yawning while he stumbled over a shoe heading to the door. He needed coffee, bad.

He swung the door open to see an elderly woman standing on his porch. He cleared his throat. "Can I help you?"

"Yes, how much is the lamp?"

Matt stared at the woman, not sure if he heard her correctly. "Excuse me?"

"How much is the lamp?"

His eyes narrowed, confused by her question. "What lamp?"

Her lips tightened. She put her hands on her hips, talking slowly as if he were a child. "The lamp. How much do you want for the lamp?" She stepped back and pointed out to his front yard.

Matt leaned forward and stuck his head out of the door. He blinked. The entire left side of his yard was packed with stuff. He scanned the yard briefly and saw a chair, pillows, blankets, and a baby stand-up toy. A table displayed dishes, books, and movies scattered on top. A lamp sat in the grass next to the table.

He noticed a sign staked into the ground by the front of the sidewalk that said, 'Yard Sale. Knock for assistance.'

Matt looked down at the woman's annoyed frown. What was going on? He scratched his head. Slowly it began to make sense. Derek. He had been played – and played well. He should have known Derek would get even.

He laughed. He might as well make some money off the prank. "Five bucks, ma'am."

Matt stayed outside with shoppers for the next twenty minutes before he put up a sign that said 'Free' and called the local second-hand store to come and pick up the leftovers. Through talking with the people that came he found out how far Derek had gone. Derek had made signs with his address and the time and placed them all around the neighborhood to announce the yard sale. Even though the prank had been on him he couldn't deny that it had been a good one.

One he wished he had thought of first.

Matt called Derek on his way to the station. By the sound of his groggy voice answering the phone, he must have woke him up. Good. "Good morning, sleeping beauty."

"Can it be considered good after only a couple hours of sleep?" He yawned. "What's up?"

"I just wanted to call and thank you. I've made thirteen dollars and twenty-five cents this morning on my yard sale."

Derek laughed. "Keep it up and you'll be able to afford that honeymoon you've been planning."

Matt stopped at a four-way, spying a sign for his yard sale that was staked in the ground near the stop sign. "I'm impressed. You got me good."

"I thought so."

"How did you do it? We didn't even leave the station until almost two-thirty this morning."

"Every good prank comes with planning, as you showed me at the Christmas party. I've had the idea for a few days but just didn't know when to do it. Since I have a truck my neighbors asked if I could drop off some of their unwanted items for them. So after we had our workout yesterday I went to their house and loaded up my truck. The SWAT emergency worked out great because I knew you'd go straight home and go to bed. Plus, I was too wired to go to sleep."

"The signs around the neighborhood were a nice touch. I got quite a few lookers."

"I would have paid good money to see your reaction."

Matt switched lanes – and the subject. "Have you decided what you are going to do about Jules?"

"Don't worry. I thought about it and I'll call her later today. Jules and I will be seeing a lot of each other over the next few days and I don't want it to be awkward between us. Just because it didn't work out between us doesn't mean that it should ruin your happiness. I'll take care of it."

Matt sighed a breath of relief. "Thanks, man. I appreciate it."

"No problem. Now go buy a house."

CHAPTER THIRTY-FOUR

AVA STOOD IN FRONT OF THE MIRROR IN HER BATHROOM FINISH-ing up getting ready for the day. Buying a house to-day called for a celebration of dressing up for the occasion. She had chosen black leggings, a long gray sweater dress with a teal belt, and her high-heeled gray leather boots. She put on the diamond earrings Matt had given her over the summer and a teal beaded necklace.

She joined Jules out in the living room as she sat on the couch drinking coffee. Jules whistled. "You look great."

Ava ran a hand through her straightened hair. "Thanks. It's a special day and I wanted to dress the part for it. Plus it's Matt's favorite outfit of mine. I hope he notices."

"I don't think you'll have to worry about that."

"You know, I'm the one supposed to be losing weight, not you. Have you been dieting?" She had been detecting Jules figuring slimming lately, but today seemed very noticeable.

"Oh, um, no, I guess I've just been under a lot of stress." Jules smiled, but it didn't reach her eyes. Ava didn't like to see her friend hurting.

Jules had come to pick her up and drop her off at the bank for their closing. They didn't need to leave for another half-hour so she joined her on the couch and sunk deep into the leather cushion. "Have you heard from Derek yet?"

She shook her head, "No."

"I'm sorry."

"Me, too. I just don't understand why he won't return my phone calls. He told me to call when I got things figured out." Her eyes welled up with tears. "I really made a mess of things."

Ava had never been so glad to hear that Jules had turned Scott down on getting back together with him. She could see a difference in Jules over the last couple of weeks. She wished Derek would get over whatever he was dealing with and talk with her so he could see the change, too.

Jules continued, "I had hoped we would talk before the rehearsal dinner tomorrow. I didn't really want my first time seeing him to be in public. Has Matt said anything?"

"I know they talked but he wouldn't tell me what Derek said, just that the two of you need to talk." An idea came to Ava. "Before you came Matt called to tell me about a prank Derek played on him early this morning."

"What did he do?"

"I guess he set up a yard sale in front of Matt's place."

"Clever."

"I think Matt thought so, too. Anyway, it sounds like Derek is at his house and not heading into the station until later."

"What's your point? Even if I call him now, he won't answer my call." Jules stood up and made her way into the kitchen to refill her coffee.

Ava followed her into the kitchen, grabbing a mug. Jules filled it up for her. "I know. That's why I think you should just go over to his house."

Jules pulled her mug away from her mouth. "I don't know, Ava. He doesn't want to talk to me. I don't want to push myself on him."

Ava opened the refrigerator, putting creamer in her coffee. She offered some to Jules but she shook her head. "He can ignore your calls, but he wouldn't ignore you standing on his doorstep."

Ava could tell Jules was contemplating the idea. "You really think I should?"

"Yes." She walked over to the counter and handed Jules her purse. "Go."

Jules took the purse from her. "I guess it's worth a try. I'll drop you off at the bank and then head over to his house."

Ava pulled her address book out of the drawer and wrote Derek's address on a post-it note for her. "You need to get to his place soon. Who knows how long he'll be there? I can take myself to the bank."

Jules shook her head. "No. I'm supposed to get you safely to the bank."

Ava handed Jules her coat. "The bank is ten minutes away. I'll be fine. Plus, I'm not quite ready to go yet. I want to put together a few boxes of decorations to take to the church after the closing." She grabbed her hand and tugged her to the door. "Really, I'll be fine. This is more important." She leaned in and gave Jules a hug. "You better listen to me before I go all bridezilla on you."

Jules laughed. "Yes, you are such a difficult bride when you put others before yourself. Sometimes you are so impossible."

Ava smiled, opening the door for her. "Go, go, go. And make sure you call me to let me know how it went."

Ava finally got Jules out the door with a promise that she would call. She walked back to the spare bedroom to collect the candles she had found on clearance. They had planned a candlelit ceremony and had been excited to find the majority of the candles on sale. Seeing it was the Christmas season they were able to find a large amount of stringed lights to hang all around the sanctuary. For not really wanting the full church wedding again, she had to admit that it would be beautiful. After the weeks of fighting the idea, she was glad they were doing it this way.

Last night as she and Matt snuggled on the couch by the light of the two-foot Christmas tree, they talked about the wedding and finalized the order of the day for the wedding coordinator. He reminded her over and over again how excited he was to marry her and that he *would* be waiting at the end of the aisle for her. She didn't think for a minute that he wouldn't be, but she appreciated his desire to make sure she had no fears.

Ava packed the last box. She decided to take the box of candles down first and then come back for another load or two. She checked the time. She could make three trips and still make it to the bank in time.

On the last trip down she carried the box of programs and gifts for the wedding party along with her purse. She walked along the sidewalk to her car but stopped when a maroon car pulled in front of her.

CHAPTER THIRTY-FIVE

JULES RANG DEREK'S DOORBELL TWICE BEFORE SHE HEARD HIS footsteps approaching the door. She rubbed her lips together to freshen up her lipstick while she gave her nerves a mental pep talk before he answered the door.

Derek's eyes widened in surprise and then narrowed. "Hey, Jules." He turned to the side and swung his arm into the house. "Come on in."

"Thanks," she said, stepping across the threshold. She hadn't been to his house before. Pulling up she had been surprised to find his house so modest. He held true to his desire to not want to be associated with his family's large bank accounts.

Derek led her into the living room. She liked his casual attire of jeans, worn t-shirt, damp hair and bare feet. She realized his slow response to the doorbell probably had to do with the fact that she had interrupted him getting ready.

"I'm sorry to just show up uninvited. Did I catch you at a bad time?" She looked around to check for any signs of him in the process of leaving.

He ran a hand through his wet hair. "Nope, I just got out of the shower but I don't need to get ready for awhile." He used his thumb to point toward the kitchen, "I made a pot of coffee. Would you like some?"

She shook her head, "I'm okay. Thanks, though."

"No problem. I'm going to get some. Make yourself comfortable."

Because his house had an open concept she could watch him in the kitchen filling his mug. A large golden retriever came out from the hallway. Jules crouched down on the balls of her feet and rubbed his ears, his soft fur slipping through her fingers. "Hi there, you must be Max." The dog's tail slapped against the floor with excitement over her attentiveness. She giggled when he licked her face.

"Watch out, he's quite the flirt."

Jules looked up to see Derek standing a few feet away, watching them with a mug in hand. She brought her attention back on Max. "Oh, you're a good boy, aren't you?" She smiled as he pushed his nose closer to her face. She hadn't realized how much she missed having a dog until right now.

"Don't let him fool you. He ate one of my flip flops this morning with no regrets. No head down or tail between his legs. If it's possible, I think he was even smiling at me." Derek walked over to the sliding glass door that led out to the backyard. "Come on, boy, go outside." Max obeyed and scampered out the door.

Jules stood, drawing herself up tall. "I hear Max isn't the only one that did something without remorse," she implied.

Derek's head snapped up. "What does that mean?"

Jules realized how he must have interpreted her statement to think she was talking about their personal situation. "I mean, I heard about the prank you pulled on Matt this morning." She gave a nervous smile, hoping she hadn't pushed him away more.

Derek walked back into the living room, smiling back at her before he took a sip of his coffee. "Yeah, it was pretty good."

Silence settled between them. On the way to his house Jules had rehearsed over and over in her mind what she wanted to say, but now that she stood in front of him her mind went blank.

He crossed his arms over his chest, his mug perched on the crook of his elbow. He was waiting for her to start. She didn't like not knowing what he was thinking. She might as well start there.

"You haven't returned any of my messages. You said to call you when I got things figured out – and then you completely ignored me when I did. What's going on?"

He looked down at his bare feet sticking out from the bottom of his pants. When he looked back up their eyes locked. "I'm sorry. I should have called. Believe it or not, I was planning on calling you later today. I was a jerk and felt sorry for myself. I couldn't bring myself to hear that you chose Scott, but I guess you're going to come and rub it in my face anyway."

Jules stepped back, blown away from his words. This is why he was ignoring her? He thought she chose Scott? "I don't know why you thought I chose Scott! Quite the opposite. I told him I didn't want to get back together with him, and if you had answered even one of my phone calls you would have known that."

Anger flashed across his eyes. "Oh really, Jules? I saw you kissing him on your front porch. Your idea of telling someone 'no' is way different than mine. I don't do love triangles and I don't play second best."

Jules held up her hand, shocked. "Wait, how did you know I kissed Scott?" She hadn't even told Ava yet – mostly out of embarrassment. How did he know? "Were you spying on me?"

He turned and headed into the kitchen while answering over his shoulder. "No, I wasn't spying. I had decided to come to your house to fight for you, only to see you with him. Trust me, I wish I hadn't."

He emptied his coffee into the sink, washing it out before loading it in the dishwasher. She slowly met him in the kitchen, not sure how to get him to understand. He had wanted to fight for her then, but was that still true now?

"Derek." She became overwhelmed with the awareness that she wanted him to hold her. The thought of being wrapped in his arms both excited her and yet terrified her in the same breath.

Derek's phone began to ring. He slipped past her and picked it up off the kitchen table. "Hey Matt, I'm in the middle of something. Can I call you back?" Derek's eyebrows narrowed as he listened.

"Hang on, Jules is right here. Let me ask her." He lowered the phone from his mouth. "Matt has been trying to call you. He's been waiting at the bank and Ava still hasn't shown up. He said that you were supposed to drop her off. Do you have any idea where she is?"

She jerked straight, checking the time on the oven clock. It was ten-thirty. Why wouldn't Ava be at the bank by now? She had planned to head straight to the bank after she had left for Derek's. An uncomfortable feeling settled in her stomach as she shook her head. "No. She told me to come here and she would drive herself to the bank." She made her way to her purse sitting by the front door. "Let me check my phone, maybe she tried to call me."

Scolding herself for forgetting she had put it on silent mode, her heart sank when her phone showed no new messages or missed calls from Ava, only Matt's. She turned a questioning eye back to Derek, shaking her head 'no.' He nodded his head in silent understanding.

"Matt, Jules doesn't know where she is. Ava had planned to drive herself to the bank. She hasn't called either of us." Derek rubbed his forehead with his fingers while he listened to Matt's response. "Okay, we'll meet you there."

Derek slid his phone into his pocket and turned to her, his face lined with fatigue and worry. She stepped forward, "Derek, what's going on? Where do you think she is?" Her voice trembled.

He leaned in and squeezed her shoulder. "I don't know, but we're going to go find out. We're meeting Matt at Ava's apartment. Let me go change and you can ride along with me."

CHAPTER THIRTY-SIX

MATT WALKED ACROSS AVA'S CROWDED LIVING ROOM, HIS frustration at its boiling point. Within a few hours of Ava being unaccounted for, they were able to go to the Investigative Agency and file a missing person's report. Being an officer complicated his part in the investigation and limited his contribution in helping to find Ava. On the legal side, he understood and agreed. On the fiancé side, it infuriated him.

Knowing how the system worked didn't help to ease his panic. Ava had been entered into a national and state database as a missing person. A team of investigators were already establishing what information they had and didn't have. His and the family's interviews had created the foundation of their search.

They had given the agency an updated photo of her and Jules was able to give them a description of what she had been wearing. From there the agency would communicate with patrol officers to check leads and locations. In a few hours, if they still didn't have any leads, they would probably use the media through a press release to get the information out to the community.

The agency promised to keep him in the loop and would let him know of any leads or aspects that he could assist with, but it wasn't enough. Sitting idly by wasn't in his DNA.

He wouldn't compromise their investigation, but he would

do everything in his power to find her and work through the possibilities on his own.

They had had limited access to Ava's apartment until the law enforcement investigators arrived and collected any evidence. Now that they had access, it had become their command center. Matt scanned the room, noting how everyone kept busy – not allowing the fear to smother their ability to help find Ava.

Lucy kept herself busy in the kitchen preparing food that no one had an appetite to eat. Ava's parents sat at the counter on their phones, calling everyone that knew Ava, asking if they had seen her.

Jake, Derek, his dad and Matt's friend, Detective Trevor Hudson stood over the table they'd set up in the middle of the living room. A laptop sat perched on top of the table, with files on Chad Taylor scattered across it.

Matt checked his watch. It had just turned a quarter to six in the evening and not only did they have no contact from Ava, but as of now, they held no leads on how to find her. Hopefully that would change in the next fifteen minutes. At the top of the hour they'd agreed to reconvene at Ava's apartment and give a report on the task they were given and if they had seen anything during their hours of searching the city. They were only waiting for Josh, and then they would begin.

Ava, honey, where are you? He swallowed the lump in his throat. He had to hold it together. It wouldn't help to find Ava if he allowed himself to fall apart.

Matt caught Jules in the corner chair talking with his mom, unable to make out what they were saying. Jules looked up and immediately shifted her eyes away from him – guilt dampening her features. He needed to take her aside and talk with her. Reassure her that this wasn't her fault and that no one blamed her.

He started making his way to her when Josh walked in.

He diverted and headed to the table. "All right, everyone is here, let's get started," he announced and then waited until everyone stood present before he continued. "Let's start at the very beginning again and then please add in any input when we reach the task you were in charge of."

Matt looked at Jules first. He hated having to put her on the spot, but they needed to make sure they had all the details. "Jules, can you tell us again how you left Ava?"

Jules stepped forward. "I was planning on taking Ava to the bank," her cheeks flushed as she glanced over at Derek, "but Ava insisted that I head over to Derek's and said that she could drive herself to the bank. I left around nine-thirty and she mentioned something about taking some boxes of decorations with her so she could drop them off at the church afterwards. She planned to leave shortly after I did. Ava was upbeat and happy when I left – looking forward to the day." Her last few words came out in a whisper as tears escaped.

"Okay, so let's talk about what we do know. We know Ava's car is still parked outside the building with the two boxes loaded in it. Her purse is missing and her door was locked. There is no indication of a forced entry or any type of robbery, and it will be awhile until we get a definite answer from the agency if there is any evidence to work with from her apartment." He looked around the room. "We all agree she didn't run away?" Yes's and nods answered him. "All right, so that leaves us with the idea that she was taken at some point between her apartment and her car."

Matt picked up a pen, ready to take notes. "Let's start crossing things off our list." He looked back at Jules, "Jules, you start."

She cleared her throat and wiped the visible tears away. "I called all the area hospitals. At this point, there is no Ava Williams admitted to any of them."

He wrote a note to do follow-up calls in a few hours. He

pointed to Ava's parents. "Steven, Grace, you made phone calls. Did you find anyone that has seen her?"

Grace held a tissue to her nose, shaking her head. Steven wrapped his arm around her. "No. We've called the school, church, family members, and her close friends. No one has seen or heard from her. Next, we plan on calling the places she frequently stops at to see if anyone has seen her."

Matt nodded. "Good idea." He didn't hold too much hope that they would find anything out, but keeping them busy would be the best idea. He looked over at Jake, "What did you find out about Ray?" His heartbeat quickened, just thinking of the man that almost killed him a few months ago. It was a far stretch that Ray had been released from jail without them knowing, but they had to cover all their bases.

"It wasn't him, he is still locked away."

"Okay, we think that Ava could have her phone with her. Dad, were you able to find a trace to her cell phone?"

"I'm sorry, son, but there is no trace. I was able to talk to a friend working with the agency. She must have it turned off, or someone turned it off for her."

With each negative answer, Matt's hope began to diminish. He ran a hand through his hair instead of pounding the table like he wanted to. He took a few seconds to compose himself before continuing. "Derek and I were allowed to be present with the investigators while they questioned the neighbors. So far no one saw anything out of the ordinary. Her next door neighbor said he had been home all day and heard nothing. There are still three neighbors that haven't returned home yet. When they do, we will question them." He scanned the circle to see who to ask next. "Josh, how's Valerie?"

Josh ran a hand down his face. "Scared. Upset. She and Aaron are locked in at her house. Erica is there also, keeping her company. Thanks for sending an officer to her house. I could see the relief in her face just to have his presence. She has not heard from Ava or had any contact from Chad."

An eerie silence spread throughout the room. The time had come that they all needed to face the facts. She had been taken and their prime suspect was Chad Taylor. What did he want with her? At first he had hope that if it was Chad, he would let her go as quickly as he had Aaron. But eight hours later and no contact from her made that realization seem very grim.

Matt placed his palms on the table, leaning forward with his head down. Derek stepped closer and squeezed his shoulder, speaking to the group. "We are going to have to go on the lead that Chad Taylor took Ava." Matt was thankful Derek took the initiative and spoke for him, because he couldn't bring himself to say it.

"What about the fact that Ava thought she was being followed?" Lucy asked. "Are you even sure that the maroon car has any ties to Chad Taylor? Maybe there is someone else we should be putting our focus on?"

Trevor took his turn to explain, "At this point, we still don't know what type of vehicle Chad is driving. Without having any other connection with the car, we have to assume that it was Chad following her, if in fact she was even being followed."

"I still don't understand why you haven't found this guy yet. How hard can it be?" Lucy didn't even try to hold back her aggravation.

"Lucy!" Grace reprimanded.

"It's okay, Mrs. Williams," Trevor assured, "Lucy, we are working as hard as we can to find him. I can understand you're frustrated, we are too. All we need is one good break. We just have to keep following the tips and hope that one of his men give him up."

Matt cut in on the conversation. "We need to stay focused on pushing forward and preparing for what is next. Time is coming up quick that there will be an alert out to the community. Jules, let's double check that we have listed her correct appearance."

He wrote what she described in her appearance. "She had on black leggings, a long grey sweater with grey boots. Teal accessories." Jules paused for a moment. "I forgot to add earlier that she had straightened her hair." She covered her mouth with her palm. "She looked beautiful." Jules rushed out of the room and into the bathroom.

Lucy followed. "I'll go talk with her."

Jake waited until the door clicked shut. "So what do we do now?"

Ava's dad stepped forward, brokenness etched in his eyes. "We pray."

CHAPTER THIRTY-SEVEN

EREK CARRIED THE THERMOS OF HOT CHOCOLATE DOWN THE steps and out the back exit onto the patio. Jules had disappeared from the apartment forty minutes ago, mentioning she needed some fresh air. He could understand that she wanted some space, but time expired long ago for her to be alone any longer.

A security light nearby helped to find her curled up on a lawn chair in the middle of the yard, her head leaning back, gazing at the stars. He grabbed a chair from the patio and joined her. "Hey, there you are." He was thankful to see she was wearing a coat, gloves and hat. December had proven so far to be a warmer month than in years past, but at two-thirty in the morning it was still cold.

Turning to him, her emerald eyes peeked out from under her stocking cap. "Hi."

Jules' whispered response gripped his heart. He traced her face, wanting to bury her red nose and cheeks into his chest. Instead, he sat beside her and handed over the thermos. "Lucy's famous hot chocolate."

"Thanks. Any new updates?"

He exhaled. "No. I'm sorry." Her eyes glassed over. She couldn't hide the pain from him. He reached over and grabbed her hand. "Julia ..."

She pulled her hand away. "Stop, don't try and make me

feel better. This is all my fault, and you and everyone else knows it." She wiped a tear away that escaped down her cheek.

"Julia, no one blames you. Everyone could play the 'what if' game all night. If I had returned your calls Ava wouldn't have encouraged you to come to my house. If Matt didn't change his plans and decide to work before going to the bank he would have picked her up. It just happened. We can't go back and change the past. All we can do is focus on the now and finding her."

She took a sip of the drink, grasping the thermos in both her hands. "I thought I was finally getting a grasp on hearing God's voice and making wiser decisions." She laughed in spite of herself. "So much for that."

Whether she wanted him to or not, he grabbed her hand back, clasping it between his own. "Jules, listening to God and walking in His will doesn't always secure an easy life. Just because something bad happens doesn't mean it wasn't a part of God's greater plan. In our humanness we want to believe that following God creates this bubble that nothing will go wrong. In Romans 8: 28 it says, *'And we know that in the all things God works for the good of those who love him, who have been called according to his purpose.'* God is not working to make us happy or give us a perfect life. He's working to fulfill His purpose. I don't know why God allowed Ava to go missing, but I do know that my hope rests in Him and He is faithful no matter the circumstances."

She stared at him a long time before answering. A small smile teased the corners of her lips. "You're a good man, Derek Brown."

"And you're a woman worth fighting for, Julia Anderson."

They shared a smile. She squeezed his hand. "I'm sorry that I've made a mess of things. I really appreciated the advice you gave me at my house after the Christmas party. I dug into the Bible, I prayed, and I even spent some time with Grace

– talking things out while she continually directed me to the Word for answers. My life is becoming clearer."

He reached over and ran his thumb across her cheek. Her cold skin reminded him he needed to get her inside soon. "I'm glad to hear it." He smirked. "I'm also glad to hear you gave Scott the boot."

Her white teeth illuminated behind her soft smile before it turned into a frown. "I'm sorry you saw me kissing him. It was a huge mistake and one I deeply regret. He caught me in a moment of weakness."

Derek couldn't deny how much he hated seeing her with Scott, but at this point she was just a friend and didn't need to give him an explanation. "It's all right. I know you are still working through things."

She lowered her gaze, lost in thought. "I am." She bit her lip and took a deep breath. "There is so much more I'm working through – something I haven't told anyone." Jules looked back up at the sky before turning her attention his way. "Until I can work through all my issues, I won't be good for anyone."

Right now was not the time to press the issue and pushing her would only cause more damage. He got up from his chair and dropped to his knees in front of her, leaning his forearms on the arm rests. "Jules, I'm not going to pressure you. We are both on an emotional high with everything going on, and discussing anything further wouldn't be fair to either of us. Right now, our focus needs to be on finding Ava. When this is all over and you are truly ready, we will discuss it again. But just know, my goal is when I do finally kiss you, you will have no regrets."

She nodded. "You're right –"

The back door pushed open with Jake standing at the opening. "Derek!"

He stood. "Jake, right here."

He ran over to them. "Matt just got a call. I guess one of

the guys gave Chad Taylor up. They have an address and they are sending units to his house. They have approved you and Matt to be there for the take-down."

Adrenaline shot through his veins. Could this be the lead they needed for this nightmare to finally be over? "Great! I'll be right there." Jake ran back into the apartment complex while Derek took a quick second for a good-bye. He turned to find Jules standing behind him.

She reached out, pulling him into a hug. "Please be careful."

He allowed himself a moment to hold her. Pulling back slightly, he then leaned back into her, placing his lips softly on her forehead. Her cinnamon scent played with his desires. "I will. Don't stay out here too long." He turned and ran off to find Matt.

CHAPTER THIRTY-EIGHT

MATT PUSHED HIS SHOULDER AGAINST THE HOUSE, MOVING slowly along the white siding, anticipation building that in a few short minutes he could be holding Ava in his arms. Derek trailed behind him. He peered around the corner of the house, exposing the backyard. He waved his hand, alerting Derek that he saw no sign of anyone and that they could proceed.

His feet grew wet from the dew on the grass. Adrenaline pulsed through his body, pushing aside his fatigue from his lack of sleep and the fact it was four o'clock in the morning.

Matt still couldn't believe that they had caught this break. One of Chad Taylor's minions was due in court later this morning and during the night had a breakdown. The fear of what his sentence could be trumped his fear of giving up Chad. Once his lawyer stood present he squealed. Within minutes he gave up Chad's location.

He tried to push down his anger over the fact that Chad had been under their noses the entire time. He had been renting a small house in a busy subdivision that stood on the outskirts of town – only a couple miles away from the police department's headquarters.

He and Derek reached the back sliding glass door. Matt put up his fist to halt their movement. They were in charge of the back exit in case Chad tried to escape. He surveyed grounds, taking note of the open yard that butted up against a small wooded area.

Matt heard the countdown for entry start in his ear piece.

He tightened his large frame against the house. Derek followed suit.

Before the countdown concluded, the door slid open and a man with the appearance of Chad raced out. "Suspect on foot heading north into the woods." Matt called out as he and Derek took off after him. Chad leapt over a small fence that bordered the grass and trees.

"Stop! Rockford Police," Derek shouted, jumping the fence first. Matt headed west, hoping to encircle around and trap Chad between them.

With only the light from the moon it was very difficult to catch a good view on Chad, but enough that he could see that they were now running parallel to each other. He weaved in and out of trees, trying to keep his fast past. An opening in the brush gave him a better chance to make up distance. He pushed, his muscles burning for relief.

Ten feet.

He jumped over a log, wincing in pain from not landing as eloquently as he had wished.

Five feet.

He was close enough now that he could see the whites of Chad's eyes widen as he lunged for him. Mid-air he grabbed him around the neck, twisted, slamming him to the ground. Matt fell on top of him as they slid a few feet.

Chad's upper-cut connecting with his jaw caught him off guard. The contact pushed Matt back. He blinked, trying to focus. Chad shifted, scrambling to get up.

Derek pinned him down, rolled him over and handcuffed him. He looked over at Matt, grinning, "Must I do all the dirty work?"

Matt smiled, rubbing his jaw. "If you think you can handle

it from here, I'm going to go find Ava."

Derek nodded.

Matt sprinted back to the house, entering through the sliding glass door.

"Clear." The officers had begun checking the rooms. "Clear." He waited, growing antsy by the second. "Clear." Where was she? He balled his fists to his sides. "Clear." Come on, Ava. Show yourself. "Clear." Dread swallowed up his hope.

Two officers came up from the basement. Matt approached them. "Did you find her?"

Officer Collins shook his head. "Sorry, Sergeant, but the house is clear."

Matt ran that information through his mind a few times. He needed to look at this from a cop's perspective, not a fiancé's. "Did you find any drugs?"

"No, sir."

What was going on? He ran through the possibilities. If Ava wasn't here, did he already move her location … or worse? He couldn't bring himself to go further on that thought … or maybe Chad never had her to begin with? Did they just get played? He thought the man they apprehended was Chad Taylor, but it was dark enough he could be wrong. Maybe this wasn't even Chad Taylor's home and they had just found themselves back at square one?

Either way, they had to pursue the lead they had until a better one came their way. Disappointment threatened to suffocate him. "Let's get the suspect into the station for questioning."

&&&&

MATT STOOD WITH HIS ARMS FOLDED TIGHT ACROSS HIS CHEST, staring through the one-way mirror at Chad Taylor. They had found their man. Now they needed to find Ava. The fear over the situation caused his chest to rise in ragged breaths.

Trevor and an investigator from the agency sat across from Chad. Trevor tapped his pen against a file as he reviewed it. Matt had insisted that he be in the interrogation room, but Trevor turned him down immediately, claiming Chad would respond better to him and the investigator. It was probably for the best since all Matt wanted to do at this moment was beat that grin off Chad's smug face.

"Mr. Taylor," Trevor began, "you've been a very busy man these last few months. We have a lot to discuss today, but first I need to know where she is."

Chad raised his head, confusion knitting his eyebrows together. "Where who is? I don't know what you're talking about."

"Ava Williams. She has gone missing and you are our prime suspect."

Chad leaned forward, "Wait? What?" He composed himself quickly. "I don't know an Ava Williams."

Trevor pulled out her picture and turned it around to face him. "You do know her and I don't have time for your lies. You are already in enough trouble as it is with your drug charges; let's not keep adding to the list. We know that on the evening of October 12th you entered the home of your ex-wife, Ms. Valerie Walker, and threatened Ms. Williams who was present in the home. Did you not?"

Chad glared across the table, and then leaned forward with a sneer of a smile "You don't have any proof, especially if she is missing."

Matt charged the door, but Derek grabbed his arm saying, "Let Trevor handle this."

Trevor didn't miss a beat. "Proof, you want proof. You should have said so earlier. We have proof that you sent Ms. Williams an unwelcome gift and a threatening note. I'd say that all signs point to you for her abduction."

"You can't prove that I sent those things?"

Matt's muscles tightened. Trevor was playing a game that he hoped wouldn't backfire on them. They didn't have proof. They could only hope to draw the truth out of Chad by implying they had proof.

"Flower shop cameras don't lie, Taylor. Where is she? Don't make this worse for yourself."

Chad pushed his frame back against the chair and ran a hand through his beard. "Fine," he threw his arms up in the air. "I threatened her and sent the flowers. Big deal. I just wanted to scare her, play mind games with her." He leaned in and jabbed his finger against the table. "But I am telling you I never touched that woman and have no idea where she is."

Matt didn't like where this was headed.

"How many times did you follow her?"

"None."

"So how did you know what ribbon to use on the box?" He referred back to the ribbons on the box that were their wedding colors.

"It's not rocket science to make a few phone calls."

"What type of vehicle do you drive?"

"A silver Impala. Listen, you can crucify someone else for this so-called kidnapping of the broad, but it won't be me."

"All right, then let's move on to your drug charges." Trevor said, shifting the conversation.

Chad laughed. "What drug charges? Did you find any on me or my house?"

"Funny thing you mentioned that. No, we didn't."

Chad smirked, arrogance radiating from the answer to his question.

Trevor leaned back against his chair. "But we did come across a small warehouse stocked with drug paraphernalia and meth ingredients. I guess you couldn't use cash forever." Trevor opened up the file placed on the table. "If I'm correct, I believe this is your signature on the lease and I also have a check here for your first month's rent. And right now we have a unit there collecting evidence and fingerprints. We also have a few guys in our custody that are ready to testify against you."

Chad's smirked disappeared, his features tightened. "I want my lawyer."

"I thought you might."

Matt stepped back, folding his hands together behind his head, unable to listen anymore. Ava was still missing. He looked over at Derek, his eyes down at the floor. He took a deep breath, "He doesn't have her, does he?" Matt's throat closed, pain slicing through his heart.

Derek looked up, holding eye contact. "No, I don't think he does."

Matt walked over to the wall and shoved his palm against it. He laid his head down on his arm, needing a moment before furthering this conversation. *Oh God, help me find her.*

He turned back to see his fear reflected in Derek's eyes. "Just say it. I know what you are thinking."

The room stayed silent a few beats as a deep scowl carved ridged lines into Derek's face. "Ava is missing and if Chad didn't take her that means someone else did." He cleared his throat, "and the fact that there is no ransom call tells us that the person who took her … isn't planning on giving her back."

CHAPTER THIRTY-NINE

AFTER MATT RETURNED TO AVA'S APARTMENT AND FILLED EV-
eryone in on what happened, he slipped back into
Ava's bedroom for some time to himself. His mom encouraged him to try and get some sleep, but he couldn't rest until
they found Ava.

He sat on the edge of her bed, breathing in the aroma of her
perfume. Their engagement picture sat perched on her dresser,
teasing him of the happiness that slowly slipped through his
fingers. His chest tightened and tears stung his eyes.

Their last night together filled his thoughts with sweet
memories …

*"Ava, we can clean up the kitchen later, just come sit with
me," he'd called to her.*

*She shut off the water and met him in the living room with
a smile on her face, "You don't have to tell me twice."*

*Matt had his back against the arm rest, watching her black
hair bounce with each step. He grabbed hold of her hand and
pulled her down to him. Placing her back against his chest,
he wrapped his arms around her, nuzzling his lips into the
crevice of her neck. Her laugh consumed the room as his kiss
grazed her ticklish spot.*

*She took his left hand and ran her fingertips over his palm
and fingers, stopping at his ring finger. "I can't wait to put a
ring on here." She turned, lifting her chin up, "you know how*

much I love you, right?"

He leaned down and kissed her nose, "I've got a pretty good idea."

"I know that I have been dragging my feet with a traditional wedding from the beginning, but I hope you realize how excited I am about marrying you. I am honored that you chose me to walk beside you, encourage you and experience life with you. Thank you for loving me and being diligent in showing me that love in the ways you know I need. With buying our house tomorrow, I know it's not only for us to start our future in, but that you did it because you wanted to give me the reassurance that you weren't going anywhere."

He tucked a piece of hair behind her ear, surprised she caught on to why he pushed getting a house so soon. "Loving you has been the easiest thing I've ever done."

She reached up and pulled his head down to hers, enveloping their lips together. He allowed himself to kiss her until his restraint began to diminish. He pulled back, reminding himself he only had a few more days to go.

He cleared his throat, needing to direct his thoughts elsewhere. "Did I hear something about an apple pie and ice cream?

She laughed. After kissing him on the cheek, she stood. "Coming right up."

Crazy how life had changed so drastically over the last forty-eight hours. A pair of Ava's shoes lay next to the bed. He picked one up and chucked it into her closet, wishing it would release at least a bit of his tension. The thud against the wall didn't sound right. On his knees, he reached into the closet and found a twenty-by-thirty cardboard box. He opened it and pulled out a canvass.

A painting of a beach, with the sun setting down over it sprang to life. He recognized this place from the summer when he told Ava he loved her. An envelope fell out and slid on the floor. He opened it to read the words, "*Matthew, may the beauty of this day continually remind us of our love for each other. Happy wedding day. All my love, Ava.*"

Matt leaned forward, cupping his mouth with his palm, as his cry erupted.

CHAPTER FORTY

FIFTEEN MINUTES LATER, COMPOSED AND DETERMINED, MATT emerged from Ava's bedroom. Everyone had cleared out from her apartment except for his mom and Derek.

Derek looked up from the table. "You okay?"

"Yep. Where are we now?"

Thankfully Derek didn't push and moved right into giving him an update. "The news is still running the alert for Ava. Since she has been missing for so long, they have now expanded the viewing area. With that, the agency has also acquired help from another agency, as well as sending the alert to all law enforcement agencies in the state and surrounding states. They have also brought in additional staff to cover the phones due to tips from the public."

"Any new tips?" Urgency laced his words.

Derek shook his head. "Not yet, but it's still early. Most people aren't even up yet to check the news. However, I did just get a call from one of the neighbors that we haven't had a chance to speak with yet. She is home now and willing to talk with us before she leaves for work."

"Great." He needed to take a shower, change into a new uniform and get some food. He couldn't remember the last time he ate, but this came first. "Let's go." Matt grabbed his notepad he had been using to jot down anything he thought would be useful for the case and walked with Derek down to apartment number seven. He knocked on the door.

A woman that looked to be in her thirties answered the door. "Hi, officers." She stood back, opening the door further. "Come on in."

They walked in as she shut the door behind them. "Thank you for taking the time to speak with us, Ms. Porter." Derek said.

"Of course," she smiled, "please call me Miranda. I'm sorry that I didn't contact you earlier. I work two jobs and leave early in the morning and get home late. I didn't even know Ava was missing until I saw the news this morning and then remembered your message to call." She lifted her hands up and shrugged. "I'm not sure how much I can help. I really didn't know Ava very well. We would see each other getting mail sometimes and wave as we passed by, but that's it."

"Miranda, any information you can give us would be helpful," Matt encouraged. "Did you see Ava at all yesterday?"

Miranda gazed down, her eyes shifting back and forth as she thought. Her eyes widened as she looked up, "Actually I did."

Matt's heartbeat raced with the thought that someone else besides Jules had seen her yesterday. "When did you see her?"

"I was heading to work later than usual because I changed shifts with another co-worker, and saw her out on the curb talking to someone in a car and then she got in and they drove away."

"What type of car? Can you give us a color or model?" Derek asked.

"Hmmm, I think it was a deep red or maroon color? I couldn't tell you what kind; I don't care much about cars."

Matt's breath caught in the back of his throat by the shock her words caused. Why had they not pushed this lead? Ava legitimately thought she was being followed by someone in a maroon car and they'd dismissed it from being anyone else besides Chad Taylor. Lucy had even brought it up last night, but they were so confident that her abduction was by Chad, they just excluded any other persons of interest.

"Could you see who was in the car?"

"I didn't get close enough to see many details, but I'm pretty sure it was a woman with long blonde hair."

A woman. He never would have guessed that.

"Did Ava look scared? Did she try to get your attention?" Matt began salivating over this new information.

"Not that I can remember. I waved at her and it looked like she was going to respond but then she looked back into the car and got in quickly."

Matt's mind raced through the possibilities. Did she know the driver? Had this been as innocent as a friend stopping by and offering Ava a ride? Had they been in an accident? In their search they had already checked the hospitals and combed the city looking for her. She would have shown up by now. No, his gut told him that Miranda had witnessed Ava getting abducted – by a woman. The thought still shocked him.

"Did you by chance get the license plate number or at least a partial?" Matt knew that was a far stretch, but he had to ask.

"No." She covered her mouth with her palm as she gasped. "Do you think that whoever took Ava was in that car? Do you think I could have stopped it from happening?"

Derek stood closer and reached out, touching her arm. "We don't know for certain, Miranda. And please don't feel guilty. You had no idea."

Matt zoned out while Miranda finished with giving a description of Ava's appearance and that she had been holding a box and her purse. His concentration lingered on the fact that they had no leads of a woman or any idea why one would take her.

Where are you Ava ... and who has you?

CHAPTER FORTY-ONE

AVA'S EYES FLUTTERED OPEN, ADJUSTING TO THE SUNLIGHT THAT filtered in around the curtain blocking the window. She coughed, gagging on the cloth that had been placed in her mouth and tied around the back of her head. When she swallowed, it felt like knives cutting into her throat. She used her tongue to push the cloth up and out of her mouth. Her cracked lips stung. She licked her lips, only to whimper from the pain and taste of blood.

Her shoulders ached from her hands being tied with rope behind her back. Lying on her side, she tightened her stomach muscles and hoisted herself up onto her right elbow. She then pushed up into a sitting position and leaned back against the wall.

The doorknob jiggled. The door opened to reveal the silhouette of Sabrina McCallum. Never would she have guessed all along that Sabrina, the wife of the man Matt shot and killed in the bank, was the one who had been following her. And that is what worried her the most. Matt wouldn't think of her either.

When Sabrina pulled up to her apartment complex she wanted to run, but the gun pointed at her changed her mind. For a second, hope rose when her neighbor Miranda walked by. Ava had been ready to call for help, but Sabrina threatened to shoot Miranda if she tried. Instead, Ava succumbed to her wishes and got in the car.

Sabrina hadn't said much to her since they arrived at her house. She had just shoved her into this back room and left without a word. It surprised Ava that Sabrina was making her presence known – and a little frightening to wonder why.

Stepping into the room, Sabrina shoved her hands on her hips. "Well, well, well, look who's awake."

Fear gripped Ava's heart with the thought of what this day would bring. "Could I use the bathroom?"

Sabrina's glare could have lit a fire. "Fine, but only because I don't want to clean up the mess if you don't." She bent down and untied her hands. Sabrina pulled out a gun from her back, motioning her toward the bathroom down the hall.

Ava relieved herself and while washing her hands, bent over in the sink and drank the water from the faucet, careful not to drink much since she didn't know when her next bathroom trip would be. She hadn't had anything to eat or drink since Sabrina had taken her. She exited the bathroom only to have her arms tied again and brought back to the same room. She sat down in her original spot, careful not to cause any problems and upset Sabrina more.

"Sabrina. I am very sorry for whatever I did to upset you so much. I know you are hurting, but –"

"No, you don't. You have no idea how I'm feeling. My husband is dead. He's never coming back and it's all your fiancé's fault." Sabrina walked over to the window, lifting the curtain to peer out.

Ava had no skills in human psychology and didn't even know where to start in an effort to calm Sabrina down and help her to think rationally, but she was going to try her best anyway.

"You're right. I don't know how you are feeling. But I was in the bank and I know your husband threatened to kill people. Matt did his job. He had to protect the hostages. I'm very sorry it ended the way it did, and I know Matt is, too."

Sabrina twisted around to face her. "Eddie was a good man. He never would have hurt anyone." Tears began to perch on her eyelashes. "Eddie had lost his job and after months of being behind on payments the bank threatened to take our house. I know what he did wasn't right, but he was trying to support me.

"Do you have any idea how hard the last few months have been for me? Not only did I lose my husband, but the media had to go and flaunt your relationship – your happiness in my face. I followed you for weeks, watching you, seeing your smile and the joy your life held," Sabrina jabbed a finger into her chest, "while I lost everything."

Sabrina paced across the floor. "I was planning on just leaving you alone, but then the paper went and made the two of you one of the highlights of the year." She grabbed a nearby picture frame on a shelf and threw it across the room. When it hit the wall, glass exploded, scattering along the ground. "Matt can't be happy, and I'll make sure of it. He took away the love of my life, and now I'm going to take away his."

With that, she turned and left the room, slamming the door behind her.

Ava waited a few minutes before moving, in case Sabrina came back. Cupboards banged shut in the kitchen, which told her she would be occupied for a while. She braced her feet against the floor and pushed her frame along the wall to a standing position. She plopped down near where the glass shattered and looked for a piece big enough to work through the rope.

Tears stung her eyes as her hands fumbled over the glass, little slivers cutting her fingers. Ava hadn't known what Sabrina's purpose in the abduction was at the beginning, but now it became perfectly clear. Sabrina had no intention of letting her go. If she didn't come up with some sort of plan soon, she would never see the people she loved again.

Her chest tightened as a cry ripped through. Would they ever find her? She brought her knees up and wiped her tears and snot on her pants. She had to stay focused. Yesterday she had spent most of her time searching the room, looking for anything to help in her escape. The broken picture frame lifted her spirits.

The television turned on in the next room as Ava started sawing the rope with the piece of glass. She pulled a muscle in her neck by trying to get a look at her hands. She'd have to work blindly. Taking her time so as not to cut her wrist mistakenly, she concentrated on one spot and hoped that if she cut through, it would be enough to at least loosen the hold.

"No! No! No! This can't be happening!" Sabrina yelled from the next room.

Ava quickly propped herself up on her knees and shuffled across the carpet to the place Sabrina had left her. She dropped the piece of glass in her haste to move, but the restraint had loosened enough that she hoped she would be able to slip a hand out when she needed to.

Sabrina burst into the room. "I should have ended this yesterday when I first grabbed you. Taking you was a last second decision and I needed time to come up with a plan, but now you are all over the news." She bent down, grabbing her arm and pulled, "Get up. We're leaving. It's time for this to be over."

"Please don't do this, Sabrina. Hurting me won't bring Eddie back or fix any of your problems. It will make them worse. My family won't stop searching for me and at some point it will lead back to you."

Sabrina's laugh held no humor. She stopped them in the middle of the hallway, "Do you think I care what happens to me? The only thing I care about is making *Sergeant Thompson* pay." Chills ran down Ava's spine from her snarl of Matt's name.

With Ava in the passenger side seat, Sabrina headed east out of town. They merged onto Ulysses S. Grant Memorial Highway and kept on course for almost an hour. Ava didn't dare speak as silent tears trickled down her cheeks. Where was Sabrina taking her? Within the next half hour they would be crossing the border into Iowa. Right after the city of Stockton, Sabrina turned on CR 10 and headed north.

Shortly after, Sabrina turned into Apple River Canyon State Park. Ava's breathing accelerated as they approached the park office building. A man leaned out the window, waving them over.

Could Ava inconspicuously get his attention without alerting Sabrina? At least if Sabrina's attention was focused on the man, she could work harder on getting her hands released.

Sabrina pulled up to the window. "Hi, there. We are just here for a day of hiking."

"Okay, that will be ten dollars for parking."

While Sabrina rummaged in her purse for the money, Ava mouthed the words, "help me." His smiled faded as he looked between the two women. He looked up into the corner of the small room and then back at them. "Is everything all right?"

Sabrina snapped her head up. "Of course. I don't have enough cash. Do you accept credit cards?"

"Um, yes." She handed him the card and he ran it through the machine. "I hope you brought warmer clothes with you. You don't seem to be dressed for a day of hiking trails."

Sabrina threw a thumb over her shoulder. "Yep, we have them back in the trunk."

The man handed back her card along with a map of the park. "This gives you a detailed map of the park and our trails. Please stay on the trails, for they can be very hazardous when you go off course. We have three designated spots for parking. Just make sure you put the parking pass on your windshield."

"Thank you."

With every second that passed as they drove away, hope diminished for Ava. Of course Sabrina found a secluded parking lot next to a trail – a perfect place to lead Ava to disappear.

Sabrina stepped out, exposing her gun tucked into her pants. She opened up the rear door, grabbing a shovel she had placed under a blanket. While Sabrina stayed occupied, Ava frantically worked her arms, tugging her hands back and forth as the rope loosened. Her left hand emerged. Free.

Without any time to form a plan, Sabrina yanked open her door. Once they were both standing, Ava charged Sabrina with all her strength, shoving her against the car as she flipped over the hood.

Ava took off in a sprint, heading toward the trail. She ran in a zigzag pattern, knowing if Sabrina started shooting at her, she would be less likely to be hit. She didn't dare look back. She passed the sign announcing the start of the trail as a shot rang out, hitting a tree to her right.

Another shot. Fire ripped through her left thigh. She looked down quickly enough to see the bullet had grazed the outside of her middle thigh. She slowed some, but pushed past the pain. The trail curved ahead and then split into two directions. This was her chance to lose Sabrina. She chose the left trail and kept at a fast speed.

Her lungs burned. Her vision blurred. Blood started to pool in her boot. She needed to find a place to sit and hide. A clearing exposed the tall limestone bluffs. Hidden within the rock wall she found a small opening a couple feet off the ground. She stopped for the first time, looking around. No signs of Sabrina, yet. She rushed toward the bluff, judging how to get herself up the additional feet into the small cave.

A couple rocks protruded out from the wall. She used her good leg to step up. Her arms quavered as she pushed her palms down against the rock, pulling her body up. She flopped forward, her chest resting on the rock flooring. With what little strength she had, pulled herself fully into the cave.

She tucked herself into the far corner. Examining her leg, she realized it was vital that she get pressure on it to stop the bleeding. The day would be warming up, but she still needed her coat. She slipped off her boot and pulled off her knee-high sock. She tightened it around her wound. It would hold for a while.

Ava lay down, trying to save her energy. Over time her breathing slowly regulated. She needed food and water soon. Dehydration had begun to play a serious part in her health. She wanted to go to sleep so badly, but she needed to stay as alert as possible.

The sun slowly creeping into the small cave gave her a good indication that plenty of time had passed. Had Sabrina given up trying to find her? Maybe she needed to try and make her way to the park office and get help.

Sitting up intensified the dark spots dominating her vision. As she tried to move back to the opening of the cave, blackness descended upon her.

Chapter Forty-two

MATT'S PHONE RANG, PIERCING THE SILENCE WITH THE WEDDING march song Ava had downloaded a few days ago. He lunged toward it, nearly tipping over his coffee in the process. "Trevor, tell me you have something."

"I think so. We just got a tip from a worker at Apple River Canyon State Park that says he believes Ava entered the park with another woman. The description of the car matches the one we are looking for. He seems certain it's Ava. He had been watching the news and saw the alert. Shortly after they pulled up, claiming they were there to hike for the day.

She was still alive!

"Do we have an I.D or an idea of who the other woman was?"

Matt noticed Trevor's slight pause. "The woman had to pay with a credit card. We have the name of Sabrina McCullum."

Matt's heart dropped to his stomach. "Eddie McCullum's wife?"

"It looks like it. Local authorities are at the park now canvassing the grounds. You all have been cleared to join the search."

He was going whether he had clearance or not. Matt made motions for the others to get their coats on. "Thanks, Trevor. We're on our way."

The drive to the park had been the longest hour of Matt's

life. The guilt stacked on his shoulders over each mile. Had this all been his fault? Was Eddie's wife getting revenge? Had he not been so focused on finding Chad Taylor, would he have seen the signs?

He ran a hand down his face. Ava had been in the park for over two hours at this point. It drove him crazy not knowing how she was doing. Had she gotten hurt? Did she get away from Sabrina, and if she did, why hadn't she gone for help yet? From the few updates they had gotten on their drive, there was still no sign of Ava, Sabrina, or the car.

Derek drove while he sat in the passenger seat. Lucy and Jules filled the back seats. Lucy reached forward and squeezed his bicep. "We're going to find her."

He faked a smile, not wanting to upset her with the doom and gloom that bombarded his thoughts. "I hope so."

When they pulled in front of the park office, Matt had his seat belt off and the door open before Derek came to a complete stop. He jumped out and jogged up to the group of uniforms and volunteers.

The lead investigator stood in the middle, barking out orders. "We have done a detailed search of the parking lots and have not found the maroon vehicle in question. However, we do have a witness that believes that the owner and abductor, Sabrina McCullum left through a different gate, by herself.

"So we are on a massive search for Ms. Williams here on the park grounds. There are five trails here in the park: Pine Ridge, Tower Rock, River Route, Sunset and Primrose. We will cover these trails first. If we don't find her, we will then spread the search throughout the entire 297 acres. Please keep in touch with your radios and report anything you find out of the ordinary. We have paramedics on hand if need be. All right, let's go."

Matt turned back to the group of Ava's friends and family that had gathered behind him during the instructions. "Let's all split up between the different trails. Jake, you take Pine Ridge. I will take Tower Rock. Lucy and Jules, you take River Route. Josh, you take Sunset. Derek, you take Primrose." He looked over to his and Ava's parents, "You guys stay here and contact us if you hear anything."

Everyone agreed, grabbing radios and splitting up to their designated trails. Matt, Jules and Lucy walked together on a combined trail until it came to a fork in the path. Matt went left while the girls went right. "Be careful." He called out to them as he split off from them.

He walked along the path with the group, calling out Ava's name. They combed the brush, careful to not get too far off the path. They came up to high limestone bluffs stretching down the left side of the trail. He scanned the grandiose rocks, noticing the God-made cuts in the outline.

Looking down at this radio, he checked to make sure it was on. Why had no one reported anything yet?

About thirty yards down the path, the rock broke up a few feet from the ground. A small cave was carved out in the rocks. As he approached, he rubbed his eyes, trying to focus. The shape didn't look right. Something black spilled out from the base of the cave floor. Almost looking like ... hair? Matt's adrenaline and hope surged.

"Ava!" He took off in a sprint, screaming her name along the way. The closer he got, the more confident he became that it was hair, but why was there no movement? He ran through the brush, stopping right under the cave opening. He found a ridge of rock for a good start to place his foot.

Before his other foot found the next foothold he noticed dried blood on the rocks. "Ava!" His throat burned, desperate to see her face.

He climbed up the rest of the rock and flung himself into the cave. Ava lay unconscious on the rock floor. He ran a hand down her pale and cold cheek. "Thank you, God!" he called out when her chest moved up and down. He pulled out his radio. "This is Sergeant Thompson. I have found Ava Williams. She is on the Tower Rock trail, half a mile in, up in a rock cave. Medical assistance needed!"

Matt took off his coat, covering her and then bent over, kissing her forehead, "I'm here, baby. Come on, Ava. Wake up so I can get lost in those baby blues."

He ran his hand over her body, looking for any broken bones. His hand turned wet along her left thigh. Pulling back, his fingers were covered with blood.

"Matt!" He poked his head out of the cave as Jules ran toward them.

"Up here, Jules." He leaned down and helped pull her up into the cave. "How did you get here so fast?"

"I didn't get very far on our trail because a volunteer tripped, breaking her wrist when she hit the ground. I stayed with her until –." She waved her hand back and forth, "but that doesn't matter now." Jules looked down at Ava and then back up at him, "How is she?"

"Alive. She's been unconscious since I found her. It also looks like she has a wound on her left thigh."

"Let me do a quick assessment." Matt shifted back so Jules could get closer. She placed her fingertips to Ava's neck. "Her blood pressure is low. By the look of her skin and eyes, I think she is dehydrated. Let me get a look at her leg." She unraveled the sock tied around her leg. "Smart girl, she was at least coherent enough to know she needed to put pressure on her wound."

Jules ripped her leggings at the thigh. "It's an open wound, but I don't think she has lost too much blood. The sock probably saved her life." She slid off her backpack, rifling through the contents. She pulled out gauze and tape. Jules worked on Ava as she talked to him. "I'll get her leg bandaged up, but she needs an IV and antibiotics soon."

CHAPTER FORTY-THREE

AVA'S BODY HURT. EVERYWHERE. BESIDES HER MUSCLES ACHING, her left leg throbbed with each beat of her heart. She tried to open her eyes but failed miserably. Had she been drugged? Where was she? The last she could remember was … Sabrina taking her to the park … she had run away … the cave. That's right; she had climbed up into the cave. But that was the last she could remember. Had Sabrina found her?

Focusing harder she lifted her eyelids enough to see she was in a room. Her eyelids closed quickly, but she forced them open again. Overwhelming hope abounded. She was in a hospital room. Looking around the room, her gaze stopped at the most beautiful sight.

Matt sat in the chair beside her bed, sleeping. His head leaned back against the head rest, his legs stretched out with his hands folded over his chest. He looked as if he hadn't shaved in days.

She tried to reach out and touch his arm, but he was too far away. "Matt." Her voice came out barely above a whisper. She cleared her throat and tried again. "Matt." Not much louder, but enough. He shifted, taking a deep breath as he began to wake up.

He ran a hand through his hair before he looked over at her. Sitting up quickly, he reached out and grabbed her outstretched hand. "Hey!" His smile melted her insides.

She gave him a close-lipped smile in return, not sure how her lips would feel being stretched. "Hi."

"It's so good to see you awake. Are you feeling okay? Are you in any pain?" He scooted closer.

She had a long list, but none of that mattered at the moment. "I'm fine, just sore." She looked out the window. "Where are we?"

"At the hospital in Freeport. It was the closest hospital from the park."

She turned on her right side slightly, her blood pressure spiking. "Matt, it was Sabrina McCullum that took me."

He rubbed his hand along her arm, "We know, Ava. It's okay. She is in custody."

Her body relaxed from the relief. "How did you know it was Sabrina? Where did you find her?"

"At first we assumed it was Chad Taylor that took you. But once we found him, we realized that wasn't the case and had to start from scratch searching for you."

Ava's eyes widened. "You found Chad Taylor?" She wanted to believe so badly that this meant it was all over. That life could finally get back to normal again.

He nodded. "We did, but that's a story for another day. Figuring out it was Sabrina started when your neighbor Miranda gave us the insight that a woman had taken you and then we got a tip from a worker at the park that saw the two of you come in. He had seen you on the news from our media alert and identified you quickly. Sabrina had escaped the park, but once we knew it was her, we put a BOLO out on her car. Within a few hours of her leaving the park, she was spotted in Iowa. She has confessed and will be transported back to Rockford."

Ava paused, leaning back against the bed, letting his words soak in. Her eyes misted. "She wanted to kill me, Matt." She turned her head toward him. "As much as I want her to pay for what she did to me, I still feel sorry for her. I kept thinking, even if I die, I still have hope because I know where I'll spend eternity. She is so hopeless, Matt. Not just in her circumstances, but deep in her soul." A tear slipped from her eye. He squeezed her hand, giving what support he could give.

Matt took his thumb and brushed the tear away. "Oh honey, your sweet spirit is just one of the many reasons why I love you. God isn't giving up on Sabrina and we won't either. Once we are ready, we will go visit her, share our forgiveness, and pray that her heart is softened enough that we can share the hope we have." He leaned in and kissed her lips with a soft touch. "But right now, all we are going to worry about is you."

Emotions tightened her chest. "I love you. I thought I would never see you again."

He dropped to his knees, his elbows resting on the bed as he clutched her hand in his. "I love you, too. I had begun to think the same thing, too, as my hope in finding you slipped away with each hour. But you are here with me now, and safe. The future we've dreamed of is still ahead of us."

Footsteps approached, stopping at the doorway. "Hey, look who's awake," Derek's voice filled the room.

Derek, Jules, Lucy and Jake filed into the room. Jules rushed over to her, bending down and enveloping her into a hug. "Ava, I'm so sorry I left you at your apartment. I never should have done that." Guilt smothered each word.

Ava shook her head, surprised Jules had put this on her shoulders. She hadn't once blamed her for what had happened. "It's not your fault, Jules. I don't blame you and neither should you," trying her best to convince her.

"We've been trying to tell her that for a couple days. Maybe you can finally make her see," Derek said as he came to a stop at the end of her bed.

Jules stepped back and found a spot next to Derek so Jake and Lucy could get closer. She looked at the three guys, noticing what they had in common. "Have you guys forgotten how to use a razor?"

Jake leaned down and hugged her. "Good to see you, too, Ava." He winked at her, his smile fading. "Don't scare us like that again, okay?"

"Okay," her voice betrayed the emotions that swelled in her throat.

Lucy stood beside her, stroking Ava's hair with her fingers. She had no desire to look in a mirror at this point and by Lucy's fussing, she probably shouldn't.

"Are you hungry? Can I get you something?" Lucy asked. "We just came from breakfast. It's not amazing, but it's not horrible either."

"Maybe in a little bit." Ava smiled, and then frowned. "Breakfast? How long have I been asleep?"

"A day," Lucy confirmed.

"You have all been here for a day?" She blinked. It was an unsettling feeling to miss out on an entire day of her life. She looked up at Jake. "Is anyone else here?"

"Matt's parents went home last night. You just missed Mom, Dad and Josh. They headed back early this morning to take care of a few things and then they will be back later today."

Lucy perked up, "Speaking of, I'll go give them a call to let them know you are awake." She reached down and squeezed Ava's hand. "I'll tell mom you'll give her a call later. I'm sure she'll want to hear your voice."

Ava nodded, not trusting her voice. Her mind went back to the comment of her being asleep for a day. Sabrina had taken her on Wednesday and then had taken her to the park on Thursday. So that must mean …

She jerked her head toward Matt, hoping she was wrong. "What day is it, Matt?"

He dropped his eyes. "Friday."

Disappointment oozed with what that meant. "Our wedding day?" She sucked in a ragged breath. "What if I get released, would we still have time to make it?"

"I appreciate your eagerness, but we aren't going to rush your recovery. The earliest you'll be released is tomorrow."

Her chin quivered. She just wanted to crawl into a ball and cry. She wasn't dead, she should be grateful, but sadness over not becoming Matt's wife today trumped all reasoning. "What if they just roll me down to the chapel? I'm sure we could find someone that could marry us." She was grasping at straws, but she had to try.

Matt looked up at the others, "Can you give us a minute?"

They agreed and slipped out from the room, leaving them alone. Ava covered her face with her palms, attempting to compose herself. She was in a hospital on her wedding day – tired, hungry and sore – nothing would seem right at this moment.

"Ava, look at me." He waited to continue until he had her attention. "You have to know that I want to marry you today. I would take you down to that chapel in a second if I thought that's what would be best. But I think if we do, we'll regret it down the road. When we look back at our wedding, do we really want it to be an all-consuming reminder of what happened?" He grabbed hold of her hand, lifting it to his lips. "Plus, I'd like you to say your vows when you're not under the influence of drugs."

She laughed. "Okay. I'll admit you're right as long as you don't say, 'I told you so.'"

He leaned in, brushing his lips against hers. "I wouldn't think of it."

Worry over all the details abounded. "So what do we do about the guests for tonight? What about the honeymoon? What about the house? Can we still close on it?"

"Shhh." He placed a finger over her mouth. "Your parents

and Josh went home to take care of guests. I already called the bank and rescheduled the closing for next week. This morning I got in contact with the travel agent and she has everything on hold until we pick another wedding date. Let's just focus on getting you healthy again, enjoy a simple Christmas with our families, and then we will get married."

She entwined their fingers together. She hated the fact that she had partially panicked because it gave him more time to change his mind about marrying her. The thoughts were ridiculous and at least she had come to the place where she knew they weren't true. "I think that sounds wonderful."

Derek knocked on the door frame. "Hey Matt, can I talk to you for a sec?" He cocked his head back toward the hallway.

"Yep, be right there." He stood, running a hand down her cheek. "Excuse me, my wedding coordinator needs me." He leaned down and kissed her forehead. "I'll be right back."

"What are you two up to?" she asked as he walked out with a mischievous smile, refusing to answer.

The nurse came in and checked her vitals. She gave her the next dose of pain pills and took her lunch order. After she left, Lucy came in and occupied the open chair. "I thought she'd never leave." She pulled out a pint of Mint Chocolate Chip ice cream and two plastic spoons from a plastic bag.

"You are a saint." Ava took a bite and let the coldness dull her aching throat.

"I don't know about that, but I'll take the 'best sister award.'"

"Done." Ava took a few more bites. "Hey," she pointed her spoon toward the hallway, "do you know what the guys are up to?"

A smile crept slowly across Lucy's face. "I plead the fifth."

CHAPTER FORTY-FOUR

Twelve days later ...

AVA DUG HER TOES INTO THE WARM SAND. SHE CLOSED HER eyes and let the salty breeze rush over her face. Today was not only New Year's Day – but also her wedding day. She couldn't think of a better way to start off the New Year than to become Mrs. Ava Thompson.

For days everyone had kept this a secret from her. And of course Derek spent the time joking with her that the wedding was planned for Chuck E Cheese. Two days ago her family, Matt's family, Derek, Jules, Erica, Valerie and Aaron all loaded onto a plane and headed to a resort on the Florida Keys.

Ava looked down at her wedding dress, thankful she picked one that worked for a last-minute beach wedding. The white satin strapless dress hugged her curves all the way to the ground. She ditched the veil and went more relaxed with her hair down, curls bouncing, with a flower clip holding the hair out of her face.

Jules had scolded her twice about not crying and ruining her make-up job while getting ready, but she couldn't help it. The day was perfect. Matt was right, this was so much better than a stuffy chapel and a hospital gown.

"Ava, it's time."

She turned to see her dad holding his hand out to her. She grabbed it, excitement causing her hand to shake inside his. Lucy, Julia and Matt's sister Sara, dressed in their deep purple bridesmaid dresses, began their walk down the path that opened up to a secluded part of the beach where the ceremony would be held.

Ava put her arm through the crook of her father's as they followed after them. When they came out of the clearing the music changed to the wedding march. The groomsmen came into view first – Jake, Derek, and then Matt's brother, Gabe. She bit the inside of her cheek in an attempt not to cry when she saw Matt standing at the gazebo waiting for her.

His smile beamed.

She let out a quick breath, blinking feverishly against the tears. Matt's dark hair and tanned skin contrasted his soft white linen shirt and khaki pants. She kept her eyes focused on him alone, as if no one else existed at this very moment. She tried to quicken her steps, but her dad just patted her hand, keeping their pace. Matt stepped out to meet them. After hugging her parents, she found her hand in his – the place she always wanted to be.

Josh started the ceremony, but paused as laughter spread through the group when Aaron's little voice said, "Look mommy, Awa so pretty." Ava waved at him, but brought her attention back on Matt. Josh continued, taking time to talk about them as a couple and how their love should represent that of God's love.

Ava handed off her bouquet to Lucy when it was time for the vows. Matt took both her hands in his as he began. "Ava, I don't believe in fate or destiny – but I do believe that God has a will for each of us and I am thankful every day that God put you in mine. I promise to not take your love for granted and will lead you with integrity, respect and a faithful heart. I vow to take care of you and put you before myself all the days of my life."

Josh turned to her, letting her know it was her turn.

Ava went to talk, but paused, pushing down the lump in her throat. "Two and a half years ago I thought my world was crashing down around me, but little did I know, it was just the beginning of our forever. You fought for me when I thought I wasn't worth fighting for. You stood by me despite me pushing you away. You love me even when I am not loveable. In you, I have found the man God created for me. I know that life isn't always going to be easy, but I don't want it easy - I just want a life with you. I promise to love you, care for you, and be faithful to you all the days of my life."

They exchanged rings. Matt didn't wait for Josh to tell him he could kiss her. He wrapped his arm around her waist and pulled her close. She draped her arms over his shoulders as his lips melted into hers. Josh announced them husband and wife. Bursts of clapping, cheers and whistles amplified as he picked her up and spun her around.

&&&&

MATT WATCHED AVA GLIDE AROUND THE BEACH, STOPPING AT tables to talk and hug their family and friends. The sun had begun to set, causing a warm glow to hover. His heart swelled to see her so happy – and finally his.

A new song started. He smiled. Matt walked over to where Ava stood with her parents, "Mind if I borrow my wife?" Man, did that sound awesome.

He pulled her into the gazebo that they had set up as a dance floor for the reception. He brought her close, not wanting any space between them.

"How's your leg feeling? You're not overdoing it are you?"

"I feel great. My leg isn't bothering me at all. If it starts to hurt, I'll sit down. Jules bandaged it up really well, so I have good support and it's protected from the sand." She reached up on her tip-toes and left a mark on his lips. A kiss that made him want to tell the guests to go home. "Thanks for always caring and for this amazing day. I don't know how you pulled it off, but it was wonderful."

"You know, you didn't have to go and get kidnapped just so we'd have to change plans to the beach wedding you secretly always wanted. You could have just asked." He couldn't stop his playful grin.

"Now you tell me. However, now that we are married, I have a few other persuasive ideas up my sleeve," she mentioned, returning a playful grin.

He loved when she flirted with him. Tightening his hold on her, they danced slowly while the soft rhythm and lyrics floated around them. "Do you remember this song?" He asked, wondering if she would.

"I do. I danced to this song for the first time with some guy I hardly knew that ended up asking me out."

He should have known she'd remember their first dance together. "And how did it turn out?"

"Perfect."

CHAPTER FORTY-FIVE

DEREK SAT IN THE SAND OVERLOOKING THE OCEAN, RUNNING the tall grass through his fingers. Within a few minutes the last glimpse of sunlight would be gone. The waves crashed against the shore in a rhythmic cadence.

"Can I join you?"

Jules' question startled him. He looked back to find her a couple feet away. "Sure." He used his arm to smooth out the sand beside him.

She plopped down on her knees, sliding her feet beneath her. He couldn't help but notice how her dress stopped just short of her knees, exposing her cream skin. Derek turned his eyes back out to the water, needing to stop noticing those things about her.

Jules handed him a piece of cake. "You missed them cutting the cake. I thought you'd want some."

"Thanks. Where's yours?"

She shrugged her shoulders. "I'll have some later." She nodded out to the water. "It's so peaceful."

He took a bite of the white cake and frosting, happy for the sugar buzz. "It is," he agreed. "Are you having a good time?"

"Yes. I wish I could stay longer, but I don't think Matt and Ava would appreciate that. You?"

He smiled, playing out Matt's reaction if he asked to stay longer. "Yes, but this is the last time Matt gets me to be his party planner."

She crossed her arms and tilted her head to the side just enough to see him out of her peripheral line of sight. "Huh, Matt tells me a different story. His version is that this was mostly your idea and you helped to fund the resort and airline tickets."

Derek's eyes widened. Matt sold him out. "Well, one thing we know for sure is that Matt can't keep secrets." He put a bite of cake on his fork and offered it to her. She shook her head. "All right, your loss."

Jules nudged her shoulder into his. "I can tell you don't want to talk about it, but it was really nice of you."

He laid down his empty plate on the sand and took a drink from his water bottle. "It's nothing. What's the point of having a trust fund that you don't use, if you can't use it for good things to help others? Matt and Ava deserved a day like this. Matt mentioned bringing Ava down here and eloping, and I just convinced him to do it this way with family and friends and let me foot the bill."

This conversation made him uncomfortable. He had been running away from his parents' money for years and the last thing he wanted was to draw attention to the fact he had just used it. He needed to change the focus of their talk.

"I noticed when I was looking through the tickets yours was just a one-way. Have you decided to run away to Florida?" He made it sound like a joke, but secretly prayed she didn't.

"After a sunset like this, I might be tempted. No, I decided to rent a car and go see my mom since she only lives a few hours from here. From Orlando I bought a plane ticket to go see my dad out in Colorado for a couple days and then I'll fly home."

He watched her shift the sand through her fingers. That had to have been a huge step for her to take and one she didn't take lightly. "How are you feeling about spending time with them?"

She shrugged her shoulders while biting her lower lip. "Nervous. Excited. Probably somewhere between happy and wanting to throw up."

He laughed – that is how he felt at this moment sitting beside her. "I hope it goes the way you want it to."

"Thanks. I'm hoping that I can repair my relationship with them both and find the closure that I need to move forward with my life." Clearing her throat, she rubbed her hand along her arms, "I'm also hoping that when I get back we could have that talk." Even in the twilight he could see a slight blush highlight her cheeks.

"I'd like that." Hope busted out through his heart, like a plant pushing through the ground at the first sign of spring. Standing, he shoved his plate and fork into his pocket and stood in front of her, arms reaching down. She took hold of hands, letting him pull her up. "What do you say we go show off our dance moves?"

"I don't know. I've seen you dance before. The eighties called and want their Running Man and Cabbage Patch moves back."

His hand clutched his chest, his mouth dropping open in mock dismay. "Jules, you wound me." Their laughter filled the night as he held her hand, leading her back to the gazebo. "Then a slow dance it is."

Natalie Replogle is a busy stay-at-home mom of three young kids and a wife to her heartthrob, Greg. She enjoys escaping the glamorous life of after-school homework, meal preparation, dirty dishes and laundry by losing herself in writing novels drenched in romance and suspense. She and her family reside in Northern Indiana. You can connect with Natalie online at www.nataliereplogle.blogspot.com.

Coming soon
Derek and Julia's story continues in:

A RESCUED LOVE

A romance starts...
Derek Brown and Julia Anderson have finally gotten to a point where being together is what they both want and that future seems to be in their grasps and full of excitement.

She witnesses a murder...
Caught in the middle of a situation that leads to death, Julia is the only eye-witness. When strange occurrences begin to happen in the aftermath, Derek takes her to his family's cabin to keep her safe until they can figure out what is going on and if there is someone after her.

Their newfound love begins to unravel...
As Julia deals with the secrets she has revealed, Derek must face his family and their different views on how he should live his life. Will Derek and Julia learn to work together through their trials or will it tear them apart forever?

Excerpt from *A Rescued Love*

DEREK BROWN'S SQUAD CAR CAME TO A SCREECHING HALT IN-side the parking garage. Trevor Hudson's phone call informing him that Jules was a witness in a murder had him rushing from his house, an uneaten supper sitting on the table. He hadn't even taken time to get back into uniform. His jeans and sweatshirt would just have to do.

He wanted to kick himself for not getting in touch with her sooner. She had been back from her trip for almost a week and he had been too scared to make the first contact. As if not talking to her would eventually make everything work out the way he wanted it to. He had dealt with rejection in the past, but to hear it from the woman he could see himself spending the rest of his life with – that rejection he wasn't sure he could recover from.

But none of that mattered now.

Trevor hadn't given him any details, just that Jules had been a witness to a murder, was alone, and he thought she could use some support.

Did Jules even want him here? She'd made no effort to contact him. Maybe he needed to get a clue. Spotting Trevor deep in discussion with the head of the crime scene unit, Derek waited to approach so as not to interrupt. While scanning the garage, auburn hair sticking out from the back of a squad car caught his attention.

He rushed forward in her direction, calling her name out as his throat tightened. "Jules!"

She heard him the second time he called. Her eyes widened with shock and then filled with relief. Stepping out from the car, she waited for him to approach. Derek hadn't expected her to throw her arms around his neck, but he welcomed it when she did. Pulling her tight against him with his left arm, he used his right hand to gather her hair and hold her head against his neck.

After a few minutes, she pulled back, using her palms to push the tears aside. "What are you doing here?"

"Trevor called me."

Her cheeks flushed pink. "I'm sorry. I told him not to bother you."

Derek pushed down the disappointment that flooded his heart from the realization that maybe he was right earlier and she didn't want him here. Using his curled pointer finger, he pushed her chin up, making her look at him. "Jules, you are never a bother."

Her shoulders slackened. Taking a step into him, she slid her arms around his chest. "I'm glad you're here."

Hope sprung from her words. "Me, too." A black body bag laid on the ground near her car caught his attention. He cleared his throat, "Have you given a statement yet?"

Stepping away from him, she turned her back to the scene and shook her head. "No. I'm waiting for Trevor." She pulled out a tissue from her coat pocket, wiping her eyes and then nose. "He's dead, Derek." Looking up at him, sadness strangled her words into a whisper. "I just can't believe he's dead."